# The Sinking of the Leonardo Da Vinci

"A beautiful book that sweeps along like a surging wave. A pleasure to read, and a joy to recall long after."
—Jack Livings, author of
*The Blizzard Party* and *The Dog*

"Italy is a real place—but it is also a dream. It is the dream of abandon, romance, and sensuality, all in Italian. In *The Sinking of the Leonardo Da Vinci*, we get a double dose of the Italian dream, as present-day romance and past love lost. Do you need a chance to escape into a sweeter world? This is the novel to take you there!"
—Eric Maisel, author of
*Choose Your Life Purposes*

"A hauntingly beautiful tale of love, loss, and second chances. This poignant, page-turning story held me spellbound."
—Åshild Kolås, Sirkel Forlag Publishing, Oslo

"Anyone who has loved, lost, and struggled to move on will find *The Sinking of the Leonardo Da Vinci* an absorbing story long after the empty cappuccino."
—Kathryn Graven, author of
*Memoirs of a Mask Maker*

"*The Sinking of the Leonardo da Vinci* is a powerful story of flawed characters in the face of tragedy, courage, and human frailty who ultimately find the capacity for love. A must-read!"

—Mark Shaw, memoirist

"What if the love of your life disappeared and you never knew why? *The Sinking of the Leonardo Da Vinci* is a sweeping tale of memory and the power to reshape the present by confronting the past—a story to savor until the final word."

—Michael Swartz, author of *Split*

"*The Sinking of the Leonardo Da Vinci* is a haunting story, a wonderful story. I couldn't put it down!"

—Deborah Bayer, author of *Rope Made of Bandages*

"The kind of story that reminds you that it's never too late to embrace who you truly are. I loved it!"

—Marilyn Raider, New York City reader

"A must-read for book lovers!!"

—Terry Levi, Rome reader

*The Sinking of the Leonardo da Vinci*
by Deborah Jeanne Weitzman

© Copyright 2025 Deborah Jeanne Weitzman

ISBN 979-8-88824-730-3

All rights reserved. No part of this publication may be reproduced, stored in a retrieval system, or transmitted in any form or by any means—electronic, mechanical, photocopy, recording, or any other—except for brief quotations in printed reviews, without the prior written permission of the author.

This is a work of fiction. All the characters in this book are fictitious, and any resemblance to actual persons, living or dead, is purely coincidental. The names, incidents, dialogue, and opinions expressed are products of the author's imagination and are not to be construed as real.

Edited by Joe Coccaro
Cover design by Catherine Herold

Published by

◄ köehlerbooks™

3705 Shore Drive
Virginia Beach, VA 23455
800-435-4811
www.koehlerbooks.com

# The Sinking of the Leonardo da Vinci

Deborah Jeanne Weitzman

VIRGINIA BEACH
CAPE CHARLES

Also by Deborah Jeanne Weitzman

*Pandora Learns to Sing: A memoir*
*Islands in the Storm: A musical*

*To Harold*

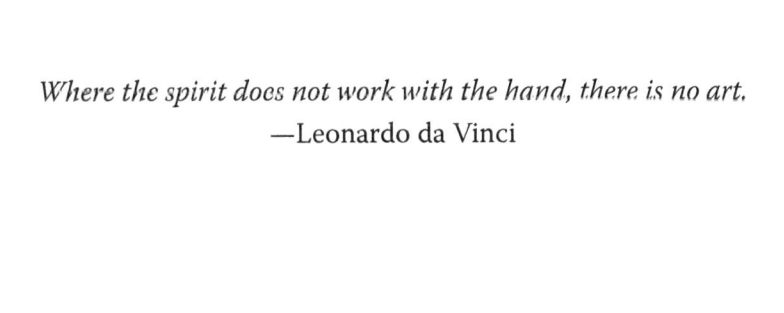

*Where the spirit does not work with the hand, there is no art.*
—Leonardo da Vinci

# 1.

## CINQUE TERRE, 2002

JOANNA LEANS OUT the window of her empty compartment and breathes in the changed air, the warmth of Italy. Hot silvery dust covers the cypress trees that whiz by like dancers, all in rhythm with the steady rock of the fast-moving train. She can hardly remember when she felt this good, this safe. Doesn't matter where she's heading, only to be free of that monstrous grip that had nothing—or maybe everything—to do with the unleashed terror and loss, the sense of powerlessness, the gaping hole where the Twin Towers remains were a smoking corpse.

Maybe in the end, everything *was* connected. Joanna couldn't directly blame her husband's death on 9/11, yet it was connected. Stuart—so robust, so steady and strong before—had become after that day a volcano of rage, raging at how the politics were playing out, raging at the Bush administration's power to distract. "Only the devil could have orchestrated this timing," he'd ranted. "Just watch what they're going to ram through. Shock people enough, and you can get away with everything." That Stuart profoundly understood the wrong road the US was now on, especially with the environment and his powerlessness to do anything about it, was finally too much.

At first, with the entire city grieving, it didn't matter that Joanna couldn't stop crying. There was such a sense of community, of caring for each other. No one judged or wondered why when, at the least provocation, she burst out weeping at yoga or at the gym or on the streets of New York. But by spring of 2002, when most people started picking up the pieces of their lives, she couldn't get past an endless sea of mourning, this suffocating fear.

Even at her work she loved, helping the old folks (like grandparents she never had), she was losing it. Couldn't sing or offer comfort to the families gathered around their dying without choking up and fleeing the room. Her colleagues at the nursing home kept reminding her that grief had a life of its own, that even if you dealt professionally with death, it was a whole other story when it was *your* husband who died. *It's not just my husband!* Joanna wanted to scream but couldn't. Perhaps she should have loved Stuart more; maybe she had, but there was never enough time. Now with him gone, there was too much time—oceans of time—and it was driving her mad.

Many New Yorkers were still hunkered down, but Joanna had to go, had to stick to the plan arranged long before of attending the music therapy conference in Switzerland. "I know it's hard," her boss had said, "but you should go, and take some time afterward. A long break will do you good."

*Will it?* Joanna had wondered then and again now on the train. Would being away give a chance to escape, even if she felt terrified of the unknown? She'd managed—miraculously—to get herself onto the flight and all the way to the conference. Yet once there, she'd fallen apart again and stayed mostly in her room. The last night she forced herself to the farewell dinner and came by chance to sit next to a friendly Italian woman who didn't seem to mind that Joanna's eyes were swollen red.

"Six months my husband has been dead, and I still can't—"

The woman sympathized. "It's okay."

"I'm supposed to stay longer, but I have no idea where to go."

"Ah," the woman said and scribbled the names *Cinque Terre* and *Vernazza* on a bit of paper. "Go there and walk. It will make you better. We therapists can cure the whole world, but not so easily ourselves."

Her warm dark brown eyes offered Joanna what she could never get enough of—the soft recognition, the gentle feeling of being okay in that ever-changing *now*. One moment *now* could be wretched loneliness, and in the next, that loneliness could slip away. And it had that afternoon on the train.

If she could just stay on this train, never arriving, forever moving, she'd be all right. She'd get through this monster of grief. It was as if her unlived self awoke with a vengeance, demanding that she, soon fifty, drop that *life-lie*, that lost vision of paradise she'd lugged through her entire married life. Time to sweep out those cobwebs, like the chicken wings of dust that hung from the rafters in McSorley's bar before they cleaned it. The oldest bar in New York she'd taken him to, not Stuart but Luca, back in the '70s when he asked to see something authentically New York. He'd hated it, how dirty it was, wouldn't even stay for a drink. And she who'd always loved that place never went there again.

Remembering this brings a fresh bolt of sadness. Now she wonders, *How will I manage without my husband? Stuart, my anchor; Stuart, my ground.*

Joanna tries to focus on the rock and sway of the train as the landscape rushes by. It had been a beautiful journey so far across the verdant Alps and past the farms and yellow fields of Northern Italy's sodden Po Valley. And now, coming close to the Mediterranean Sea, the air grows bright with color and the overwhelming scents of lavender, sage, and pine. She can almost taste the mix, stirring something old in her, so old it feels brand new and brutally alive in the awakening. There's a whisper of shame in the longing to feel wild again, that abandon of being in love.

Almost in response, the train surges into a cold and seemingly endless tunnel. Then, flooding with light and a burst of heat, the train roars out of the tunnel and screeches to a stop at the next station. Joanna looks out the window and watches a mother and four children struggle off the train with a mountain of luggage. A large man who'd been waiting on the platform leaps forward to help and then sweeps the children into his expansive arms. Impulsively, Joanna reaches her arm out the open window, yearning to be part of this family, to be held like a long-lost child in the father's arms. Stuart was like a father to her, the father she never had.

The tears come fast and hard. She doesn't want to think about her mother or what happened between them after the funeral, a vague competition for who had suffered more. Her mother, Lillian, was stubborn as a mule and wouldn't reconcile with Joanna in the months before she left for Italy. They'd never gone this long without speaking. Joanna could have pushed more, as was her habit, but this time she didn't even phone to say goodbye, only a brief email that Lillian, uncharacteristically, hadn't responded to. Joanna knew her mother would suffer, was suffering; they'd always been each other's everything. It was killing Joanna as well. With Stuart gone, there was no one to talk to or confide in—not really. But she was sticking to this. For once in her life, she was taking real distance from her mother.

*\*\*\**

The last hour whizzes by and Joanna's startled when the train's loudspeaker shrieks: *La Spezia*, the station Joanna has on her paper of instructions to change for the *Cinque Terre* local. She rushes to gather her things, nearly hits someone with her guitar as she leaps off the train. Though it's very hot on the platform, she feels a chill. The sound of Italian and versions of Luca's face—his dark eyes, his curly hair—seem to be everywhere. She can't help but remember how it felt waiting at the harbor for the ship to return from the Caribbean. The *Leonardo da Vinci*. The first glance of him, his face brown from the sun, his *ciao bella* breathless with excitement. Larger-than-life and so unlike anyone she'd ever met.

## LUCA OF THE SEA, 1976

Who am I this dark wintry day? Not who Leo, my boss, sees as he rushes toward me, seducing me with his eyes. "Guess where you're going to represent our Anchor Travel agency? Though you hardly look the part."

He's right. I'm a question mark of fear in the seething quicksand of living. But Leo is worse, with his belly hanging to his knees.

"This is good news." He laughs. "You hate winter. It's warm where I'm sending you. Here." He hands me a wad of bills. "Go buy some sexy clothing."

Twenty-one years old, and those words creep along my skin. Sexy—ugh. Makes me more ashamed than I already am. Though it's my seductive voice that got me this job, I hate all that wormy, girly stuff. I hate when the sleazy businessmen come in person to meet the voice they love. Ironic that I, who yearn to be a singer yet panic in public, have an appealing voice when unseen.

Leo leans back on his heels. "I don't know if I should do this. Send you off for eleven days to the Caribbean on the *Leonardo da Vinci* with a hundred Italian crewmen. Mmm, mmm." He hands me a brochure of the cruise with everyone flashing the cheap smile we're trained to believe is what happiness looks like. Yet I can't deny I'm thrilled to go—anything to get away from my lonely life in New York.

"What if my professors won't reschedule my exams?"

Leo quickly writes why I must go on the official agency paper. "Here," he says. "They won't say no." Then he hands me another wad of bills. "Buy some new shoes as well."

All my music professors smile a *lucky you,* sign the paper, and reschedule my midterm exams. It's with my geology professor, Mr. Karpel, the course I'm taking to fulfill requirements for my music therapy degree, that I feel guilty, as if betraying the cause of protecting the earth by going on a cruise. After every class, I linger to listen to him those few extra moments as he expands on his vision of the earth and nature, and the wrong road we humans are on. Watching his large rock-holding hands move excitedly as he speaks, I feel certain there's a purpose in my existence, a reason I am here.

Surprisingly, he signs the paper. "Years from now," he laughs, "you won't remember anything you've learned here, but you'll remember the cruise."

"I . . . I love your class."

"I know," he says, "still, you won't remember it."

\*\*\*

With everything rescheduled, I'm high from the excitement of going away. And my mother, Lillian, what a mood she's in! Like she's the one going off, rounding up clothing from friends she hasn't seen in ages. She opens a bottle of bubbly as we fashion-show the clothing: a strapless evening gown with matching shawl, a chiffon negligee and matching robe that twirls in ripples as I turn, and sequin slippers. I want to bring everything and pack two huge suitcases.

The day arrives and my mother drives me and my bulging suitcases to the *Leonardo da Vinci*. She's thrilled when the captain invites her to join us in the special room set up for *me*, the travel agent who will sell the cruise, with roses and chilled champagne and tiny sandwiches too beautiful to eat. God only knows how much champagne she guzzles with the stunning Italian crewmen refilling her glass to overflowing again and again. When the captain comes to escort her off the ship, she looks perplexed, as if *she's* the one meant to stay. I secretly wish she could. Though my mother drives me mad with her alcoholic moods and demands, she'd know how to behave in this context, despite never having been on a cruise. I have no idea; the entire show of social interaction terrifies me. Once my mother's gone, I feel a sinking hole and rush to the outer deck with the other passengers and spot Lillian, both of us crying hysterically like we're in the saddest movie. I wave until she's a tiny speck, and when I can't stop crying, it hits me that I've never been away from her more than a few days. *What's wrong with me?* rumbles through my head. I should be thrilled to be on this cruise, not dreading the task ahead. Just thinking of representing the agency, of having to act normal and adult for eleven consecutive days, sends me into a tizzy. I'm about to panic when, suddenly, the Statue of Liberty looms before me. So close, I can almost reach out and touch her face. Her eyes are filled with compassion; she understands how scary it is to be judged, how easy to get it wrong. I try to keep her in sight as long as I can. When my neck is about to snap, I turn and face the prow and gasp at the vast undulating sea. I grab hold of the rail, not trusting my impulses, until my fingers turn white with cold, then slip unnoticed through the hallways to my cabin.

    I want to unpack to ground myself, but one of the porters has already done it. Puffed up my pillows, turned back the sheets, spread the chiffon nightgown on the bed with the waistline tucked in the middle like someone sophisticated is lying there. *A hint of how I'm meant to be!* I grab this impostor, this negligee, place it against me, and dance a stupid dance around the room. I must become her—*a woman!* I fall to the bed, let the nightgown slip to the ground. *I can't do this!* But I must. I must pull myself together; there's no getting off the ship now, no going back. I am stuck here for eleven days.

    I force myself up and into one of the new dresses bought with Leo's money, the sleek peach wraparound, and the new beige high-heel strapless pumps that I practice walking in, as I rarely wear heels.

I put in the dangling gold earrings and twist my auburn hair into a bun to look older. I hardly ate the last few days and feel slimmer. With my shoulders back and down, I set out to explore the ship.

It's enormous, with dining halls, salons, and shops, and all the cabins divided into five decks. There's a swimming pool with lounge chairs set up like a beach. Most of the passengers seem ancient and startled to see a young woman alone on a costly cruise. I don't wear a badge, so my job isn't obvious. I begin to enjoy how the passengers and crew are curious. I strut with false confidence until a swift jerk of the ship knocks me flat. Mortified, I crawl to the nearest rail and pull myself up.

The sea has settled when they announce dinner. At my assigned table, I'd imagined meeting incredibly interesting characters, like in a Hemingway novel. But the passengers are stiff and boring. Except Stella, the live wire at the table. Way older than my mother, but she says she doesn't feel a day over thirty. She makes fun of all the people at our table in a husky, comic voice, like Joan Rivers. "Just because they dress up in a fancy gown, they're still their same dreary selves." She's been on this ship many times since her husband passed away, because of the crew, she says. "Where else could I afford all this pampering from such *gorgeous* men? I don't really care where we're headed, only that we get there slowly. Very slowly."

We hit some swell, and I'm about to fall over again when Stella grabs my arm and helps me balance. "Come," she says, leading us to the nearest bar. We slip onto the steadfast barstools with a railing beneath that I grasp. The ship dips and rises like a living thing.

"Two whiskey and sodas on the rocks, if you please," Stella orders.

She hands me my drink. I hesitate. "I've never tasted whiskey before," I tell her.

"Then sip it slowly. Everything slowly." The ship pulls strong to the right, and my stomach lurches. "Drink," she says. "It helps. You have to embrace the rocking, my dear. Don't fight it."

We sip our cocktails until the swell calms; then I follow

Stella outside. We gasp aloud at the blaze of stars, the night air crisp and pure.

"It's wondrous!" Stella says. "I never tire of this first day leaving New York. Sailing past Liberty and into this, this majestic sea, this spectacular night sky, the gentle spray like soft kisses. Ha!" She sighs deeply. "Don't look at me like that. I'm not dead yet. Oh, listen... the music has started. Do you like to dance? I do."

We head back in and rush to the ballroom, to the edge of the dance floor where she gets swept away instantly. The room is straight out of a Fred Astaire movie, with gold curtains and sparkling chandeliers. I watch silver-haired men dance. They look great, like the best at Roseland Ballroom in New York where I sometimes go. Then I too get asked to dance, and when my partner feels I can follow, he ups his lead, and we're soon swirling across the floor. After a few rhumbas and foxtrots, Stella takes my hand and leads me to the bar.

"Don't waste your time with those oldsters. You gotta meet my favorite of the crew. Marco!" She waves at a strikingly handsome officer with piercing blue eyes. He rushes over, says her name like a song, and lifts her hand delicately to his lips. "Wonderful to see you again. *Come stai?*"

"I am very fine, thank you, Marco." She turns toward me like I'm a gift she's brought especially for him. "And *this* is Joanna."

He has what my mother calls bedroom eyes. The way he gazes at me, sensually undressing me, sending ripples through my body. He takes my hand to his lips. I don't want to feel what I feel, don't want to like it, and quickly pull my hand back. He looks slightly insulted but intrigued. The moment he's left us, I feel him searching me out but try to ignore him. Stella nudges. "I can tell he likes you. He's the best, if you get him and if he's free."

"What do you mean?" I ask.

"They all take turns on the watch," she says. "Four hours on, four hours off. They keep rotating, so you never know who'll be free on any evening. And for the rest"—Stella scrunches her face in a scowl—"you know exactly what I mean."

That's just it; I'm not sure I do. Years of witnessing my mother's fiascos with men makes me squeamish. I've had sex but still don't get what the fuss is about. Yet, I can't deny the hot currents that shiver through me as Marco holds his gaze. Luckily, I get asked to dance and dissolve into the undulating world of music and the swish of my fabulous new dress.

When next I look, someone new is standing at the entrance. Mysterious and intense, his curly hair falling to his collar. He seems on fire. Our eyes meet, and he doesn't cheaply undress me with his eyes like Marco had; rather, he searches through me as if he's waited forever to find me—only me.

And then he disappears.

## 2.

## CINQUE TERRE, 2002

THE TRAIN FROM La Spezia thunders in and out of tunnels as it weaves through the mountains. It pulls in at the first three of the Cinque Terre towns—Riomaggiore, Manarola, Corniglia—then screeches to a stop at the fourth of the *five lands* in Vernazza. With trepidation, Joanna walks down the staircase of the station. Smack in the middle of the cutest town she's ever seen. More than she hoped for, she exhales a huge sigh of relief. Bathed in a golden light, a labyrinth of narrow streets and pastel-colored houses weave down to the sea. Not a single car on the too-narrow streets, and from every window, laundry hangs like impressionistic art. Nearly every house has rooms for rent, yet with the train blasting through the station every fifteen minutes, she explores streets farther away.

With less light but noticeably quieter, she finds a simple studio with a desk, bed, and tiny kitchen. The room feels snug and safe, and she books it for a week. She drops off her things and hurries out to explore before it gets dark. Just as she turns the key, a wave of anxiety hits, and she rushes inside to check everything, including the stove. Her hands tremble as she locks the door again, checking several times that the key is safe inside her knapsack.

*Come on,* she urges herself. *You can do this.* She wishes the Italian woman who'd told her about this place could be here. Longing for that sense of acceptance she felt in her presence, Joanna's eyes smart with tears. She thinks of what that prophetic woman had asked—whether she ever sang for herself, and not just for work.

"Not really," Joanna had said. The last time she'd allowed a real depth and gusto into her voice had been with Luca, a million years ago.

"Then you must. You must walk and sing until it doesn't hurt anymore." With a soft murmur, as if granting a wish, the woman continued, "In the hills, you can find paths where no one will hear you. Sing for the trees and the sky, sing your feelings, just for yourself. It's our singing voice that shows who we really are."

Emerging from her tiny street into the square, she's stunned by the amount of people. In the short time since she arrived, the town is now overflowing and giddy with celebration. Cafés are filling with meticulously dressed people, mostly Italians, as she overhears their excited and loud conversations. It seems there are many Americans as well, young and old, more casually dressed. At window-like bars, a rougher crowd hangs out—raisin-skinned fisherman, boatmen, and farmers dusty and tired and relieved for the day's end. And all the pedestrians pouring in from the vertiginous surroundings energizes the town. Faces sweaty and glowing from sun and exertion, boots covered in dust. Boots, Joanna keeps noticing, not sneakers. Curious if she'll manage with what she has, she stops one friendly walker and inquires. The woman assures her sneakers will do.

"If you've just arrived, you'll want to take a quick peek before sunset," the woman says, pointing to the opposite side of the square from where she'd come. "Just follow the signs up a bit. It's worth a look. If you're planning to stay, I recommend starting with this side." She points again to the left. "The other goes to Monterosso, more beautiful but brutal, with a ton of steps up and down. The beach is great, so take a bathing suit if you go, but I'd start with the path to Corniglia so your legs get adjusted." Joanna thanks her and heads in the direction she recommended.

The climb is steep, but her sneakers do fine on the gravel and small stones. Not in her best shape, she stops often to catch her breath. Up and up she goes, conscious of the waning light, but she can't turn back, not yet. With each step, the breathtaking views expand into lush, undulating mountains; the sparkling blue sea all around and the intricate web of Vernazza and the other Cinque Terre towns dangle in the distance like jewels off the mountain.

Alone on the trail in the tender light, she thinks of those old biddies, her favorites from the nursing home, and how they told Joanna, now a widow like them, that she'd soon be speaking aloud to her husband. She hadn't felt ready before, but now she cautiously tries.

"Stuart?" She waits to hear a strand of his voice in return, but there's nothing, just the whoosh of the wind off the sea. Maybe as in life, Stuart needed to be alone, and not hearing him is a good sign. That she'd been a good wife after all, or good enough. Most of the time, she'd left him to do his work, his climate-change work. She hopes now, in death, he won't mind communicating more. How she longs to hear him, that deep, resonant voice he never lost.

As the path flattens and the twilight softens the sharp contours, she stops to pick up a rock. A layered rock of many elements, the kind Stuart loved to study. He lived for the touch of the earth, the feel of dirt, soil, the sand of creation. She'd been his student. His unwavering conviction and the timbre of his voice had ignited her. He who'd changed the course of her destiny, would he guide her now with an invisible touch? Can she sense him with her as present as the ancient path beneath her feet? Suddenly, she feels a gust of wind across her lower back, like a gentle, supportive hand. Like the way he'd give a gentle push on their hikes when she grew tired.

"Stuart. That's you. I know it's you." With a sharp sting of regret, tears blur her vision. "Forgive me . . . forgive me for—" She's not ready to name it and can only whisper, "I promise, I'll get your book finished."

She shudders to think of the huge stack of papers just where he'd left it. He'd been writing at his desk. She thought he was sleeping; he often fell asleep while working. She'd leave him and come back with a cup of tea and gently wake him. Except this time, he didn't wake. After they'd taken him away, she couldn't go near that room, that desk, that daunting manuscript—his treatise on actions needed to prevent the worst of climate change—reminding her not just of his sudden death but his inability at the end to find the right words, he who always had the words. He'd never asked her to finish the manuscript, but then he hadn't planned on dying. The heart attack came out of the blue; one moment, in the full of life, a fit seventy-five, and the next moment gone.

The sound of distant church bell startles her to the present. She turns to head back and gasps when seeing the sky, ablaze with reds and golds so brilliant, it grabs all her attention. And then she, who barely had any appetite for months, is starving. With her stomach growling, she hurries back along the path and down the myriad steps into town.

*\*\*\**

The evening is warm and balmy. Lively restaurants line the harbor with everyone outside eating, drinking, and laughing. Yet the idea of sitting alone with all the joyful couples and families seems too much, so she enters a small street tucked behind the church and finds a simple *osteria*, a place for the locals to eat without fuss. She sits at a tiny corner table and orders a bowl of minestrone, a simple pasta and salad, and a glass of local white wine. When it comes, this Vermentino, it is so delicious, she drinks it down and orders another. How long has it been that she's sat by herself enjoying a drink? A delicate buzz comes over her, and she takes out her diary, like a companion, to tell it all to. When the food arrives, she savors each delicious bite. She has to get used to this, this taking her time. Her bill comes, and she pays it, then goes back out and joins the crowd, strolling up and down the main street, licking cones of gelato. Back and forth with the flow until the crowd starts thinning, and then, as if by curfew, the street suddenly empties. The restaurants shut, the cafés close, the steady soundtrack of the train ebbs, yet she keeps walking, the air still balmy like a caress, and if she could bypass going to bed, when Stuart's absence feels most acute, she'd keep walking till dawn.

The next morning Joanna dresses quickly, grabs her diary and sunglasses, and goes out into the bright and now again-busy streets. Tons of hikers off for their strenuous walks, and tourists heading for trains and boats to other towns along the famous coast. The sound of *Buongiorno! Ciao!* is everywhere, and the scent of freshly baked bread, *cornetti*, roasted coffee, and the aromas of the restaurants preparing for lunch swirl between the ancient walls. Captivated by the theatrics, she searches for a viewing spot to sit where she can take it all in. She sees a stoop of brick steps overlooking the harbor where people sit with their espressos. She orders a cappuccino, happily plunks herself down, and takes out her diary. Perhaps it's the smell of the sea, the delightful entertainment around her, and the good night's rest that makes the coffee taste more delicious than ever. She lets her pen rest on the blank page, not wanting to write, not wanting to miss one moment. *Basta!* she thinks, smiling to remember an Italian word. All those years ago when she tried learning Italian for Luca, *basta* was one of the few words she remembers. *Enough with words!* She just wants to look and smell and float in this sense of wonder.

\*\*\*

The week flows by, and she settles into a sweet rhythm—each morning at the brick stoop with her diary and a cappuccino, then a long hike in the afternoons. The hottest time, but the trails are less crowded then and she can try her voice here and there in little humming tones, a beginning. Every day the locals greet her with friendly smiles, happy she's still there, as most tourists only stay a few days. Approving of how she distances herself from the noisier, young Americans, with their shrill conversations and seemingly endless means. She's learned from some locals who speak English that ever since the tour guide, Rick Steves, raved about Vernazza, the place has become a zoo. They need tourists, but not *that* many, and some they like more than others. Which makes her more and more protective of this little paradise.

She becomes resentful when, during her evening ritual at a tiny unfrequented nook by the harbor, an unruly crowd of youngsters upsets the whole vigil. It's been so peaceful here all week, with the waiter already knowing her order, and with a nod bringing her a chilled glass of Vermentino and a bowl of tiny Ligurian olives. The other patrons are, like her, enjoying the peaceful meditation of the setting sun. There are tons of boisterous cafés. *Why do they come here?* The waiter swiftly puts three tables together and sets up the chairs while Joanna discreetly slides her table away. She can't stop watching them, her annoyance escalating at how they order one at a time, making the waiter work harder. One of the young men, with a loud nasal voice, rushes to the edge of the water and dramatically tosses his gum. "It doesn't matter what you throw in here; the Mediterranean is already filthy!"

Goodness, she wants to slap him. Like an old righteous woman. Hot tears spring to her eyes. She's been doing so well. *Why did this annoying crowd come here? They never come here.* Why is she so intolerant? But she is and she can't stand to be there a moment more.

She walks a few rounds between the station and harbor, calming down. On the third round, she hears a friendly whistle and recognizes one of the local patrons from the osteria where she eats each night. He waves so welcomingly from the window-bar to come have a drink that she impulsively joins him. He orders her a Vermentino, and when it comes, he raises his glass in toast. He gets back to a lively conversation in Italian with his mates, and she gratefully loses herself in the music of the language, catching a word here or there that she understands. She offers to buy him a drink, which he declines, and she says the ubiquitous *ciao* and leaves for the osteria for dinner. When an hour later this same man arrives there with an even bigger smile for her, she realizes the foolish thing she's done. *Should never have accepted the drink.* She quickly signals for the check. *Oh no*, his body language indicates, *you can't leave yet. You must have another drink with me.*

She declines his offer, pays for her meal, and gets up. But he is adamant and gestures with his hands that it doesn't work like that. Within seconds, a fresh glass of wine appears.

"*No grazie*," she says, explaining with her limited Italian and gestures that she's had enough, that she's hiked several hours and is very tired. Now the man doesn't look so friendly. He shakes his head, sucks in his lips, and makes a clicking sound with his tongue as if to say, *You can't first say yes and then say no.* Then it hits her; Italians are never alone. Even on the walks, they're always in groups. The lone walkers are from other countries. She has aroused suspicion. All those friendly smiles she's imagined welcoming her, maybe they thought she was looking for a man, and now at last she's chosen one. She's been there long enough to notice the widows in black, waiting, sitting, looking out the windows. Her style of grieving, by gallivanting all over the mountainside like a goat, is not the norm. That she's living her Italian fantasy, has stayed longer than the usual tourist, doesn't exempt her from the rules of this traditional society, rules she didn't even know.

## LUCA OF THE SEA, 1976

By the third morning on the *Leonardo da Vinci*, I'm finally getting used to the rock and sway of the ship, but not to all the drinking. I never drink this much. With my head pounding, I get a brilliant idea to jog around the top deck. It's going well until the fifth round, when I nearly throw up. Peevish and green, I stagger down to the pool deck and order a ginger ale. Stella, lounging nearby, has watched the whole thing. Laughing, she pats the lounge chair next to hers, signaling for me to join her.

"What were you thinking," she asks, "circling the top deck like a mad seagull? Of course you feel sick."

"I had to clear my head," I moan, "and get some exercise."

She gives a lewd look. "There are better means, my dear. You're a foolish thing. Marco would have taken good care of you. Instead, you spend your time swooning over that moody fella. You're not going to have much fun with *him*." I fling my arms across my chest defiantly.

A few minutes later she nudges me. "Hey, guess who's looking for you." She points to the higher deck, where the man of my dreams is holding onto the rail. For an intense instant, our eyes meet. Then he's gone. A moment later he appears on our deck but walks right past me. A thousand knives stab at my heart.

"Boy, does he like you," Stella says, letting her glasses slide down her nose. I turn to her, perplexed. "Of course, he likes you. Why else strut past like a peacock? Men! Why doesn't he just say hello and ask to meet you later? I'd be careful with him. At least with Marco you know what you get, and he won't bother you once the cruise is finished. What's he called, this new one?"

"Luca," I say. It's the first time I've said his name aloud. "He's one of the navigators. He told me last night."

"He seems awfully young." Stella pushes her sunglasses back up with a smirk, like she'd never trust him for a second. I slink down in despair.

"Don't get all temperamental. If you want him, you can have him. Look around. You see anyone else your age? These men don't have that much to do. Half of their job is to pamper us. You're the most fun they're going to get. Enjoy the game!"

"The game?"

"Yes, *the game*. Don't you know anything? Jeez, Louise."

*It can't be a game! I've never felt this alive.*

After dinner, I'm watching Stella dance when Luca appears. He beckons me to follow him outside. I'm so excited, I can hardly breathe.

"Do you mind that I don't dance?" he asks, lighting a cigarette. "When you work this ship, you hear the same songs over and over."

"That's okay," I say, trying not to show my disappointment. If we could dance, we'd be closer. I so want to touch him. His broad shoulders, his sculpted hands tanned from the sun, the way his hair laps over his ears and curls onto the collar of his starched white shirt, his navy-blue uniform. The power he contains. Unable to keep still, I weave around Isadora Duncan-style. He grabs me in my hysterical pirouette so I don't fall overboard, then lets me go and puts his hands back into his pockets.

"You are a crazy girl," he says. "Let's go to the bridge. I will show you where I work." He takes out an impressive ring of keys from his pocket, like the keys to the world. When he grabs my hand, I again can't breathe. We climb higher and higher to the top of the ship, to the bridge, then outside to the highest point on the ship, the top of the world so it seems, to the roar of mast and rope, to a maze of stars so bright, so close. I reach my arm out like I could touch them but then get dizzy with vertigo and pull my arm back.

"Are you scared?" Luca asks, laughing. "I won't let you fall." He wraps his arms around me but doesn't kiss me. That's probably good. I'd explode if he kissed me. "It doesn't matter where we are born," Luca says with a luscious voice, the vowels slow and deep. "You are my soulmate, my other half." He sings in beautiful, broken

English. "We are the same, you and me. We are not of this world."

That he sees me, really sees me, is the most wonderful feeling in the world. And I believe him! My body tingles as he stares right through me, weaving us together.

"You feel me," he says. "And you feel *this*." He again stares deeply into me, like he needs first to make love to my spirit. "I can see the stars in your eyes."

A miracle to let someone see me and not feel ashamed, me who's always ashamed, always changing myself to please the other. I can be fully in his gaze, in his love, with no need to pull myself back or change anything. I throw my arms around him, holding him so tight that soon we're one body breathing.

"But," I cry, for this is too good to be true, "the world will find us and stop us and take this away."

"Not here," Luca says. "They won't find us here."

# 3.

## CINQUE TERRE, 2002

AFTER A GORGEOUS week in Vernazza, the rain comes and with it a wrenching feeling, raw and unsettling. Tentatively, Joanna opens the curtain. A gray chill creaks through the window as the rain pours steadily down. No doubt the dry Mediterranean needs rain, but without sun there'll be no sitting at her stoop, no lively morning of distraction, no long walk or swim. She crawls under the covers, shivers from the damp, and aches something fierce for Stuart. She can't sense his hand on her back, that reassuring hand she's felt every day. Even if she did, it's not enough. Her anxiety mounts like something terrible is about to happen. *Come on, come on*, she convinces herself, remembering she's taken care of everything back in New York. Paid someone to keep an eye on her apartment and water the plants, but she gasps; no one is looking after her mother. *I should go home.*

She lugs herself out of bed, determined to shed this mood. She puts on her warmest clothing, her skimpy summer jacket draped over her head as an umbrella, and makes her way through the empty, rain-drenched streets. Vernazza seems abandoned and totally unsuited for inclement weather. In a bizarre attempt to stay calm, she rips a bit of paper from her diary and rolls it into a makeshift cigarette. Never a smoker, she does this at times of stress. The deep inhale, the sucking and holding of breath, and the slow exhalation soothes. She paces along the harbor, puffing on her imaginary cigarette, waiting for the doors of her regular café to open.

With the rain, the staff is busy setting up the inside dining room. A waiter recognizing her points to a small table against the wall. She wishes she could speak with him like a friend, off-load the silly happenstance from last evening with the fisherman, maybe help in the kitchen. She needs something to do. Suddenly, being a tourist seems banal and useless. She's fidgety, feels like making a scene. She puts her fingers to her lips, continuing the pretext of smoking, trying like mad to calm herself. She takes out her diary and writes furiously, then scratches out everything. The waiter comes, and she orders a cup of steamed milk, still too jumpy for coffee. He rushes back with the milk and looks questioningly at her, like maybe she's sick. Who drinks a cup of hot milk in Italy? That horrible feeling of being a kite in the wind with no one holding the string. She's losing it. With Stuart, she lived a tight ship. Everything scheduled. No downtime. *Ever.* That was the key. It's her fault she never learned to be in her own skin.

She keeps taking desperate peeks at the waiter, then looking away. He smiles seductively as if inquiring if she might want more than hot milk this morning. She drops her head and squirrels her hands through her hair, then scribbles in her diary:

*This is Italy; this is what the men do. The way Luca had looked at you so long ago. You want that, you still want that, that hungry eating through to the soul, the joining together. You are so homesick . . . but if you keep looking at the waiter with your needy, dog eyes, he will assume you want more.*

"Is anyone sitting here?" a woman with an American accent asks. Joanna jerks in her chair. "Sorry, I didn't mean to startle you. This looks like the only table free to have coffee. I'm dying for a cappuccino. I have a book to read, so I won't disturb you."

Joanna tries to suppress her delight that this woman has suddenly appeared. "It's free. Yes, please have a seat."

"Don't let me stop you writing." The woman signals to the waiter.

Joanna knows she's too excited. This hole inside her. She counts one more second, then responds as normally as she can muster, "It's just a diary. I've been writing all morning."

"I'd be happy to write in mine," the American says, pulling a small notebook from her knapsack. She flashes the empty pages. "You see, nothing! Zilch. I carry it everywhere, but I never write. Much easier to talk."

"Yes. Talking is easier." Not true for Joanna, but she can't help herself, like being thrown a life raft. "Until today, the weather's been so good," Joanna says, apologizing as if it's her fault.

"I don't mind the rain. In fact, I love it." The woman's voice is boisterous, not at all concerned how it punctures the air around her. Yet, Joanna is grateful for this sudden arrival. This strong personality, her blond curls bouncing around a freckled face, blue eyes sparkling with mischief and daring. "I've had endless sun for months now. It's killing my skin. I used to live in California and now Greece."

"So why did you come here, to Italy?"

"For green. It's much greener here, and the wine, and, well, a change. My name's Terry."

"I'm Joanna, and—"

"Is it okay to be a woman alone here?" Terry goes on, looking around at the still empty restaurant.

"I'm not completely sure." Joanna shrugs. "My diary's been a sort of cover."

"Are you recently divorced?" Terry asks, tapping her chest. "Like me."

"No. I'm a . . . my husband just passed. Well, actually six months ago, but it still feels recent."

"Oh, I'm sorry. You don't look like a widow. I hope it's not like Greece here, where all the widows sit like black crows. Well, whatever, I sure need to talk to someone who *really* speaks English or I'm going to lose my mind."

"Me too!" *Did I create this person? Is she really sitting there?*

"Don't you wish you could switch places with someone, like maybe that waiter—he looks content—for like a day?"

"Or forever," Joanna says.

"Probably not forever. Eventually we'd be homesick for ourselves."

"Maybe." Joanna sighs, relieved her anxious mood is lifting. She wants Terry to keep talking. It's like watching a movie, the best distraction from a lost self. "Did you leave the US because of your divorce?"

"You could say so," Terry says. "The divorce was the kick I needed, that's for sure. I left before September eleventh, and I'm glad I did. Not sure if I would have managed to get away afterward. I had tried to go home when it happened, but there weren't any flights, and then I kept staying. I felt safe in my little village. It's so cheap there, and my money stretches like mozzarella. I'd never been away this long. With my husband, we'd do those package deals where you'd whiz through ten European cities in a week. The amount of money we spent, Jesus, I live on that for months now. That's why I've treated myself to a little holiday in Italy." She stops and smiles at Joanna. "It's been good though, being away from the US. Even before the divorce, I was fed up with everything, just didn't know it. Probably why my husband left me."

Terry takes a long sip of her cappuccino and licks the foam from her lips. Her hands touch the wooden table as if to appraise it. "My ex, he still craves all those nice things. He even found himself a Barbie doll of a wife, or so I've heard from my kids." Terry shakes her body as if covered in a swarm of bees. "My husband is obsessed with making sure no one has more than he has. It's exhausting, like a dog chasing his tail. Have you ever watched a dog do that? It can drive you mad. Chasing his tail but never catching it." Terry thrashes her arms in a circle, nearly hitting the passing waiter. "I was pissed off I didn't even *know* my husband was having an affair. I mean really, is that not the cliché of clichés? You can fool yourself for a while when it all looks good on the outside. He did me a favor, I suppose, and I've never been happier, even when I'm angry. At least I know it's *my* anger."

"You must be furious with him," Joanna says, enjoying Terry's life growing wild and sumptuous around her. She doesn't mind that it's still pouring, that they're stuck inside, the rain like a gift.

"To be honest," Terry says, "I don't know half the time what I'm furious about. So much a part of me. My plan, if I even have a plan, is to try to live more simply." Joanna thrills at such words. *Maybe Terry will stay and we can find this simplicity together.* "But there's hardly anything to consume in my village in Greece, so I'm not sure it counts. It's changing there too; the capitalistic paradigm is irresistible. It's like you first have to eat way too much; then you can push away your plate. Speaking of which, I'm starving. It smells great here. Have you eaten here?"

"Not yet," Joanna says. "I usually have a cappuccino outside, but I still feel, you know, strange, eating alone in the busier restaurants. All those sorrowful looks."

"Takes time to get used to, you know, being alone. Maybe that's why I talk so loud. I'm overcompensating, like I'm two people. Just like how I've been hogging this conversation."

"No, it's great, honestly. I don't have that much to say."

"You'll be surprised, just wait. It's like you become a dam, and when the river has a chance to flow again, it gushes. The hardest part is being away from my kids. I really miss them. Do you have any?"

"No. I never had kids, but I can imagine."

"They're in their twenties, so don't think I left them high and dry. It's just having the chance to live my own life, not serving their every need, has done us *all* good. I keep wondering what I did to make them so demanding and self-centered. It's easier to give them what they want."

Joanna feels the urge to tell Terry about her reaction to the noisy crowd last night, but she doesn't want to stop Terry's flow. If she stays, there'll be enough time to share. "At least you can see it," Joanna says.

"Yeah, that and fifty cents, and I can get a coffee! That's an old joke. What does fifty cents even buy these days?" Terry laughs and her face softens, revealing how pretty she is. "Sometimes I make a ritual of my suffering. Go high into the hills behind the village in Greece and scream. I tell you, it feels great. I don't know why the doctors don't prescribe that! Have a day off to go in the hills and scream."

*To scream*? Joanna thinks. Joanna's just finding courage to sing again. Maybe she should find an empty path and let it rip. Could she dare?

"Do you think you'll stay for a bit?" Joanna blurts. "I've found some empty trails. You could have a good scream there."

"Who knows. No plans yet," Terry says, eyeing her watch. "These smells are to die for! Aren't you starving?" Not waiting for an answer, Terry signals the waiter, with her shoulders curling seductively. He flashes a generous Italian smile and sets their table.

The lunch ends up being a huge meal since Terry wants to try many dishes. She insists on paying as compensation for Joanna's attentiveness. "Do you know how much I'd pay a therapist in California for such devoted listening?" she says, eating with gusto, ordering more glasses of wine. When they finish, the rain has stopped, and the day is brightening.

"Could we do one of the walks you spoke about?" Terry asks once they're out in the sunshine. She's unsteady and holds onto the brick steps, the place where Joanna usually sits. "Is there an easy one we can do tipsy?"

Joanna smiles. "Sure."

***

The sun pours down, and vapor rises from the old cobblestones. Water runs in small brooks and splashes along the funneled sides of the quaint streets. Everything sparkles, freshly cleaned.

"God, it's beautiful," Terry says over and over, like a refrain in a pop song. Joanna doesn't mind. The afternoon with Terry has made her feel normal again. She rarely feels this comfortable around women her own age and delights in this ease. The duo walk the trail to Corniglia, slowly, until the sun begins to set. They return to town and keep talking by the harbor until the church bell strikes nine chimes.

Terry looks at her watch. "Wow! I can't believe how many hours we've been together, but I really have to go . . . haven't even unpacked."

Before departing, they arrange to meet at ten the next day and hike to the beach. When Terry leaves, Joanna watches after her until she turns the crooked street and disappears.

## LUCA OF THE SEA, 1976

The *Leonardo da Vinci* anchors by the harbor of Martinique, the first port of call, and Luca is free to come with me. The moment I step from the tender to the wooden pier, I fall over. After all the days on the undulating ship, my legs forgot how to balance on solid ground. "Some sailor you are!" Luca jokes and helps me up. "Come quickly. There'll be a long queue for taxis."

We arrive at a breathtakingly beautiful beach with not another soul in sight. Luca pays and tells the driver when to come back. He appears incredibly important in his pressed white uniform, the one for outside use, brilliant in the sunshine. The turquoise water laps onto the white coral sand, soft and sensuous. He removes his shoes, and I do the same. Then he takes my hand, and we run along the shore until the silky sand shifts, and we fall, because we want to. We fold into each other's arms and finally kiss. I, who spent my youth watching movies while babysitting, who learned to French-kiss alone by imitating the actors, practicing on the neighbor's vinyl couch while their children slept, never imagined love this good. And for a thousand years or so it feels, we kiss.

He still hasn't seen my body, and I tentatively unwrap my tie-dyed skirt to the bikini beneath. Shy to be so exposed, I get up and run into the water. He strips off his uniform to his bathing suit and follows me in. In the calm water, he gathers me in his arms. No need for words. Just kisses and strokes and the unbelievable swell of love between us. Such happiness makes me wild and unsettled, and I dive under the water to slip away. He swims after me and catches me, and we kiss and fondle for another thousand years. I'm about to explode and again swim away. We play like this, belly-to-belly, undulating, and I'd have gladly turned into a dolphin and lived with him in those tranquil waters forever.

"Why," I ask later, as the sun begins to wane, "must the time go so fast?"

"Ah," Luca says, gesticulating with his hand. "*La vita* . . . the life."

I love when he says, *the life.* I think he means *that's life*, but I prefer his translation. I start to feel he means more than just daily life, like a magic door leading us to our real selves. Mostly, I'm too shy to look anyone straight in the eyes, but I do with Luca. I look right into him while he stares deeply into me. His dark brown eyes become large, and his face opens. "Joanna," he says, "please do not worry. . . . You must never worry. I am here, and I love you. Do you have any idea how long I've searched for you? Now that I have found you, I will never let you go." I'd follow him anywhere for this, this universe he's unraveling in me.

"*Bella, bella!*" he cries when we are back on the ship and in his bed. "Come closer." Though I am as close as a person can be. And when we finish (though we never really finish; I still feel him inside me), he shouts in his beautiful accent, "We shall be together until the end of time."

# 4.

## CINQUE TERRE, 2002

JOANNA WAKES LIKE a child, eager for the first trip to the beach after a long winter. She leaps out of bed, leans out the window, and smiles in delight to see the sky a perfect blue, not a cloud in sight. The warm breeze ruffles the curtains, and the scent of morning fills the room, all welcoming her: coffee and flowers, sage and lavender, and birdsong so lovely. For the first time in ages, instead of the howling ache for Stuart, she feels whole and ready to join the day.

The plan is to meet Terry for coffee at ten, do the walk to Monterosso, and spend the rest of the day at the beach. By the time Joanna weaves through the busy streets to her morning spot, it is well past ten, and Terry isn't there. *Is she an early bird? Has she already left?* Pretending all is well, Joanna sits on her stoop and opens her diary. But she keeps bobbing her head like a Chinese doll. Finally, she sees Terry, her face flushed from running.

"Sorry I'm late," she pants. "I haven't slept this much in ages. What a bed! I really splurged on my room here. My mattress in Greece is like a sack of potatoes. And I woke so hungry, and the smell of, what's it called—*focaccia*—it's to die for. I had to get some, but the line was, like, *so* long. Where did all these people come from? Here, have a bite. This one is with olives. God knows how many calories, but we're going to do a long walk today, right? There's time for a coffee?"

"Of course!"

"Cappuccino for you too?" Terry asks.

Joanna nods a happy yes.

"I love it here!" Terry says, returning with the coffees. She plunks herself down beside Joanna. "I wish they still built like this. Everything charming and close together, no need to drive. Jesus, in America you're sentenced to be a taxi driver for your kids. It's like the happiest day when they start driving. And the first thing you do is buy them a car."

"Manhattan, where I live, is better. My husband and I used to complain how most places in the US are set up so you have to drive."

"Like most of the world," Terry says, noisily enjoying the cappuccino. "God, this is so good! So what was he like, your husband?"

"He had an unusual way of seeing the world." Joanna stops for a moment, noticing a soft brush across her back.

"You're feeling him near you now, aren't you? Your face just changed."

Joanna nods, grateful that Terry confirms her experience. "He was a geology professor and environmentalist. I remember sitting on his lap, after we were married, while he told me about the earth, like a story. About the fossil fuels, and why it was so wrong to dig them up and burn them." She feels Stuart speaking through her, her voice growing deeper and more confident. "Plants used the sunlight to capture carbon from the atmosphere. Over millions and millions of years, this ancient plant life turned into fossil fuels and was stored deep in the earth. This process created a livable, breathable atmosphere perfect for animal and human life and a climate that's served us so well. Burning up these fossil fuels in a few centuries is like burning us back to an atmosphere and boiling-hot climate where life as we know it can't exist."

"Wow, you're really smart. I've never thought about it like this, though in truth I try not to think about these things."

Joanna feels her cheeks burn but awkwardly goes on. "Did you know that, once upon a time, the bicycle was used all over America, like in Holland and China? The oil industry did away with that. Bicyclists were fined if they were on the road . . . roads meant for cars only."

"Is that true?" Terry asks. "If you live in LA, you'd die without a car. It's so weird when you wonder what started what. And all the things you think you can't live without."

Terry stops eating and shoves the rest of the *focaccia* in the paper bag. "Sitting here, loving this town . . . maybe it isn't as grand as we think. Maybe it's great for us because we don't understand a word of Italian and can enjoy the best and leave when we want." Abruptly, she stops and smiles. "*He's* really cute."

"Who?" Joanna asks.

"The waiter over there, setting up in the next restaurant. A bit skinny, and probably fifteen years younger than me, but he's got those burning black eyes, oh my God *so* Italian."

Joanna hadn't seen him before. It was a much older man setting the tables up all week. This younger waiter dances as he works, making a show of juggling plates and silverware, sensually sweeping his black hair from his eyes. Terry can't take her eyes off him. Joanna is drawn to him as well. With the two women staring, the waiter smiles and runs over in a flash.

"Did you just arrive here?" he asks.

"No" and "Yes" come out at the same moment. Joanna lets Terry's *yes* ring louder.

"Do you also work dinners?" Terry asks with a voice Joanna hasn't heard before—breathy and high-pitched.

"Yes," he says. "It's my aunt's restaurant, and *o Dio* she works me too hard!" His hands wave through the air to show how much. Just then, an older woman charges out of the restaurant, arms flailing, her shrill voice indicating this isn't the first time her charming nephew has left his post to flirt with the ladies.

"My name is Gino, and that's my aunt, and I gotta go. Come tonight. Eight o'clock. I make a special table. *Ciao*!"

Joanna rubs her temples, feeling the start of a mean headache, and lets out a noisy sigh.

"Are you all right?" Terry asks. "I'd thought you'd like it. To try another restaurant, to not eat alone."

Joanna forces a smile. "Come on," she says. "Let's do the walk."

The first part is steep and narrow, and all focus goes to walking, single file. Terry is agog at the beauty and stops often to snap pictures as the landscape changes with each step. Joanna keeps steady on, like a stubborn tour guide. When the path flattens out, Terry catches up.

"What do you think he's like?"

"Who?"

"Gino, that charming waiter. Would one night do, or would he get under your skin? It's been slim pickings in Greece. God knows I could use a flirt." On and on she goes about his sumptuous limbs, his graceful hands, his intense gaze.

"I . . . uh . . ." Joanna exhales, wishing they'd never seen Gino.

"Sorry, crude of me. Ah man, I've been alone too long."

The path turns into an endless row of mounting steps, like a ladder, and with the sun baking down, it's too hot to talk. In the silence, Joanna recalls a story she'd heard at a yoga retreat about two monks on a pilgrimage. Along the way, the monks come to a gushing river. There stands a lady in distress, unable to cross. Without pause, one monk lifts the woman on his back and carries her to the other side of the river, then calmly puts her down and proceeds walking. Several hours later, the second monk can hold his tongue no longer.

"I can't believe you carried her! We made a solemn vow never to touch a woman."

"Yes, that's true," says the first monk. "I carried her ten minutes across the river, but you, my friend, have carried her for fifteen miles."

It infuriates Joanna to realize which monk *she* is. Terry could have Gino. No struggle, no competition. Yet, his being there has already come between them. Terry hasn't come to Italy just for the greenery and the wine.

Joanna walks ahead in a daze, slipping further into her own world, back to Stuart's funeral with all the people kissing her, giving condolences. To her own apartment with the smell of quiche, of bread and cheese and wine. Platters of sandwiches and salads and cakes, all so pretty, so well arranged.

Then it was over and everyone had left except Lillian, alone on the couch with her cigarette dangling. That dangling cigarette, the sign of her mother getting drunk, had infuriated Joanna. She had grabbed the cigarette and smashed it inside the paper cup of Lillian's wine.

"Hey," Lillian protested, like Joanna was a waitress in her local bar. "I wasn't finished."

"Mom. You promised."

*"Promises, promises, I'm all through with promises, promises now . . ."*

With the urge to slap her mother, Joanna had turned away. But Lillian's skinny arm had clutched her and pulled her back.

"Will you just talk to me? Will you just for once get me a nice glass of wine and talk to me? Stuart was a good man. I really am sorry, Joanna. No one deserves for their good man to go."

Joanna had walked to the cabinet, her body shaking. Stuart wasn't there to be the buffer. She had needed to negotiate her overly dramatic mother. She had gotten an open bottle of red and two glasses and brought them over.

"Here," Joanna had said. "I'll have a glass with you, okay?"

"It was always strange for me," Lillian had said, "that Stuart was older than me, but I liked it. Sometimes, just he and I . . . we could have a nice little exchange about the other times. He was good like that, your Stuart. He had time for a loser like me."

"Mom, you're not a loser. Why do you always say that?"

"Because it's true."

"Because Dad left us? You have to let that go."

"He didn't leave us," Lillian admonished with a solid voice Joanna hardly recognized.

"Do we need to talk about this now?"

"Your *real father*, he didn't leave us."

"My what?"

"I never told you."

"You've had a lot to drink."

"No, actually, for once in my life, I haven't. But I can't keep this in any longer. It's killing me."

"It's killing *you*?" Joanna had shrieked, putting down her wineglass as if any minute she would crush it with her hands. "What the hell are you talking about?"

"You have to understand. I was young. It was a different time. I ran away before he knew, before he even knew I was pregnant. We were better off without him. He was violent . . . dangerous." Lillian had taken a nervous drag of her cigarette, her shrillness meek. Joanna had suspected she was telling the truth. "Recently, I tried to find him, but he . . . because he . . . I never told you about him to protect you. I'm so sorry. He died a few years ago."

"So why are you telling me now?" Joanna had felt her voice, the voice she had always searched for but never found, roar in her chest. "What sort of twisted person tells her daughter this, at the funeral of her husband? You're a monster, that's what you are! No wonder most of my life I felt invisible. My so-called *father* in all those photos who you told me abandoned us when I was three, he never was my father, was he? Just one of your many boyfriends? God, I hate you!"

"Joanna, listen, please listen. How long does it take to make a baby? A few minutes. But to raise a child, that, my darling, takes everything you have. I was there for you. I've always been there for you." It was not convincing, had never been convincing, those words Joanna heard her whole life. Just because her disaster of a mother had failed to reveal this detail, Joanna had spent her entire life wondering why her supposed father never came to see her, never loved her, and why every goddam scene between a loving father and daughter makes her seasick with longing. The impulse to harm Lillian was so intense, she ran to the kitchen and drank glass after glass of water, as if washing away a curse. She didn't hear when her mother crept out of the apartment.

Deep in remembrance, Joanna jumps when Terry calls out, "Hey, is this the beach? It's great!"

Joanna nods, shaking out her fingers, still in tight little balls of rage from thinking of her mother. She's surprised how far they've come, the inviting Monterosso beach before them with a broad sandy beach and glistening water. Terry runs the rest of the way to the shore, strips to her bikini, leaves her things on the sand, and rushes into the sea. Joanna hesitates, then does the same. The water feels good, and she desperately needs to swim, to loosen the monstrous grip upon her. After several laps, Joanna looks out to the beach and spots Terry chatting with some travelers. She's laughing and holding a drink, without a care in the world. *Ugh*. Joanna sighs in disgust. If she can hardly bear herself, can she blame Terry for seeking other company?

## LUCA OF THE SEA, 1976

I am a painted pony on a merry-go-round that, instead of the normal up and down, only goes up! Higher and higher, into the stratosphere. This can't be okay; this is too much love. I yearn to speak to Stella, to ask her advice. But all she gives me is the evil eye, like I've broken a sacred code on the *Leonardo* by falling in love. She no longer saves a seat next to her in the dining room, instead chats merrily away with those monkey-brains at our table who I know she despises. Won't even look at me for a second. How can she have lived so long and still be so stupid? I thought there was a time when people finally learned. But then, I keep hoping the same with my mother. *Can't Stella understand what's happening? This isn't just some shipboard romance.*

I hardly eat. Just show up at mealtimes for a few bites and a chat with the captain, the piece I must do each day for my travel agency job, though for the rest, I hardly remember who I was before meeting Luca. The captain smiles graciously, seemingly approving of how slender and radiant I've become. The second he leaves, gawking ladies shoot me arrowheads of loathing. I wish everyone could get this kind of attention and not hate me. Especially Stella, so she could be my friend again.

Luca works the midnight-to-four shift, and he's still sleeping when I sneak out of his room for breakfast. I'm starving this morning but don't want to miss a second of being with him, so I run all the way there and all the way back. When I return, he is awake and beckons me into his arms.

"Where did you go?"

"To get food," I say and toss him a croissant and a banana. With a big smile, he covers me in croissant-flavored kisses.

He must work again for just a few hours. We agree to meet by the pool later. Stella is lounging there, reading. I sneak up on her.

"Is it a good book?" I ask.

"No," she says with a sinister stare. "But it was light, so I packed it."

"You never talk with me anymore." I try to sound mature, but my voice is a wimpy mouse.

"Ah, you've missed your Stella."

"Yes." I nod.

"We can't have everything now, can we?" She returns to her

book, but I don't go away.

"Will you go ashore today to visit Antigua?"

"Nah, I never leave the boat. I like it best with everyone gone. It's calm and quiet, and I have the waiters all to myself." Then she looks up. "Someone is waiting. Your moody sailor boy is ready to go. Nice to see you, dear. Have a lovely day."

I try to hug her, but she shoos me away.

\*\*\*

The beach on Antigua is even more astonishing than Martinique. Another magical, untouched place with not a soul in sight. The gentle breeze through the palm fronds feels like heavenly kisses, and the water and sand seem untouched. This flawless beauty, this perfect day, is a blessing and torment, for each moment with Luca is one moment closer to never seeing him again.

Just when I fear I shall cry and spoil the day, Luca takes my hand and leads me to the water's edge.

"Here," he says, handing me a stick. "Write your name in the sand." I carve JOANNA ever so slowly, ever so deeply. Luca does the same next to mine and then exclaims with noble certainty, "The sea shall swallow us and remember us forever. Do you believe me?"

The answer comes with all my heart. "Yes, yes!" It aches to watch the waves scoop the letters until nothing remains. Suddenly, I wish for the sea to take more than just our names. To take us entirely, for it won't be possible to be with Luca forever or live without him. Oh, to be like the lovers in the DH Lawrence story who bond eternally by drowning in each other's arms.

We stand mesmerized by the softly lapping waves for a lifetime. Alas, the taxi arrives to fetch Luca. He has to work early today and will arrange for the taxi to get me later. He gives me a hug, and I watch him diminish up the slope toward the taxi. An unbearable ache crashes through. I can't stay here without him.

"Luca, wait!" I shout and gather my things and run toward him. Without a word, I jump into the back seat.

"You're a crazy girl," he says, wrapping me tight in his arms.

Once onboard, I can't bear for him to leave. It's just for an hour, he assures me, and then we'll meet up again at the bar. I rush to my cabin to shower and change, afraid to breathe, afraid if I exhale, I'll blow away our perfect love. I change into a strapless sundress and stare in the mirror at this new woman with glowing cheekbones and golden-brown shoulders. *Who is she?*

# 5.

## CINQUE TERRE, 2002

AFTER SWIMMING MANY laps along the Monterosso beach, Joanna sees Terry waving for her to join the group. Exhausted from the intense hike and long swim, she hopes to suppress her grief and disappointment in Terry to not contaminate the others. As Joanna approaches, Terry takes a large floppy hat from her bag and places it meticulously on her head, creating a flattering angle. She makes all sorts of funny and seductive faces that, despite Joanna's dark mood, gets her laughing. The handsome Australian couple Terry has befriended joins in her silliness. They start a sort of hoedown dance, link arms, and sing with such infectious cheer that strangers close by start clapping in time. The bright sunshine, the clear blue sky and sea, and overall good cheer transforms Joanna's mood, and she can't help smiling.

"These guys are so cool," Terry says. "God, I love traveling. You meet the most amazing people."

"Ah, my love, we're just ordinary folks," says Mick, the male half of the couple.

"You are so not. Not where I come from," Terry says and then turns to Joanna. "I hope you don't mind, but I told them, you know, about your husband. I've been lousy at helping you feel better."

*Maybe I should dress in black as a warning. Maybe it's not such a foolish tradition.*

"Ah, no you don't," Mick says, swooping in and taking Joanna for a turn. "No feeling sad on my watch."

"I can't imagine what you've been going through," Glenda says in that singsong Australian way. "Grief is ghastly. You mustn't be on your own. The mind can be a dangerous neighborhood."

"And we won't let you go there," Mick adds. "Starting with a beer." And with that, this man built like a surfer gets a beer from their cooler for Joanna. "Here you are, mate, the Australian remedy for all that ails you."

"Mick could charm the snow off of igloos," Glenda says, giving him a soft punch. "Be warned, ladies, be warned!"

Without missing a beat, Mick licks his lips, then cocks his head apologetically. "Glenda, my love, haven't I been good as gold?"

So large of being, these two, with their jingle-jangle Australian lilt, entirely comfortable *in* themselves. Joanna can't help feeling better. Not wanting this gregarious gathering to end, Joanna impulsively asks Mick and Glenda to join them for dinner. An offer Terry completely approves of.

\*\*\*

They meet up later in Vernazza at sunset. Drinks in hand, they relax into the softening light, chatting away. By the third round, Joanna, who thought Mick and Glenda's company would have smoothed whatever awkwardness had come between herself and Terry, notices that whenever she jumps in with a comment, Terry cuts her off and steers the conversation away. It's getting so obvious that Glenda gives Joanna a not-so-subtle glance of wonder. There's no question Terry's behavior has changed again. Joanna can only assume by the low-cut dress and hair done up with seductive tendrils falling across her face that Terry has big hopes for the evening. By the time they're seated at the restaurant, even Mick can't get a word in edgewise. Terry is a one-woman show, no longer interested in the group. Only Gino, the waiter. Each time he passes, she curves her shoulders back and makes her bosom rise. Gino, with a full house to attend to, seems oblivious.

"My God," Glenda whispers, "someone needs a shag!"

"Don't I wish!" Terry says.

"He is a cutie-pie." Glenda scrunches her lips. "Wouldn't mind a nibble myself."

"He's mine!" Terry cries. "I found him first. *Mmm* . . . look how he moves!"

They all turn to watch Gino swiftly weave between tables.

"Oh stop. He's not that cute," Mick jibes. "My God, Glenda, have I been remiss? Didn't realize you were still hungry."

"Don't worry, darling, just having fun."

"What do you think, quiet Joanna?" Mick turns to face her, his long arm filling her wineglass. "Are you in love with him too?"

"No, I hardly—"

"I'm not in love with him," Terry shrieks, cutting off Joanna. "No more love for me, thank you very much."

"Just community service? Is that it?" Mick says. Glenda gives him a shove, to which he responds, "I didn't mean *me*, darling."

"That's a good one!" Terry says. "Community service. I'll drink to that."

"You're drinking to *everything* tonight," Glenda says.

"Gotta grab those firecracker moments before it's too late," Terry shoots back.

"There's time, my love," Mick says. "You're a good-looking woman. He'd be a fool to let you slip by." Joanna can't tell whether he's enjoying Terry's outrageous behavior or just placating her.

"Thank you, Mick," Terry says, smiling so big Joanna can see the gums of her teeth. "Can you please fill my glass?"

"For God's sake, take the bloody bottle!" Glenda says. "Someone's just come through the desert, or what?"

"I have, I so have," Terry says, reaching for Glenda's hand. Joanna is amazed to see Terry this drunk. She tries to turn away but can't stop watching her. Mick and Glenda have also consumed a lot, yet they seem to handle it better. Terry keeps getting louder, her arms moving this way and that. Joanna fears she'll knock the plates out of Gino's arms as he passes; it's embarrassing. As if Terry can read her thoughts, she grabs her hand and shouts, "We're making a toast!"

"I've had enough," Joanna says, placing her hand over her glass. There's no stopping Terry. She pours anyhow, forcing Joanna to move her hand. Terry shoots her a hard look, like it's Joanna's fault that her hand is splattered with wine. "Raise your glass, goddamn it."

With a forced smile, Terry cheers, "To the end of boring! I mean, *really*, is there anything worse? If I have to climb to the rooftops and shout it so God in his deafness can hear . . . I mean come on now," she says, urging the others to lift their glasses. "To the end of BORING!"

"TO THE END OF BORING," Mick and Terry cheer.

"And NO MORE TRYING TO DO THE RIGHT THING!" Terry shrieks. "I'm sick of it."

"There's no right thing," Mick says, his voice seductive. "Isn't that so, my darling?" Mick wraps an arm around Glenda, who pushes him away. Stubbornly, he grabs her and kisses her, and Joanna can see she likes it. With his other arm, he lifts the empty wine bottle and signals Gino to bring another.

Gino takes his time and doesn't look at anyone directly as he uncorks their bottle. Joanna suspects his somber expression reflects contempt for this crass behavior.

"Joanna, I forbid you to cry," Mick says.

"I'm not going to."

"I can tell when a girl is about to cry. Can't I, darling?" Mick reaches for Glenda and kisses her again and then says to Gino,

"Better give her a bit more. The girl's sinking. We've got to save her."

All at once, completely out of sync with the others, Joanna feels desperately alone. She must get up. Her legs are unsteady, a feeling she remembers from the *Leonardo* when Luca took her ashore after days on the ship. Those first steps from the tender to the solid landing, when she fell over, and Luca caught her. There's no one to catch her now. Carefully, she rises, steadying herself as she makes her way to the restroom. Once inside, she leans over the sink, turns on the tap, and drinks the water, letting it splash over her face.

Opening the door to exit, she hears a crash of breaking glass and sees Gino crouching on the floor, gathering up broken stemware. Their eyes meet in a flash and he stands. Like a traditional folk dance, the delicate brush across the line of contact is more powerful than an actual touch. There's a zing, a bolt of felt connection. He, with vulnerable puppy eyes, and she, completely off guard. Flooded with feelings, they tumble through the cracks of the world. Her body shakes and her knees quiver, but she can't pull her eyes away. And Gino, he too can't look away. For an endless moment, they melt in longing. Their lips nearly touch, so close, so terribly close.

*No!* Something screeches in her. *This can't happen!* Unable to move, tears fall. Tears with no place at the table. Gino cries as well—or so it seems. The world stops for that endless moment. The pause ends, and the world moves, and she, who can't bear for Terry to see her reddened eyes, rushes back to the restroom.

She washes her face, blows her nose, and peeks out to see if Gino is still there. He isn't, though a part of her wishes he was, that they could break out of the world forever. She spies him back outside clearing the tables. Most of the guests have already left. Only her table is still in full swing.

"You were gone a long time," Terry says.

"My stomach is a bit . . . I'm not used to drinking so much."

But Terry isn't interested and turns back to Mick and the story she'd been telling. Joanna hears her words but can't follow. Gino comes to clear their table. Terry turns abruptly away from Mick, pulling out a chair for Gino and cooing for him to sit. "You've worked *so* hard!" she says. "Surely you can join us for a drink."

Joanna can't help but watch Gino's reaction as he spins theatrically up and out of Terry's arms with the grace of Fred Astaire. "*No, grazie,*" he says. "It's been a long day, and I have to set up early tomorrow."

"You're working lunch again?" Terry asks.

"And the day after and the day after that too," he says, showing a look of weariness. So effortlessly, he gets back to work without seeming to reject Terry, not looking at Joanna or any of them. Their bill paid, his services no longer required, he disappears. *Truly a pro,* Joanna thinks. He knows exactly how much Terry wants him. *How boring it must be for him.*

Joanna struggles to her feet. "Goodnight, all," she says coolly before vanishing into the narrow streets.

She's a mash of feelings. The way Gino looked through her was like Luca had done that night he saw the stars in her eyes. *Maybe a trick of the Italians,* she considers. A seductive way to make the other melt. The sensation of being seen fully with recognition and love is intoxicating. It felt so real that night with Luca, and now with Gino, too real to be dismissed. *The thing we long for, whether we know it or not . . . no, no, no*, she chides herself. *The wine, surely the wine, and the balmy night.*

She keeps walking, no way to fit inside her small room with her head a swirl of emotions. She follows a path behind the restaurant, up a jagged hill to a cliff overlooking the dark sea, and inches as close as she dares to the edge, to the roaring surf. Much windier than down below, her skirt whips against her legs, her hair blowing wild, the sky ablaze of stars. She grabs the top railing of the nearby bench to steady herself. For a moment, she feels like a sailor on the bridge of a ship. But she's no sailor, just a foolish woman indulging in memories and that excruciating mix of happy and sad and breathless infatuation.

All her married life, she'd felt guilty for never feeling *that* for Stuart, not able to give herself fully, not again. Joanna forced herself not to think of Luca over the years, yet how could she not think of him here? The way Gino looked through her, turning her inside out. It's foolish, she knows, longing for love and to sing again as she had that night with Luca. Is it inside her still? And writing songs? She hasn't written a song in ages and misses it, the out-of-control madness that creates a song. Is that also dormant in her?

## LUCA OF THE SEA, 1976

The sunset from the deck of the *Leonardo* puts me in a dreamy state. Luca arrives and sweeps me into his arms. I'm bursting with happiness and can't help myself from singing. My voice is deep and rich, and it feels so good that I can't stop. He's never heard me before, and his face opens in delight, which makes me sing even better.

"Come!" he says, grabbing my hand and leading me back inside the ship and through the halls. He takes his keys and opens the door to a music room where the band practices. "No one needs this room now. We can make as much noise as we want." Luca heads for the drum kit, takes hold of the sticks, and starts drumming like a pro. The rhythm pummels through his hands, swift-changing patterns, a waterfall of sound. I clap and dance around him.

"Ginger Baker," he shouts. "I am Ginger Baker!" He sees quickly, though I try to hide it, that I have no idea who Ginger Baker is. "The best drummer in the whole wide world, that's who he is! And right this second, he is me, because I AM GINGER BAKER!" He's on fire. Sheer ecstasy. His verve and drive ignite me. Before I know it, I'm dancing and singing madly around the room with my voice pouring out like honey. "*Mamma mia!*" he cries. "*Quanto stiamo bene insieme!* How good we are together!"

I can't believe I didn't know Luca was also a musician. *This is the key to unite us.* And why we almost exploded before. Because we *have* to play music. Only with the music will we be complete and whole. I'm not crazy as I've always feared; I've never been crazy. I get crazy if I *can't* be in the music. For hours, we continue, one riff following the next, bursting with inspiration.

We're both covered in sweat and collapse on the floor, soaked in triumph. We laugh and laugh, and I kiss him hard and fast. "Don't you see!" I shout. "We must be together. Only together can we help each other be completely in the music." I never find this place on my own, and by the way he looks, neither does he. "Luca, you play so great. As good as anyone I've ever heard in New York. Why don't you work as a musician?"

Instantly, he rolls away, his voice hard as steel. "Because my father would kill me."

"Then don't tell him."

"No," he says. "He already knows everything."

"He doesn't know you're here right now."

"You have no idea of my father."

I coax him back to the drums and place the sticks in his hand.

"No!" he shouts like a broken man and lets the drumsticks fall on the ground. "I can't play anymore. I'm no good."

"That's not true. I just heard you."

"*That* was Ginger Baker."

"Maybe if you start playing again, he will return!"

"No, he won't. I wait and wait for him. Only once at the death of a pope does he land on my head. That's not enough. I need him all the time." He leaps from the drum stool, grabs the sticks from the ground, and tries to crack them in half. In a nick of time, I pull them away. I tap him on the head, as if holding a magic wand. "*Abracadabra, pow!* You are now Ginger Baker." It thrills me that maybe I really am a witch, for he grabs the sticks from my hand and starts playing. We find it again, the miraculous music. I am sure, surer than anything, that we must stay together.

# 6.

## CINQUE TERRE, 2002

JOANNA WAKES WITH a brutal hangover. And the noise outside, what a racket! The screech of delivery vans, voices yelling, and the pigeons. *Where did these pigeons come from?* She leans out the window and claps her hands, aggressively shooing them away, nearly gagging from the stench of fried onions and meat. *Must get moving. No lingering today.* One coffee, then a long, long walk to clear her head and decide what to do. No more feeling ashamed of her grief. Sad and lonely, she misses her husband and the old folks at the nursing home. *It's time to go home.*

She forces herself to her morning ritual. At the restaurant, she orders a cappuccino, opens her diary. No peeking to see if Gino is setting up.

"Hey, Joanna, how's *your* head?" It's Terry. She's slumped over and diminished with a different floppy hat, this one covering her face.

"Not as bad as yours, I suspect."

"Wish I could shoot the coffee directly into my veins."

"Sit here," Joanna says. "I'll get you one." Waiting for the coffees to be brewed, she realizes how fast she jumps to be caretaker. Such a strong habit. Terry's unsteady hand as she takes the cup also reminds Joanna of her mother.

"Look at him," Terry says, pointing to Gino. "Flirting away. You'd think he earns extra on the side, that his auntie encourages him so they'll have a full house each night."

"Probably," Joanna says. She hadn't yet looked at Gino, but when she does, she feels a swoon in her belly.

"Won't even come over to say hello. Oh look, he's waving. Day one, you get the whole of him, day two, just his hand . . . like a prince."

"I suppose he has to work some of the time."

"He sure liked *you* though. After you left, man, he was like a dog who lost his bone."

"I think you're exaggerating."

"How I wish I were. You can't see yourself. How attractive you are. All that grieving, no offense, is sexier than anything."

"But I—"

"I know, you laid low, and that was kind of you. But it didn't help. He was smitten, couldn't stop looking for you after you left. And me, the royal fool, couldn't leave him alone." Joanna looks down, with a lump in her throat. She should get up, not hear any more, but she stays. Terry goes on, her voice choppy. "Don't tell me you didn't notice. I was all over him. I *should* know better. Nobody wants a dog panting for them. Sorry if I was a shit to you last night. You looked so beautiful, your eyes rimmed with tears, like the Madonna they worship all over this country. And me, the whore."

The words sting: the dark side of alcohol. Joanna knows that well. The day after a binge, her mother was a roller coaster of confession and abuse. It all jams up, along with a strange relief, and she hadn't made up what transpired between herself and Gino. But she also feels sad that it went so wrong with Terry.

"Please, Joanna," Terry whines, "don't start crying. Gino will come over and comfort you, and I couldn't bear that." She drinks the rest of her cappuccino. "Just wanted to say goodbye."

"You're leaving?"

"You've no idea how obsessed I can be." She slowly gets up. "Funny how the parts in yourself you hate and thought you left behind come running after you like a stray dog. Well, I gotta go. I'm catching the next train."

Joanna watches Terry walk away. *Should I, too, pack up and go?* Such a little town like Vernazza, one mustn't stay too long. She'll do a final long hike and then prepare to leave. She finishes her coffee and gets up.

"Wait," Gino calls, running over.

Joanna avoids his gaze, unsure what to say.

"Do you want to stay in the most beautiful room?" Gino points to the other side of the square, to a terrace smothered in bougainvillea. "It's a very special place," he says, circling his hands to accentuate how much, "and it's free now. The best place to stay in town, and it's never free for long. He's my friend, who owns the house, and he told me this morning. Because you're also my friend, he'll give you a good price. Follow the road behind the station to number thirty-six. There are many steps, but it's worth it. Beautiful, like a paradise. At least go see it."

The landlord is waiting at the entrance, expecting her. He smiles and opens the front door of what appears to be an apartment house built into the side of the hill. There are many steps, more than five flights up. When the landlord unlocks the door of the top apartment and the light pours in, she stands in awe. Instantly, she sees what makes this room special—French glass doors of the little studio open to a lavish garden. The room itself is modest, with a double bed, a kitchen, a table, and a few chairs. Joanna follows the landlord out into the garden with maritime pines, cypresses, palm trees, and a shade-giving fig tree in the center. At the far edge is a breathtaking view of the sea, steep sloping vineyards, and an enormous sweep of sky.

"Who else uses this garden?" Joanna asks, almost too excited for the chance to stay in such a place.

"Just you," the landlord says. "And sometimes my wife, to give water and take the figs that are ready. Eat as many as you want. Too many for us."

Joanna can't imagine this sumptuous garden just for herself, or that she can afford to stay for as long as she suddenly wants to. The price the landlord quotes if she stays at least a month is well within her budget, and she quickly says yes.

"When can I move in?" she asks.

"Today." The man smiles and hands her the keys. He leaves her alone now, and for a moment, she panics, wondering if Gino expects something in return for telling her about this amazing room and garden. *How can I say no to all this?* To wake each day to this view. To sit under the fig tree almost biblical in proportion and eat ripened figs, sweet and lush, to revel in the calming scent of pine and lavender, the soothing breeze through the palms, this chance of healing.

She walks to the garden's left wall and looks straight across to the other side of the horseshoe-shaped town, to the cliff where she'd stood the night before, and down to the harbor and Gino's restaurant. He's there, setting up for lunch. She can watch him and feel his presence. All from a safe distance.

The church bells ring loud and clear, startling her. *Already eleven-thirty!* She must check out of her other room. And she's starving. Most days, she'd buy just a few things for her daily hike. With her decision to stay longer, she'll stock up. In a happy swirl, she runs down the steps.

In Italy, the midday meal is an elaborate affair, and it's so close to lunchtime that the shop is full. Joanna observes how the women chat intensively while waiting their turn. Though food is clearly important, this sense of community seems even more so, and the conversations are loud and vivid. When it's Joanna's turn, everyone gives advice as to which coffee is best, which wine with what food, which fruits and vegetables are ripe just now or *domani*; food samples whizz by with smells and tastes so delicious that her basket soon overflows.

Entering the apartment, it already feels like home. Unpacking her purchases, she smiles in triumph. *Just like Thoreau.* She laughs. *Well, not exactly wild nature but more than I'm used to.*

*It's a start, Joanna. A good start.* She gasps. It's Stuart's voice, his deep resonating voice crackling through as if being played on an old recording. Memories flood in of their years together, their trips deep into the woods, into real nature. Stuart, blessedly safe in his being, found the most remote places to camp. He'd laugh gently at the thousand things she worried about. "Joanna, when are you going to trust me? Has anything ever gone wrong?" And she'd respond, "I'm a New York City girl. For me, Central Park is big nature!"

With Stuart's voice fading, she shakes off the mirage. Whether it was really him or not, she'll take this as a sign to do an even harder hike, to a place she's not yet been. Hoping her dead husband will teach her how to be alone. She prepares a few sandwiches, two bottles of water, some fruit, and heads out.

At the entrance, the landlord calls to her, "*Signora*, don't go far. Bad weather is coming."

The sky looks a bit murky, the air heavier, but nothing serious. "That's okay," she says. "I need to walk."

✳✳✳

She takes the train to Levanto and follows the markings to a higher trail, one that should be five hours and leads back to the familiar Monterosso al Mare. Dark clouds loom on the horizon. She notices there aren't any other walkers. Still, she continues, hypnotized by the rhythmic sound of her feet on the dirt path. Without Terry's incessant picture taking, Joanna keeps a fast pace and begins to feel better. After a few hours, she comes to a viewing point and sees white-capped waves in the distance. She tries to feel Stuart, thinking he'd be proud of her, all alone on the trail. The way he'd look out to the sky, loving the earth in the most extraordinary way. He'd say, "It's a miracle, in that tiny layer between the deadly cold and radiation of space and the mass of magma under the earth's crust, we have life!" Then his face would fall. "But we can easily destroy it."

"Why?" Joanna would often ask. "Why are there not more people who think like you?" She loved to lean against his broad chest, his arms around her, while they spoke of the earth like a love child.

"Most people prefer hiding in the illusion of safety, in the familiarity of busy everyday lives, in our man-made cities and towns. Nature tries to get our attention, but it's drowned out in the noise we make."

The sound of distant thunder gets her moving again. The path turns away from the coast and its orienting view, and the forest grows thick and ominous around her. She hurries her pace, exhilarated by the vital presence of the approaching storm. The wind picks up, and the sky turns a menacing gray, as thunder roars closer. She's running now, with the trees thrashing about and leaves blowing every which way.

With a deafening clap and a mighty gush of wind, the sky opens and rain lashes. In seconds, she's soaked and cold and must find shelter. There are a few houses scattered in the woods, but they all looked shuttered. She spots a shed behind a group of trees and runs for it. To her relief, the door is unlocked, and she quickly ducks inside. In the pitch-dark, she finds a dangling string for light that miraculously works. There is hardly anything in this tiny room besides a shovel and a few folding chairs. She finds a burlap bag and wraps it around her for warmth while the rain pounds relentlessly on the roof. She postpones eating her sandwich, not sure how long she might be stranded. She was foolish to not have listened to her landlord, to have been seduced into going by Stuart's imaginary voice. He would've seen the bad weather coming, would've been better prepared or not have gone. But she's here now with no phone and no one to call and must make the best of it.

## LUCA OF THE SEA, 1976

I wake on the *Leonardo* with a feeling of dread. Only a few days left on the cruise and Luca has to work nonstop. So not to mope all day, he sends me off alone to the last port of call, St. Thomas.

The moment I arrive at the pier, I want to turn back. This island is horribly commercial, the worst of Times Square, with palm trees, and my mood only darkens. Without Luca, I'm not sure where to go. He knows the islands so well. The weather isn't great, and I want to stay close to the harbor, to leave as soon as possible. Several cruise ships are docked nearby, so the harbor is packed with tourists. God, look at them, frantically shopping with their vacant faces and shrieks of shopping-glee like it's the last chance ever to buy anything. I fear I'll strangle the next person who squeals about how cute the straw dolls are. I pull myself away and walk some backstreets to restore my sanity. It hits like a meteorite that I've made the whole thing up. Luca doesn't really love me; it's all part of the package, the tourist machine. He finds a weak, gullible one like me and has his fun, because he's so handsome and convincing. And then I go back to the travel agency and sell this product, this cruise, because of the wonderful time I've had *with him*. It's all been a show, a con. Stella's been trying to warn me. Why in heaven's name would someone as gorgeous as Luca fall in love with *me*?

I'm alone on the tender back, with the crewman who won't even look at me, a stupid girl who can't stop crying. I rush to my cabin, not wanting anyone to see me. Ever. And later, when I'm meant to meet Luca, I'll tell him everything is off.

He, too, seems in a dreadful state, and before I can say a word, he blurts, "It's no use trying to play the drums. Without Ginger Baker, I stink."

I've no energy to cheer him up, drowning in my own foul state. "That's how it goes," I tell him blandly. "Nothing is how we think."

Luca nods without looking at me. Like a contest of who can make the other most miserable, he adds, "Will you do me a favor and throw away all the photos you took of me?"

I can't help myself; hate rises like steam from my skull. "I'll go one step further and throw my camera overboard and forget this whole stupid trip. How about that!"

Like the ping in a game show when the contestant answers correctly, his face lights up and he lets out a full-throttle laugh. My anger seems to have pleased him. His eyes completely change, and he grabs me passionately. In an instant, our fury melts, and I shower him in kisses. He sweeps me up in his arms and takes me to his room. After we make love, he goes to his porthole to shout to the stars how much he loves me. I leap out of bed to wrap around him and hold so tight until there's no border between our naked bodies.

Suddenly, there's a loud groan and a mighty vibration as the engines rev up. We're preparing to leave the harbor and head back for New York. *No, no, no! We can't go back. We just can't.* A resistance builds in my chest; my legs burn with the pressure, as if trying to stop the ship.

Luca gathers me in a bundle and lays me on the bed. I feel his hand brush across my back as he writes on my skin with his finger, *I like you very much*, and then, *I think I love you*. Getting dressed into his blue uniform for his night watch, he says, "It is not for us to know what will be. It is in the stars! But I know we are meant to be together."

With absolute certainty, I respond, "I'll come to the pier each time the *Leonardo* sails back to New York. The ship returns every eleven days, right? That's not so long to wait for love."

"You will wait for me? You will come every eleven days to see me?"

"Of course I will. We must be together."

# 7.

## CINQUE TERRE, 2002

"HELLO?" A VOICE calls out. "Can I help you?" A woman with a sun-wrinkled face in a shroud of red hair opens the door of the shed where Joanna has sheltered.

"I'm so sorry," Joanna says, startled. "The rain was coming down so hard."

"Indeed, it still is. Was the door open?" Joanna nods. "Lucky for you. It usually isn't. I saw the light on and was wondering."

"Forgive me, but there was nowhere else to go."

"Come up to the house," the woman says without hesitation. "Have some tea and get dry. The storm is far from over."

"Are you sure?" This stranger seems almost glad about Joanna's intrusion. It feels spooky, like in a Grimm's fairy tale where seemingly good things go terribly wrong.

"Just come. Really, it's fine."

The tempting thought of getting warm and dry wins over Joanna's doubt. She follows the woman to her cottage hidden in a cluster of trees. A blazing fire, a scent of incense, and soft chanting music welcome her. Pastel-colored weavings and African masks line the wooden walls, and the furnishings seem to be from everywhere, creating an earthy enchanting mix.

"Come in, come in. I've a pot of ginger tea going. I'm Grace, the other *nutter* who loves a storm. I almost went walking myself. Here's a pair of socks and slippers. You can dry your wet socks by the fire."

"I'm Joanna . . . and thanks for being so kind. My landlord warned me not to go, but I really needed to walk. I didn't think it would get this bad."

"Always a delicate line, isn't it? Take no risks and nothing happens, yet too much can be *deadly*." Just as Grace says deadly, a blinding flash lights up the room, immediately followed by a burst of thunder. "Wow, that was weird. But life *is* weird, isn't it? I'm beginning to believe there are no coincidences, even if we don't know yet why our paths have crossed. I mean what were the chances of our meeting? I'm hardly ever in this cottage, the shed is usually locked, and it rarely rains this hard. I bet you've never done this walk until today."

"No." Joanna says with a shiver. "I hadn't."

"So strange. I made a huge pot of soup, like I knew someone was coming. I'll be right back. You must be starving." While Grace goes to the kitchen, Joanna looks around for clues about this fairy tale of a woman she's stumbled upon in the woods. The beautiful cottage seems barely used, with no family photos or other specific items of daily use, all of it so tidy. Joanna can't place her accent, perhaps a rich eccentric from England or Australia here on vacation.

Grace returns with a tray of Japanese-style bowls of steaming soup and mugs of tea and leads them to a rustic wooden table. The soup is delicious, miso with chunks of tofu, something you'd imagine at a yoga retreat or a Japanese restaurant.

"Where did you get this?" Joanna asks. She hasn't seen any tofu in the shops, nor any Japanese restaurant.

"We make it on our farm up in the hills."

"Your farm? Where?"

"It's a bit hidden, not easy to find. If you're curious to drop by, we can always use a hand. Someone can fetch you from the station at Levanto. How long are you staying around?"

"I'm not quite sure. Maybe a month," Joanna says, thinking of her new room and the quick decision to stay longer.

Grace seems to read her thoughts and smiles. "Strange, right? All part of the *mystery school*."

"The what?"

"The one all around us," Grace says with no pretense. "I don't know your plans. But I sure could use some help."

Joanna gets up. "No, not here." Grace laughs. "Sit, sit. This little cottage and I, we're an easy team. First, some more soup." Grace heads back to the kitchen to refill their bowls. She comes back with a ripe avocado and a steaming loaf of brown bread, also not common in the shops, so Joanna imagines it, too, was homemade.

"This is so good," Joanna says.

"We grow most of our vegetables and fruit."

"Is that the help you need? On your farm?"

"Actually, yes. If you could spare a few hours tomorrow, if the rain lets up, that would be grand. You can stay here for the night."

Joanna hesitates. She's meant to be in her new room tonight. If she doesn't return, will the landlord worry? And what about Gino? The sound of the teeming rain and the warmth from the fire and soup create an unexpected calmness, and a sweet tiredness overtakes her. She couldn't possibly summon the effort to leave.

After they finish eating, Joanna follows Grace into the kitchen to clean up. She hands Joanna a cloth to dry and begins washing up. "Can I ask a personal question?" Grace says. "And stop me if it's too much. I seem to have lost all social skills since my husband died."

"Yours too?"

"Now I don't have to ask," Grace says, taking the bowl carefully from Joanna with both hands, like a child afraid to drop it. "I had a feeling you'd recently lost someone close."

"My husband passed away six months ago," Joanna says, with a feeling of warmth and connection. Now she understands why Grace was so welcoming; that's exactly how Joanna was with Terry.

"Mine went five years ago. Insane man, my husband, thinking he could fly."

"Is that what you meant before when you said *deadly*?"

Grace nods. She concentrates fully on putting the things away, as if new at cleaning up, then wipes the counter and rinses the cloth. Her hands suddenly free, she rustles them through her disheveled hair. "Just listen to that rain! You definitely have to stay the night."

"You sure you don't mind?"

"I'm glad for the company." With a fresh pot of tea, Grace leads them back to the living room. She stirs the fire and invites Joanna to the couch, handing her a blanket. Joanna leans back, giving over to the warming fire. Grace, however, seems suddenly restless. Her milky-blue eyes twitch nervously, and she keeps turning a twig in her hands.

"Are *you* okay?" Joanna asks.

"Yes and no." Grace lets out a loaded sigh. "And thanks for asking. There's some writing I'm meant to do tonight that I keep putting off. It's why I'm here in the cottage. Impossible to get any writing done on the farm. Would you mind if I just ramble? Maybe if I talk to you, I'll be able to come up with something." Grace laughs. "Do you know anything about the twelve-step program, like AA?"

"A bit," Joanna says. "I've heard of it from my mother, who refuses to go."

"Yeah, that's typical. I fought going for years. I do it long distance, as there are no meetings here. I'm supposed to send my sponsor, that's the one in the program who guides you, some writing by tomorrow."

Joanna, pulled in by Grace's sincerity, leans forward with the blanket draped around her. "Go on."

Grace lifts her mug of tea. "*This* was not my drink of choice. I've been sober four years now, and I really like this sponsor, and I don't want to lose her. Why are you smiling?"

"Just thinking of my mother, who'll never give up her alcohol."

Grace cocks her head, one hand weaving through her hair. "It's not easy to do, that's for sure. You must, as they say, hit bottom. And to stay not drinking, you're meant to look at your life and clean the wreckage of your past."

Joanna feels a chill. She thinks of the strange reveal at the funeral, this father of hers, a father she will never meet. Maybe Lillian won't stop drinking because of this, of not wanting to clear the wreckage of her past.

"You're really courageous."

"Thank you, but it hardly feels courageous, more like I have no choice. Not anymore. I used to be very rich, stinking rich. Funny to say that, the *stink* of our money. Took me time to enjoy a simple evening like this. Even if our stinking money bought this cottage, there's nothing luxurious here. Washing my dishes by hand, I never did that before." Grace nibbles her bottom lip, glancing time to time at Joanna. "The way we used to live, my husband's work, I never really thought about it, didn't want to."

"What did he do?" Joanna asks.

"Ah, he was one of those bastards that keep the wars going, selling weapons. Didn't matter who wins. All the while, I was too busy decorating our many homes and guzzling expensive wine to ponder where the money came from."

Joanna looks discreetly around the cottage. Tidy, yes, but not fancy. Still, to have a cottage in this location must have cost a fortune. She noticed while washing up that Grace's hands were blistered and cut, her face weathered like a farmhand, hardly a millionaire's wife.

"I'd be lying," Grace went on, "if I said I didn't sometimes miss my old life. Skiing the Alps, the French Riviera, islands in the sun, and yachts in between. All the comfort, and someone else doing the dirty work. Not for nothing, wars are fought defending that opulent lifestyle, keeping the beautiful places just for the rich, not caring how ugly the rest of the world gets." Grace holds her mug to her chest. With her other hand, she takes the metal rod and pokes the smoldering logs, bringing them to blaze once more.

"Wasn't easy, trading my gorgeous glass of wine for a cup of ginger tea. And now, to stay sober, I *must* look at my part. Always thought I could skip that part of the program, that looking at your past, because I hardly saw anyone. Who could I have possibly harmed? It was my husband to blame. I, the innocent bystander." Grace puts down the rod and presses her mug to her lips, as if hiding behind it. Joanna can see she's trying not to cry. She turns to Joanna.

"That's it, isn't it? I let things happen. I let everything happen. I'm sorry. I must sound pathetic to you. The poor, rich girl."

"Not at all," Joanna says, as comforting as she can.

"Oh man, I was never there." Grace exhales deeply. "When I think of my kids, the quick peck goodnight, the insignificant hug before handing them back to their nanny. Sending them off to boarding school with their little faces streaked with tears, their unheeded cries." Grace collapses onto the edge of the chair, her head in her hands, weeping. Joanna gets up and touches her gently on the back. Grace reaches a hand around her back and squeezes Joanna's hand.

"I'm sorry. I'm really sorry."

"It's okay," Joanna says, feeling her own tears swell.

Grace sits up and wipes her eyes with her sleeve. She takes a tissue from her pocket to blow her nose. "I shouldn't miss him, but I do. Especially at night. Awake, he was a piece of shit. I didn't mind his affairs. I drank too much to notice. And he'd always return at some point, God knows why. He got bored with the affairs and started with mountains, climbing those fucking mountains, each time higher and higher. Those deadly peaks got on my nerves, worrying he'd freeze to death. Which he finally did."

Joanna feels a shiver, imagining such a dreadful death. She wraps the blanket tighter around her.

"It's my kids I owe the most amends," Grace says after a few sighs. "Bloody hard to admit what a lousy mother you've been. Especially to my son, Connor, letting his father abuse him and doing *nothing*, nothing to stop it. God, the fights they had. Connor wanted to be a painter, and he wasn't half bad, but my husband couldn't stand it. Thought it was girly and sensitive, determined he follow his tracks in the corporate world. Wasn't enough that my daughter, Emily, did. They're twins, but as different as can be. My daughter, she's changed her career now, thank God. I couldn't stand for her to be like him. My kids are amazing. Not my doing, that's for sure.

"But my son's resistance was more than his father could bear. Once, between climbs when he was back drinking, he took my son's best painting and smashed it over his knee. 'If you were a real man,' my husband roared, 'you'd climb Everest with me.' And my son roared back, 'You're a thrill junky. Go climb your fucking mountain. I hope it kills you.' My husband was warned not to go, but off he went in his typical defiance." Grace bites her lip, trying not to cry more.

"It wasn't Connor's fault his father died, but he blamed himself. Went off to live in a cave on the Canary Islands, in Goa, even on the streets for a while. Emily and her brother are very connected. She could feel every twist of his pain and got him into an Outward Bound group, deep in the mountains of the Pyrenees. The leader was brilliant and shrewd and so unlike his father. The extreme experience, a sort of organic shock treatment, saved his life."

Grace pours more tea into her mug and then fills Joanna's. "He stayed on as a counselor, and when he finally came home, he was totally changed. He didn't want to paint anymore. Wanted only to make up for the horrible things his father had done. To devote his life to changing the system. Because of my son, we have the farm. I know, we can never really make amends for all the damage caused, but it's a tiny start. And why I finally stopped drinking. Not immediately, of course, first had to try every quick fix out there.

What Connor called fast food for the soul. I burned through a ton of money going to every workshop, reading every book. It helped, but not enough. Something foul had erupted in me. Couldn't stand it anymore and swallowed a barrel of pills. Connor found me."

Grace turns to face Joanna. "You sure this isn't too much for you, hearing this whole sordid tale?"

"It's okay," Joanna says. "Go on."

"My husband left us plenty, and Connor had big plans for that *dirty* money, including getting me well. With his Outward Bound experience in nature, softened for his mother, he dragged me everywhere, walking. When Emily could, she joined us. I laugh now, but those walks saved my life. Then I got into AA, back in England. Meanwhile, Connor had learned about permaculture and living sustainably and wanted to try his own place, something smaller. An *intentional community*, as they call it. Then we found the farm, on one of our walking visits. We already had this cottage and could stay here. Three years ago, we got the farm, and"—Grace bangs her knuckles on the table—"it's still going strong. By far, the best way to make amends for my . . . silent consent."

Grace gathers the finished tea mugs and heads for the kitchen. She stops at the doorway to face Joanna. "That's what I have to write about, my silent consent, my not being there. Not very original. At least I have something to send my sponsor. You've been grand to listen."

"Thank *you*," Joanna says. "I mean it." She thinks with a twinge about Terry, how alcohol removed from the equation makes a huge difference.

"Right!" Grace says, back to the whimsical eccentric of the earlier evening. "Now to get you sorted. Something to sleep in, and I'll show you the guest room."

***

By the next morning, the rain has cleared, and in bright sunshine the two women drive by moped to the farm. Along the road, hidden by lush foliage, Joanna spots a faded *Agriturismo* sign on a ragged piece of wood. Following a dirt road, they arrive at the farm, to a few large rustic buildings surrounded by several acres of cultivated fields. With the backdrop of lush and steep green hills of the Levanto area, the air feels fresh and clear from the rain, and it looks beautiful. Grace points to rows and rows of tomatoes bursting red on the vine.

"You see how ready they are to be picked."

There were about ten other people around, some who lived there in exchange for work, others who rented rooms and did their own work yet participated in the community. Still others, like Joanna, came to help for a day or two. She'd hoped to meet Connor, but he was with his sister in England. The overall atmosphere at the farm feels welcoming, like a small kibbutz, yet with so much needing to get done, there's not much time for socializing. Joanna enjoys the vigorous activity and sense of purpose and completely immerses herself in the hands-on work.

"You've been grand," Grace says, coming over much later with a big smile. "Look how many bushels you've filled! Come, it's getting late. I'll give you a ride to the station."

Though Joanna looks forward to her sweet new room, it's done her a world of good to be around Grace and the farm, and she's a bit sad to leave.

"Hey," Grace says once they're at the station. "You're welcome anytime. Here's my card with my cell number and email. Whenever you feel like coming by, just give a call and someone will fetch you from the station."

"Thank you so much, for everything. What do I owe you for the food and lodging?"

"Are you kidding?" Grace's face could change so quickly. "It's me who owes you. Here, take this." She hands Joanna a cloth bag of tomatoes, peppers, and zucchini. "That's the deal. You work in exchange for vegetables. And if you ever want to stay over another time, you're always welcome. Thanks again for listening to me last night. I finally wrote to my sponsor."

## LUCA OF THE SEA, 1976

Luca must work again, and I rush to the dining room before it's too late for dinner. I'm starved for everything—food, talk, drinks, laughter—the resilient human show. So happy I haven't made the whole thing up, that Luca really loves me. I plunk down loudly in the empty chair beside Stella so she can't ignore me. In a gregarious mood, I make everyone laugh, including Stella, with my witty anecdotes.

When the captain comes over to greet our table, he drapes his arm around me and sings out that I'm the sweetest travel agent they've ever had on board. By now, everyone knows. So elated, so maniacally high, I nearly tell the captain that I'm hopelessly in love and don't care a hoot about the travel agency or money or the material world. Stella catches my mania and tells the captain, "She's had a heck of a good time. I'm sure she'll do her best to sell this cruise."

After dinner, it's me who links arms with Stella like we did the first night, ten lifetimes ago, me who invites *her* for a drink. As a sign of trust, I use up the rest of my money, the money I've saved for my taxi home in New York, believing Luca will be coming home with me as he's promised. He keeps showing me all the money he has, wads of dollar bills in his pockets, all the money he has no time to spend. He says that when we arrive, we'll take a taxi with all my things to my apartment, then go out to a very expensive restaurant. I sit high on the barstool, feeling sassy and confident, my hair bouncing on my carefree shoulders.

"Where's lover boy?" Stella asks, her eyes looking around.

"He has to work," I say.

"Ah," she says with a sourpuss look, realizing she's second fiddle. "Till when? It seems his friend is coming over." Stella signals with her eyes to Luca's mate, the one with the mustache he's often hanging around with. He's a great dancer. I wave hello and motion that we should dance. Stella squishes her forehead in warning, as none of Luca's friends have dared ask me for a dance. But I laugh it away.

He's a whirl on the dance floor, and Cole Porter's "Begin the Beguine" is playing, impossible to resist. It's one of my favorite songs they play at Roseland ballroom. I was really born in the wrong time. I close my eyes and let him twirl me and turn me in perfect time with the music. The song isn't over, but the mustached friend yanks me off the dance floor. He points to Luca, brooding at the entrance, then vanishes. I rush over.

Luca's mood is rancid. He whips his hand through the air. Though he doesn't touch me, I feel a burn.

"Why did you dance with my friend?"

"It was nothing, just one dance."

He turns angrily and heads down the hall to his room. I run after him, refusing to let the darkness win, not when my mood's finally so good.

"It's because of you!" I grab him to stay still and listen. "Because of how much I love you. I felt so happy, I *had* to dance. Can't you understand?"

"I understand nothing!" he shouts. He opens his door and nearly slams it shut in my face. I keep knocking until my hand is sore. Finally, he opens the door. "Go away," he says. "My mood is too bad. No fixing it, not tonight." He closes the door, but not completely, and I slip in. He's at his desk, with papers all around. I stand behind, watching him write furiously.

"Can I see?" I ask.

"What? You read Italian now? You can understand?"

"Your words look so pretty." I rush to get my diary out of my bag. "Here, you can read what I've written."

"Why . . . why should I?" he asks with disgust. "We are the stupidest people who ever lived." Just then, the ship jerks severely to one side, and I lose balance. He leaps up and catches my fall. "You are no sailor," he says. Then he bites his lip with a mischievous smirk and says wickedly, "It's going to be very rough for the next few hours. I love to think of all those rich passengers falling over, drinks spilling on their expensive clothing."

"You're terrible, Luca!"

"Why are they even on this ship? What do they want? The sea gets angry, you know. It's like a horse stung by a dragonfly."

"How do you know a word like dragonfly?"

"I know a lot of words!" he shouts. Both his shouting and the turbulent ship seem to ease his mood, and his eyes glow impishly. He grabs my arms, and we start dancing.

"Now?" I ask in disbelief. "You want to dance now?"

"Yes! It's great when the ship is wild. If you can dance on the waves, you can live."

We dance hysterically around the room, sometimes in each other's arms, sometimes apart, all in time with the crack and roar of the sea. The wilder we became, the easier to balance the sway. All at once, I start singing, *I could have danced all night*. Luca tries to sing along, making up his own words, and soon we're both drenched in happiness.

"Look!" I shout. "I'm a real sailor now! I can get a job singing on this ship, and we can be together!"

"So, we better get married," he roars.

All at once, I remember a time from childhood when me and three friends pierced our fingers and mixed our blood, vowing eternal friendship. I explain this ritual to Luca. His face lights up. "*Sì, sì!* It's a wonderful idea. But I only have this," he says, getting scissors from his desk. Going first, I take the scissors gently to the middle finger of his left hand, wait for the ship to steady a bit, and then pierce delicately, yet enough that his finger bleeds. But when it's his turn to cut me, the ship lurches abruptly. His hand slips, and he cuts me deeply, blood gushing everywhere. We quickly touch our fingers together in a river of red.

"I'm sorry," he says, rushing to the bathroom to get more tissues and some aftershave (he has nothing else to disinfect it with). He bandages my finger. It takes forever to stop bleeding, but I don't care a jot. I'm so happy. He holds my other hand while we both swear eternal love. Tears flow down his cheeks, and he seems happier than I've ever seen him. Though he's completely forgiven me, he makes me promise to never dance with anyone but him ever again.

"We shall have many children," he sings out, "and they will sing and dance and write silly poetry just as we do. I shall never let you go again! My love, my true love. Now that you're my wife, can I tell you my big question?" He grows quiet. "My father spent his life on the ships. I hardly saw him. He thinks I am crazy to have other ideas. 'It is a good life to work the ships,' he says over and over. Maybe it was a good life for him, but not for me. I really want to play the drums."

"And you must, Luca, you must!"

"We will live in Roma," he says, grabbing me tightly, "and we will be happy, very happy!"

# 8.

## CINQUE TERRE, 2002

JOANNA HEARS A loud knocking at the door. She springs up, completely disoriented; for a moment, she hasn't a clue where she is.

"It's me, Gino. Are you there?"

Gino? Then, getting her bearings, she realizes she's in her new room in Vernazza. "Just a minute," she calls out. Groggy, she throws on some clothes and opens the door. She can't suppress a smile.

"Where have you been?" Gino barks. He seems both relieved and irritated. His hands swirl about, adding dynamic and accent. "The landlord said you went for a walk before the storm. He didn't see you come back, and that was two days ago! I know from my mother who works in the shop how much food you bought, but then nobody saw you! Don't look so surprised. In this town, everybody knows everything. I missed seeing you this morning having your coffee."

What could she say? Had it all been a dream meeting Grace, her cottage in the woods, the farm? Joanna feels the blisters on her hands from working the garden, sees the sack of vegetables Grace had given her on the table. She doesn't know where to begin.

"Well, you're here now, and I'm very happy to see you. You like your new room? It's nice, huh?"

She smiles. "It's wonderful, like out of a novel."

"Is that what you're doing here?" Gino cocks his head to the side. "Writing a book? The last time I saw you, you wrote so hard, I thought your arm would fall off."

"Not a book, just my thoughts, like talking to myself."

"Why do that?" Gino smiles so unreservedly that dimples appear on both cheeks, dimples she hadn't noticed before. "Today you can spend the whole day talking to *me*! I have the day off, and I want you to come with me to Monterosso, to my favorite restaurant, and have lunch. *Per favore?*"

Joanna laughs nervously. She's still not awake, doesn't know what to think, only that it's lovely to see him, the way he leans back with his arms high on the doorjamb, swinging to and fro. Endearingly awkward, yet confident and full of life. He drops both arms, then lifts his open hands toward her, inviting her. "You have to come! The weather is great today. And don't worry, just because I told you about this room, you don't owe me anything. Okay? Half an hour, at the harbor." His dimples appear again. "*Ciao, bella!*"

He's gone, but his *ciao, bella* ripples through her. She feels dizzy with excitement, then catches herself. Is she just like her mother, or Terry, wooed by a handsome man? *It's not just that*, she tells herself. *This is you rejoining life, even if it makes you uncomfortable.* She was afraid at first, with the unusual meeting of Grace, but it had all gone well, more than well. This is the new Joanna, taking risks, trying new things, being spontaneous, even if it doesn't always work out. She hurries now to get ready.

*\*\*\**

The harbor is a maze of boats and tourists—a boisterous mix of Italians and foreigners queuing to get onto the various charters, yachts, and party boats. Joanna searches frantically for Gino in the crowd.

"I'm here!" He waves from the corner kiosk, his torso bent over as if at full height he'd be too tall for the town. Relieved to see him, she runs over. "I've ordered you a cappuccino," he says, pointing to her cup. He held an espresso. "Foreigners always drink cappuccino. I hate all that milk."

"Thanks," she says, out of breath. "I was afraid you'd left."

"Why would I do that?" His hands open so wide that his espresso nearly tips over. "Ah, there's our ride," he says, taking her hand.

The boat taxi is small and basic, ferrying locals between the towns. Gino helps her onboard, still holding her hand. Such a little thing, holding hands, yet it feels surprisingly good, like a soothing current. To not think and not know. The warm wind in her hair, blowing loose strands as the boat cruises across the water. After all the years with only Stuart, strange to have another man so close. How two strangers can open something in the other just by being close. A few lines of "Moon River" come to her, and she hums under her breath. *Two drifters off to see the world. There's such a lot of world to see.* A longing only grasped in the brevity of song. For the briefest moment, that unabashed yearning gives a catch in her throat. She looks past Gino to the sea, to the light and smell and soft spray of coolness in this perfect day.

They arrive at the harbor of Monterosso. She's come several times by foot and train; it's a new experience to arrive by boat. She delights afresh at how pretty it is, all the quaint pastel-colored buildings and charming restaurants and cafés, the light. Gino continues holding her hand as they weave through a crowded maze of picturesque streets.

A voice calls out, "*Buongiorno!*" followed by a barrage of Italian.

"My friend invites us for an aperitif. Is it okay?" Gino asks.

"You don't have to drink much, just to awaken the appetite." *Just to awaken the appetite. Sounds so lovely.* Joanna orders a drink she's only seen but never tasted—Martini Rosso. It comes in a tall glass with ice and a slice of orange. She sips the savory-sweet cocktail and enjoys Gino's voice like music, chatting with his friends, his hand reaching for potato chips brushing softly past hers. Not knowing, not ever wanting to know. They finish the drinks, say goodbye to the friends, and meander once again through the crooked streets.

She wants just to keep moving with this sweet feeling of nothing to decide and no chance to get it wrong. Gino seems to feel this as well, this desire to just float as if for him too, that's more than enough. No looking deep into each other's eyes, no chance to evoke that strong feeling they'd first shared.

At the restaurant, she keeps looking at the menu, though he's already ordered. When the waiter takes the menus away, she shifts her eyes to the street and flowers and finally to the food when it comes, almost too pretty to eat. The *risotto ai frutti di mare* arrives in a yellow and blue ceramic bowl with a mountain of creamy rice full of shrimp and clams and mussels. It comes with a large basket of steamy country bread. She's starving and savors each delicious bite. This isn't just food—it's art! Seducing the eyes, the nose, the lips, the tongue, mixing with the balmy sea air and the wine.

"Just one tiny sip more," she tells the waiter, who refills her glass.

"You're going to get drunk!" Gino says. "I'm twice your size, and you drank most of the bottle. I'll have to carry you home."

She lifts her glass in cheers with Gino. Now their eyes meet, and she blushes. Then quickly looks away. If only to play the whole sweet morning again and not go beyond this point. It can only get complicated, being at least ten years older than him, their different cultures, and goodness knows what else.

"What are you thinking?" he asks.

"It's a long time since I spent a day like this."

"*Che è bene sapere!* Good to know." He gets up to pay. She

reaches for her money. "No," he says. "My treat."

"Can we walk back?" she asks.

"Are you crazy? I never do those walks! I still can't believe people come from all over to walk here. Can't they walk at home?"

"There aren't hiking trails between charming little towns like this back home."

"After that American wrote us in his book, it's become a zoo. Too many people come, and everyone feels like they're being . . . what's that word?" Gino jerks his body back to demonstrate being hit by a powerful force.

*"Bombarded."*

*"Bom . . . bar . . . ded?"* he asks, contorting his face as if eating a lemon.

"Yes." She laughs. "Bombarded."

He moves his lips repeatedly to learn the word. Nearly at the harbor, he abruptly stops and asks, "Am I *bombarding* you? Like how your friend was the other night with me?"

"Terry?" Joanna asks. "She really liked you."

"That's not liking." He puts his hands around his throat to mimic suffocation. Joanna starts laughing. She ducks under his raised elbow and darts away. He runs after her, playfully. Out of breath, she slows, and he catches up with her. He wraps his arm around her shoulders, making all sorts of comic faces. "You still didn't answer my question," he says.

"You're right. I didn't. Maybe I'll never answer another question again." Joanna is on a roll of giddy laughter, the full impact of the wine and his playful presence.

"You're a funny girl."

"I am, but not funny enough." She feels the urge to sing but stops herself. Something she would have done when she was young but feels too foolish now. A wave of sadness descends, the brutal passage of time.

"What?" he asks. "What is it?"

"It's nothing," she says, moving her hands to erase the thought.

"Okay," he says. "You don't have to tell me, but you're not allowed to be sad. Today nobody can be sad." He looks at his watch. "Come, we have to hurry to catch the boat back."

Once they're under way, she asks Gino if he gets sad sometimes.

"Me? Oof! Too much! It's why I like you." He leans his arm over the railing, letting the water splash his skin. "I only like people who get sad, even if I don't want you to be sad today. People who can feel sad are the most true."

Being with Gino reminds her of Luca. Not that they are so much alike, but Gino's accent, the way he moves his hands, his emotional bursts, brings back that unsettled, unfinished story. She never understood what made Luca so sad. Sadness is private, intimate, and she never really knew him. Not enough. You need language and time to know someone, and they had neither.

"The *too* rich people who eat at the restaurant," Gino goes on. "I can tell you they are . . . how do you say in English, a pain in—"

"Pain in the ass?" Joanna says, grateful to smile again, how easily he could make her laugh.

***

The boat nears Vernazza. Joanna hasn't seen this town either from the sea before. It seems so fragile, the way it hangs onto the mountainside.

"I saw a guitar in your room," Gino says. "You must play or you wouldn't drag it here."

"I do, for my work. I brought it here with the hopes of playing some, for myself. So far I haven't."

"Maybe," he asks, "you can sing for me?"

"Maybe," Joanna whispers.

The engine slows as they enter the harbor. "It's so hot," Gino says, getting out of the boat. "Let's jump in the sea by the rocks.

Have you been swimming here yet?"

Joanna shakes her head in a vehement no. "I'm way too scared with the rocks and the cliffs. I prefer the beach in Monterosso, where you can feel the sand under your feet. I brought my bathing suit. I thought we'd stay at the beach over there."

"The beach is boring. Here is better, and it's calm today."

They walk to the rocks, and Gino strips down to his swimsuit, then slides into the water. Joanna moves away and changes into her bikini.

"Come on in," Gino shouts, then dives under the water. When he surfaces, she's still standing there. "Don't be afraid," he says. "I'll help you."

She takes her time letting the towel drop, feeling self-conscious and afraid to swim in such rough, deep water. Gino reaches out a hand to help her. She takes it and slides down the slippery rocks into the water. Back and forth they go, swimming laps. She's doing fine until a strong wave takes her by surprise, and she swallows a gulp of water. Panicking, she flails her arms. Quick as a dolphin, Gino's lanky body wraps around her. "You're fine," he says. "I'm here." Joanna clutches his arm. "Swim some more," he urges. "It's good to keep going, to see there's nothing to be afraid of." Gino leaps up from the water to look behind the rocks. "That wave came from a big boat. There isn't another one coming. Let's swim."

Gino is lithe and nimble, scampering up the slippery rocks like a seal, and helps Joanna up. Safely back on the smooth, warm surface of the higher rocks, she lets out a deep sigh.

"What are you afraid of?" Gino asks. "You're a good swimmer." He seems to suspect there's more. She likes that about him, his many layers, his curiosity. Very different, she realizes with a sting, from Luca, who never was that curious.

"I almost drowned when I was a kid," she says. "I was quite small for my age. We used to go, a bunch of families, to a lake outside New York City. We kids would swim to a rope at the far end where it was deep, grab hold of the rope to catch our breath, and then swim back. One time, too many people sat on the rope, bringing it way down so the water went over my head. With nothing to hold onto, I panicked. I tried to swim back but swallowed too much water. The next thing I knew, someone was on top of me on the shore, pressing water from my lungs."

"And your parents came running?"

"No, my mother hates the water. She wasn't there."

"And your father?"

*My father!* She shudders. "I didn't know where he was."

"But still, you're a good swimmer."

"Now. Not then. I was terrified of the water for years until I took a swimming class in college. Still, I prefer a pool or a calm beach. My husband didn't like to swim, so I—"

Gino jerks himself up. "Your husband? I didn't know you were married."

Odd how she'd said *my husband*, without thinking. "I was married. He passed away some months ago."

"You're a wid—? . . . He must have died young."

"He was twenty-five years older than me." The air between them squeezes into an awkward staccato. All so new to be a widow and spend the day with a strange man flirting. Even the word *widow* sounds old and finished, and she doesn't feel finished.

Gino sweeps his hand through his wet hair. Black strands fall across his forehead, his dark brown eyes, and handsome face. Joanna feels him processing this new information. "So, in New York"—he cocks his head to the side like how he does when asking about a new word—"you don't wear black? You can just come to another country and walk and swim?" Not waiting for an answer, he continues, "Do you miss him?"

His eyes seem beckoning, as if asking more than just that question. Their starting points and cultural assumptions are so different. Now she's forced to feel her maturity, that she's lived longer than Gino, a maturity she happily left aside the entire day. He looks so young, can't be more than his mid-thirties. She has no idea what this day might mean to him. Gino, waiting for an answer, takes a pebble and scratches noisy chalk lines on the rock.

"I do miss him," she says. "But I've really enjoyed this day with you. Does that sound terrible?"

"Am I the first man that—"

"That I've been with since my husband died?" she interrupts.

Gino's eyebrow rise.

She nods.

"Ah," he says, tossing the pebble out to sea, like he's getting rid of something foul. "You don't think your husband would mind you spending the day like this?"

Joanna shakes her head. "I think he would be happy for me. Where I'm from, we don't have to keep wearing black."

He raises his arms to the sky. "*Allora*," he says. "There's enough black in these towns."

And with that, he stretches out on the warm rock, closes his eyes, and falls immediately asleep. She watches him, so easily at peace, clearly able to shift and change even with the news of Stuart and return to the moment. In that way, he's also completely different from Luca, and Joanna, not plagued by moods and torturous judgment.

Unable to sleep, she leans back, rolls onto her side, and watches him. She yearns to touch him, to feel his heat, the softness of his skin. To kiss him? Could *she* allow this, this suspended moment connected to nothing, as frightening as swimming off the cliffs? Could she live like this, floating through her days? Seeing what comes up, for things have certainly been coming up. *Be with Gino, try to sing, do her walks, help Grace on the farm?* She tries to quiet her mind, concerned her thinking is loud and raucous, like someone rustling a plastic bag in church. As if on cue, he wakes, stretches his arms, and smiles at her.

"I'm so thirsty," he says, smacking his lips and slowly sitting up. "Hey, why don't we go up to your room and drink some water and you can sing for me?"

"Now?"

"Why not? I have the whole day free."

"My voice will be awful."

"What, do you think that everyone sings so great here just because once upon a time they made a lot of opera in Italy? Believe me, the answer is no. No, no, no, no. My father, since he stopped working and stays all day in the apartment with his canary birds, *he* started singing. And I can tell you, if those birds had hands, they would put them over their ears. It's a lot of noise up there between my father thinking he's Pavarotti and the birds trying to stop him. But I'm sure *you* can sing."

## LUCA OF THE SEA, 1976

We are sailing back to the cold and gray, past the grim smokestacks of the New Jersey skyline, where functional modern life shrieks its venom and lies, its desperation. The sea rages in protest; even the sky morphs into one gray endless void. Sailing past the Statue of Liberty, she's but a shadow in the mist. I can't see her eyes, and she can't see mine, can't see how utterly miserable I am.

We arrive at the Fifty-Fourth Street pier, and I wait for Luca, just as we planned. Suddenly, he appears, running by with his mustachioed friend. "Luca, wait!" I call out. But he doesn't stop; he doesn't turn back. The two of them laugh like they pulled off the biggest heist in the world. Can't even run after him, loaded with bulging suitcases. He knows I've not a penny left to my name. How can he do this? I thought he loved me. He, with his pockets filled with cash, convincing me how excited he was to spend his free weekend with me, to see where I lived and stay with me. My cut finger throbs in this freezing air. *God, what a fool!* Our ridiculous make-believe marriage! Still, I stand there, hoping he'll return. All at once, I see despair on everyone's faces. The fancy *Leonardo da Vinci* that pampered and fed all our desires can't protect us in the end, for none of it was real.

Stella sees me and waves. She, of course, is sensible and arranged a friend to pick her up. He's there now, helping her with her luggage. She rushes over to say goodbye, and I burst into tears that feel like frozen icicles.

"Oh, for God's sake," Stella says. "I warned you. Come with us. We'll drop you off."

Outside my apartment on East Eighty-First, Stella writes her number on a card and gives a hug like she is after all not a bad sort. "Try not to think," she says. "Unpack, take a bath, and go to bed. You'll feel like death for a few days, but it will pass. You're a sweetheart but naïve. . . . It was bound to happen. Chin up, and on you go. Years from now, your sailor boy will be no more than a tiny leaf in a huge forest of memories."

I'm grateful my three roommates are all out. I couldn't bear for them to see me like this. There are two entrances to our apartment—one to the kitchen that leads to my bedroom and the other to the living room where the bathroom and other bedrooms are. We don't lock the two doors, as it costs more to replace the locks when we get broken into, and none of us has anything worth stealing. I slink into my large but dismal bedroom and stare at my piano and guitar like abandoned friends. My mostly empty room seems uglier than ever. Just my mattress on the floor, a tattered rug in the center, and an old wooden chest of drawers.

Luca made me feel large and mighty. Under his spell, everything was vibrant and beautiful—our dream of being musicians together. Without him, the ugly dragon of reality spits in my face. Impossible to get back to my tedious life now. I'll never manage to concentrate and get through this last killer semester and graduate.

Without unpacking, I build a fort of suitcases, crawl between them, and fall into a dark, dreamless sleep.

Kathy, one of my roommates, finds me. Not sure where I am or what day it is. My head throbs, and my finger is in agony. Shit, I suddenly realize I'm not dead and will have to finish university and go to work and see Leo and sell the *Leonardo da Vinci*.

"Are you okay?" Kathy asks.

I lack the strength to hold back, and it all pours out.

"Oh my God." She laughs. "You fell in love with an Italian! They're the worst. You'll recover. We all do."

I shake my head that I won't. That I fell outside the universe and there's no hope. Kathy makes all sorts of faces; her lips are putty and reach to her nose, and one eye sinks down to her chin. A facial gymnast, she's so funny that I start laughing against my will.

"He took me beyond the world, to where everything is beautiful. But when we arrived, he walked right past me like I never existed!"

"People do the stupidest things," Kathy said. "Maybe his friends made fun of him. I bet that's what happened. They're the ones he has to work with every day. Maybe they teased him that you'd be heading back to your life in New York and that *he'd* be a fool to go after *you*."

I hope with all my might she's right. "Tomorrow is my first session with a therapist I *have* to see. It's all part of my training to be a music therapist, and she can't see me like this! But if I don't go, I won't graduate."

"We are all actresses when we need to be," Kathy says. "Just pretend you are fine."

If only it were that easy.

# 9.

## CINQUE TERRE, 2002

"GOD, YOU ARE good," Gino says, rising onto his elbows. He's lying on the ground in the garden outside her room, listening to Joanna play the guitar and sing. The sun is still warm but not as hot as earlier. Joanna is amazed how effortlessly it pours out, as if it has waited all these years for this glorious release. To sing like this feels so good, she can't stop. One song after the other, with Gino applauding and asking for more.

"Why haven't I heard you on the radio?" he asks. "I mean it."

She hesitates to answer, to break the spell. "I never sing like this."

"Eh?" Gino shrugs. "I don't understand. You *are* singing like this."

"It's hard to explain. Can I just sing you another?"

"You can sing to me forever." Gino walks over to the table. He takes hold of a chair, turns it around, and sits with his legs straddling the side, his chest against the back. "I still want to know why."

She's reluctant to stop, afraid the ease of her voice will disappear. "Did you ever want to accomplish anything so badly that you always messed up when people were watching?"

"No," Gino says, skillfully rocking the chair like he's riding it.

"The only thing I'm really good at is waiting tables, and there are always people watching."

"I care too much what people think that I'll—"

"What?" Gino laughs. "You're afraid they'll throw tomatoes at you?"

"It's not just that. I often can't sing at all. I freeze up. My voice gets strained and sounds horrible. You have to feel safe in yourself to sing freely in front of people. I really wanted to be a singer-songwriter and tour, but I was always too afraid." She sighs. "Do you know Janis Joplin?"

"Yes."

"*She* didn't care what people thought."

"But she's dead!" Gino says, his hands in the air for emphasis.

"I can't even practice without torturing myself, can't bear how terrible I mostly sound. Only once in the bluest moon do I sing like this." She remembers how Luca complained that he only played well once a year, when he felt Ginger Baker take him over. "You need to be confident you can sing well, at least most of the time, before letting others hear you."

"Oh man, you should hear my father. If you heard him and then heard yourself, *that* would cure you. Anyway, why do you care what people think? People are mostly stupid. Don't you know that?"

Joanna laughs, and with the laughter comes the flash of connection between them, that erotic pull, that charge. Maybe that's why she sang so freely all afternoon with Gino. She has to stop thinking, just do one more song before this rare opening slams shut. She quickly tunes her guitar and begins one of her own compositions from ages ago. He can't possibly get all the words, yet she can tell he likes it. When she's finished, he stands and claps.

"Thank you!" She feels a strong urge to kiss him but resists. He must have felt her impulse, for he reaches gently over to take the guitar from her arms. She tugs the guitar back and puts it in its soft case.

Gino touches her arm. "Why are you afraid?"

"I'm not afraid," she says without looking at him. She gathers her song notes, puts them into the pocket, and with a jerk of finality zips the case shut.

"You are! You should see your face. Like I am holding a knife."

"It . . . doesn't get better than this."

"What?"

"Before it gets ruined." Her voice is already hoarse, the magic gone.

"*Non capisco!* Please tell me what you are so scared of."

"You'll probably think I'm crazy," she says. "I'm no good at this."

"Joanna, please don't be upset. Maybe we're all crazy. I am, that's for sure. Your songs are so pretty, and your voice, I could listen to you forever. It's just that I also want to kiss you. Is that wrong? Maybe I am not good at this either. Most of the women who come here are like your friend."

"Like Terry?"

"Yeah. They just want a night. But you . . . this. It also makes me nervous. I've never met anyone like you."

She turns away from him. "We kiss, and then what?" Joanna says, going toward her room. "Like in the movies, we leave a trail of clothing and have wild and incredible sex and live happily ever after." She shakes her head. "I can assure you, it won't go like that, not with me."

"What, what is it?" Gino asks.

"Please forgive me. . . . I just can't."

Gino comes closer, lifts her face in his hands to study her. "It's okay," he says.

She pulls herself away and goes inside. He stands for an awkward moment at the door, then with the infamous *ciao*, leaves.

\*\*\*

Once he's gone, she misses him. She misses him terribly. The only thing she wants is to do it all again, with a better ending. The way he held her on the boat, her tipsy carefree mood during lunch, how he'd dared her into the water, and the way she sang. There'll never be another day like this. She's had her chance. Should have just gone ahead and kissed him. But she's forgotten how. That door has been closed too long. Stuart always seemed fine that they were more friends than lovers. He'd been married before, had kids and another life. They filled their days with other activities, perhaps *sublimating*, as Freud called it. But it worked, and they were happy.

Why is this all happening? Is she falling in love with Gino? They make it look easy in the movies, but it isn't, not if you haven't slept with anyone, not even your own husband, for ages. Can Gino possibly understand?

*＊＊＊*

Joanna now thinks of the brick steps outside the café as her stoop, her perch to begin the day. No one has yet claimed the spot, so she plunks her knapsack down and gets a coffee. When she returns, she opens her diary yet can't stop peeking to see if Gino has arrived, wondering what his first reaction will be when he sees her.

"You mind if I sit here?" a man asks. She doesn't want him to sit next to her but can hardly stop him; it's a free space. This man seems all at once eager to speak with her, perhaps to practice his English. But it isn't really English he speaks, more a melody of sounds with a few recognizable phrases supported by gesture. Or perhaps he wants to complain to her. She understands enough that he's distressed about his mother, whom he's visiting, who lives in a grand house too big for her but refuses to move.

As the man rambles, Joanna wants to move away but can't without being rude. She glances over at Gino, who is now there setting up for lunch. He seems more agitated this morning, his movements disjointed. He drops silverware, breaks a plate, then goes inside for longer than usual. The man sitting beside her finishes his espresso and his diatribe and, with a flippant *ciao*, is gone. She opens her diary and starts writing.

Gino's voice startles her. "Hey, you talk to too many people! You won't have time to write." He's smoking a cigarette.

"Since when do you smoke?" she asks.

"Since when I'm angry," Gino says, trying to form smoke rings.

"Angry?"

"At you speaking with everyone," he says.

"That man?" It surprised and, in a way, touched her that he was jealous. "He just wanted to complain about his mother."

Gino pulls hard on the cigarette, the other hand twisting through his hair. "But why did you have to listen to him?"

"I had no choice. I don't want to make enemies in this town."

He takes a few more drags of his cigarette.

"I had a great time yesterday," Joanna says.

"Me too. I wish I didn't have to work today so we could go somewhere."

"Really?"

"Why are you surprised? Just because you kicked me out in the end? Oh boy, there's my aunt. Can we meet later, on the rocks?"

"How about tomorrow?"

"*Domani*?" Gino's hands lift so far in the air, they seem to leave his body. "You sound Italian. What do you have to do today that's so important?"

"I, um—" She hoped to do a long hike, maybe go to Grace's farm in the afternoon.

He looks at her so endearingly that Joanna can hardly stop herself from hugging him. Just then, a sharp scream pierces the air.

"I can't talk, my aunt. Come to the rocks, today. *Per favore*. You have to swim with me again, so you get better at it."

"Okay." Joanna smiles. How can she resist him? She'll do a

shorter walk, go to Grace another day. "I'll see you later."

***

She follows signs to a monastery, a trail she's not yet taken. It leads steeply up and then opens to a startling vista of Vernazza directly below. Exposed, like a naked woman—the cluster of houses a pelvic mound and the V-shaped coastline her thighs opening to the sea. With boats coming and going and the swell of waves, it feels somehow erotic.

Charged with sensation, she climbs higher and starts singing, hoping to find the free voice from yesterday. There it is, that wonderful click inside, that elusive door opening, and her voice pours forth. Every sinew, bone, and cell resonates with sound. Nature full and lush around her, she feels like Maria in *The Sound of Music* and sings full throttle. Her voice reverberates off the trees and sounds beautiful to her ears. She dares to give over more and more, and unexpectantly, a new song arises. She grabs her diary, scribbles down the words, and notates the melody with arrows. A new song hasn't come to her in ages. What is she getting herself into, awakening all this? Not to forget this new melody, she sings it again and again.

Then comes a familiar reaction—clutch to the brain, a slam of the brakes as if forbidding this liberating expression, this glorious but dangerous release. She chokes, and that powerful, free voice is gone. The way it always happens, her killer critic just too strong. What she didn't tell Gino yesterday was that she'd never have managed a life as a performer; all that *exposing herself* would have destroyed her. Furious with her lifetime of crippling fears, she rages up the craggy incline.

Entering the courtyard of the monastery, the air feels cool and mysterious. She can almost hear an ancient hum from spirits of hundreds of pilgrims who sought salvation here. She circles the empty walls, challenging the pretense of who she's always been, her beliefs. Always convinced something would steal her voice. It wasn't only lack of daring that stopped her, but a strong conviction that deep down she wasn't any good. And where had that begun? It surely didn't help that her mother never told her the truth about her real father. All the nonsense excuses over the years of why that impostor father, whose picture was on the mantelpiece, would always let her down. How pathetic the way her mother would get her worked up and all dressed up for a visit from this *father* who, of course, would never show. And Lillian, always the actress, would be as dreadfully disappointed as Joanna. Finally, when Joanna was about ten, she put an end to the charade. Refusing to feed the secret hope that maybe this time he'd show, maybe this time she was worth it. When you shut one door in yourself, you tend to close the others.

Slinking down against the cool wall, tears of another sort stream down her cheeks. From a strange, twisted happiness that maybe, just maybe, she can learn to be there, just with herself. She closes her eyes and falls into a meditative sleep.

*** 

Several hours later, when she makes her way back down, Gino is already there on the rocks.

"How was your day?" he asks.

"Different," she says.

"Because of me?"

"Maybe."

"Because of you, I dropped two plates and three glasses, and my aunt would have killed me if we weren't so busy. To make up, I promised to help earlier this afternoon, so I can't stay long now. Ever since my father got depressed, he—"

"Your father's depressed?"

"Yeah, that's why he's all day in his robe, singing to his canary birds. He never leaves the apartment. Don't look so surprised. Just because this town *looks* pretty doesn't mean everything is."

## LUCA OF THE SEA, 1976

I'm at the first obligatory therapy session, sitting in a tiny, overheated room across from an overly smiley woman who's very thin except for a small bump around her belly that could be either the result of a huge lunch or the start of a baby. She radiates that blond cool Midwestern just-moved-to-New-York smile, and her hair bounces like in a shampoo commercial.

"Even though you're doing this for credits so you can graduate, it's important that you value this time. Not just about learning to be a good therapist for others, but to be in your own process." When I still don't say anything, she eggs me on. "I can see something very strong has happened to you. Tell me. You can trust me."

Her darling blue eyes and soft cooing voice become dangerously seductive, and before I know it, I spill out the whole story, about Luca and falling in love. Though nervously touching my infected finger, I refuse to mention *that*. I say way too much and probably won't graduate, but it was exploding in me and actually feels good to tell someone.

"Not to worry," she assures me. "I won't report any of this. It's confidential. What happens in the therapeutic situation is just between us." We eyeball each other, like a quick ping-pong game. "I mean it," she says.

Still, I carefully choose my words now that the explosion has passed, to sound sensible, reasonable. "You know, how some things you just have to feel," I say, trying to sound calm and mature. "When I was four, despite my mother telling me not to put my finger in the flame, I did. I had to know what burning felt like."

"And?" the therapist asks, listening closely. I get the feeling she's new at this; she keeps looking at her notes.

"It hurt a lot, and I screamed. My mother came running and yelled at me for not listening. In a way, I was glad because, from then on, I *knew* what being burned meant and why I shouldn't put my finger in the flame. How can we know a situation without the experience?"

"Good insight," she says.

"So I really know that Luca fell in love with me. Even if he ran quickly away yesterday, I understand why he had to do that, to keep our love separate from his work. He will write me, and I will see him again, and everything will be fine."

She starts scribbling hastily on her yellow pad. *What is she writing? Why can't she say something, that yes, everything will be okay.* Instead, she bites her lower lip, stares down at her pad, and sighs. "You must be realistic."

"I AM!" I yell. "Didn't you hear what I just said! I understand why he wasn't there to meet me yesterday. I really do."

She shakes her head, sucks in her lips. "That's not what I mean. I'm sure you had a wonderful trip. But you can't really imagine a stable relationship with a sailor on a cruise line who lives in Italy. That's not realistic."

"He was the navigator! Not a sailor."

"Even so." She's tricked me, and it's too late to take back my words. Just because she's living a normal life with money and a husband and a baby probably growing inside her, she gets to decide what's real.

The session ends, and I've never hated anyone so much.

✱✱✱

Once outside, on the cold, unforgiving concrete of New York, I panic. Why can't she approve of my love? Not write it off as a silly romance. It was the strongest love a person can ever know in this dreary, monotonous life.

Still no letter from Luca. Why hasn't he written? I feel like Cinderella who has lost not just a slipper but everything. *She* was at least warned it would all vanish at the stroke of midnight. But like her, I've fallen madly in love, have tasted a life I can no longer live without.

I take the train to my mother's place to return the suitcase and borrowed clothing for the cruise, and Lillian sees immediately that I'm drowning in sorrow.

"Oh boy," she says. "The apple doesn't fall far from the tree. God knows I've tried chopping down that tree. Come here, you." She wraps me in her arms, and we both cry.

The next day, with my head slumping and my heart as heavy as a planet, I begin the miserable trek to the Bronx State Mental Hospital for the six-month music therapy internship. Three mornings a week, until June. Luckily, the aides I meet once I arrive laugh easily, giving me courage.

On the way to class later, the wind rips down Broadway, and dark thoughts torment like vultures: *Luca is in the warm tropical sun with another girl on that magic beach, writing THEIR names in the sand. She is very rich and can buy a big house in Rome, where Luca can play his drums as loud as he wants. He wouldn't dare run past* her *laughing with his friends when the ship pulls in, because for her he'll quit the* Leonardo. *THEY will have a real marriage and live happily ever after. He will think of you at the briefest seconds when he feels the pain in his finger. But his cut was shallow, and he will soon forget you ever existed.*

Good thing I have Mr. Karpel today. He always lifts me up and away, into something far more important than my stupid life. Today, he stands at the blackboard for ages, as if waiting for higher instructions. Everyone's so still, you can almost hear the earth move. Slowly, he takes a bit of chalk and writes the timespan of the dinosaur age. Then, in large capital letters, adds, *MANKIND* with a starting date followed by a dash and four question marks. He turns around with his arm pointing to the four question marks and dares us to fill in this date to mark the end of our lifespan.

"What do you mean?" a boy calls out. "Are you implying our time here is limited like the dinosaur?"

And Mr. Karpel, with that amazing voice of his, says, "Did you just assume we would be here forever, no matter what we do?"

"But we're so different from the dinosaurs! The world is perfect for us, for humans, I mean."

"Ah," says Mr. Karpel, "but are we humans so perfect for the world?"

The class ends, and everyone rushes out—except me.

# 10.

## CINQUE TERRE, 2002

JOANNA WAKES FROM a shockingly sexual dream in a pool of sweat. She doesn't want to remember it, but certain parts persist: *She visits her mother, who is very drunk. Joanna tries to ignore her and goes to her old bedroom. Lillian barges in. "Someone's here to see you." A man as big as the door pushes past her mother and grabs Joanna's arm.*

*"Come," he commands. He drags her down the stairs and out to his car, a convertible with the top down, though it's November and very cold. Joanna screams and tries to stop him, but she can't. As they drive, the scene shifts to the Mediterranean. The man stops the car in a shady spot overlooking the sea. He touches her and her limbs grow weak with desire.*

*"You are beautiful," he says. "But your mother fears for you, fears she's ruined your chance for love." The man reaches over to embrace her. Joanna wants to lose herself in him but is terrified.*

*"I won't hurt you," he says. "I'll give you what you wish for." His body comes in closer, grabbing her...*

Arousal swarms her. In a terribly unsettled state, she goes straight for the station and onto the first train. She doesn't want anyone to see her, not like this.

She gets off at Corniglia, a town she's walked toward several times but has never climbed the myriad steps to. Very differently situated than Vernazza, perched precariously high away from the sea, like a hat on the cliffs. Impatiently, she pushes past the tourists and enters narrow, claustrophobic streets. Like a trapped rat starved for space, she follows signs down a thousand steps, or so it feels, to the harbor.

It's a tiny cove with no beach. No one is there, no Gino to guide her in the rough, unsettled water. A few fishing boats bang restlessly against the concrete pier. Without hesitation, as she can't bear the feelings crushing through her, she strips off her sundress and jumps in. She dog-paddles, going far away from the concrete ledge with its iron rings. Swimming in a frantic swirl, she tries to purge the threatening erotic dream. Exhausted, she climbs out of the water and dries off. Still, that raging feeling torments her. As if a black claw reaching out to grab her, she must keep moving. She slips on her sundress and scampers up the endless steps back to the town and then down the other thousand treacherous steps, the only way to the trail back to Vernazza. She runs like a goat, not caring if she slips and falls.

Who was the man in the dream? Luca, or—?

Halfway back to Vernazza, she sees a large crowd outside a café she hadn't noticed before. CNN is blaring from inside. Foreigners, mostly Americans, stand watching the news. Joanna hears snippets: The build-up of a new war... Saddam Hussein... weapons of mass destruction. "We will protect democracy—!"

Joanna hasn't been following the news. Maybe that's why she's felt so triggered, so out of sorts this day, not just the dream. She remembers Stuart's concern that another needless war would shove aside urgent needs like climate change and give neoliberals *carte blanche* to escalate turbo-capitalism.

She watches the mostly young crowd grow excited about this

looming war on terrorism—yet another war to end all wars. *How can they get excited?* she thinks. *Can't they see the manipulation? Why aren't they outraged?* The timbre of George W. Bush's voice, of Dick Cheney's, makes her skin crawl. A young American man notices her scowl. "Hey lady, chill out. None of it matters anyway. It's all a game."

Joanna is livid, trembling. "It does matter! It's not a game."

"You're gonna tell me about the Vietnam War and the marches you went on. I know that look from my mother's face. It's a different time now. Don't you get it? This time we'll win. We're gonna get those mother fuckers, those terrorists who did this to us. And it'll be over in a second."

She can't stay there a moment longer. The thunderous music behind the news, like it's a show. She rushes out and heads back to the trail. With her mind distracted, Joanna slips on the loose gravel and falls over. Her hands sting from the scrape, her knees bruised.

"Are you okay?" a voice beckons.

Kneeling, she turns and recognizes a face from the café, one of the reticent observers.

"I'm okay." Joanna gets up and brushes herself off. "It's nothing."

"Wait," he says, catching up with her. "I want to tell you I agree with you. It *does* matter. I don't understand what's happening in the US. After September eleventh, the whole world felt such empathy for America. Now they're pushing for this war on Iraq, and it doesn't feel right."

So surreal these days, this whole week. She wants to touch this person, have him pinch her, make sure she's not still dreaming.

"I'm from Holland," he says. "Are you from the States?" He's nearly as tall and slim as Gino, his hair a mob of dirty-blond, with a generous smile and grayish-blue almond-shaped eyes. His voice is a bit raspy, like Tom Watts, but easy to understand. "I love coming here. Too many Americans, but still, so easy to get here by train from Holland, the combination of mountains and beaches and little towns with delicious food. Vernazza's getting too touristy, but what can you do. I'm Pieter." He reaches his hand over to shake. He seems younger than Joanna, but lately everyone seems younger. He has a nice face and seems comfortable in his skin, but his nails, she notices, are bitten to the cuticles.

"I'm Joanna, from New York."

"The city?"

She nods.

"Wow. I'd love to talk with you more. To hear how it was for you, the whole September eleventh thing. I have to get back to my work, but please come by. I'm staying at the guesthouse behind the café, close to the road. Just follow the path. You can't miss it. That's where I usually am, working. I'm a writer, but this whole thing has poked a hole in my brain, all the misinformation and now this war coming, can't get anything done."

"I haven't been watching or reading the news," Joanna says with her habitual shrug of shame. "Are you staying for a while?"

"I am. Please come by. I'd love to speak to a real New Yorker." He bids her farewell and heads in the opposite direction.

Once back in Vernazza, she heads for the harbor. She hadn't planned to see Gino, but somehow after speaking with Pieter, this sensible, well-informed Dutchman, she feels calmer. Gino is waving like an eager dog when she arrives.

When she comes closer, he steps back, startled. "Are you okay? You look terrible."

"It was a strange morning. Then I heard the news that there may be another war."

"There's always a war. Just now it's not here. The life is too short to think of every war every minute."

"Gino—"

"Shh."

"I can't stop thinking of it."

"Yes, you can." He learns over to kiss her, and this time she doesn't stop him.

"Ah!" Gino laughs. "I am happy for this war." He kisses her some more.

"I'm not good today," Joanna says, letting him hold her in his arms.

"Okay. Listen to my plan. You're on your own too much. You need to be with people, especially where I can keep an eye on you! There's a couple living here sometimes. They always order the best fish and the most expensive everything, and they asked me to invite someone, someone interesting to join their table tonight. I think they get bored with each other. They travel a lot, so they speak English."

"But I look terrible. You just said so."

He gently strokes her cheek. "Go home and have some sleep. You'll be fine. Do you have something nice to wear, a bit more"—he cups his fingers together—"Italian? The dinner is at eight, and after we can talk, okay?"

"You mean kiss."

He laughs; his happiness is contagious. "My English gets better when we talk. I'm already good at kissing."

"Okay." She nods. "I'll come have dinner. You're right, it will do me good to be with people."

"No kissing in front of the others. My aunt would kill me. She wants all the girls to think they have a chance."

## LUCA OF THE SEA, 1976

The days go by and still no letter. Yet, I stubbornly stick to my plan and study Italian during the long subway rides to the hospital in the Bronx and back.

On the way to my piano lesson, my head hangs so low, it's banging against my chest. I get right to the piano, to the Chopin piece. *He* knew this heartache; his music reeks of heartache.

"You have music in you," the teacher says encouragingly.

"Or is it suffering?"

"That helps too." He laughs and pats me on the shoulder. "You're a fine player. Don't forget that."

If only to glue those words to my head, to convince my brain that I'm okay. For the rest of the lesson, we speak about confidence and the trick of believing.

"You can," he says. "You have everything you need."

Except I don't. Why can't he see how afraid I am? I've never learned how to do this life. And why it's urgent to see Luca again. With him, I was okay, actually more than okay. Even if it's been nine days since Luca sailed away, and still no letter, even if I'm dying in the cauldron of doubt, I can't give up the slim hope of seeing him again.

*\*\*\**

The next morning, distracted as I am by my manic moods, the hospital door slams shut on a finger of my right hand, my strumming hand. I shriek in pain, fearing the tip has been severed. The aides rush me to another ward, and they stitch me up. The doctor drugs me to a stupor and promises I won't lose my finger. He also treats my other finger, the one Luca punctured in our foolish marriage ceremony that is hopelessly infected, then rebandages it. Now I'm wounded on both hands, a casualty of love.

My supervisor at the hospital is not happy. How can I lead the drumming circle or play the guitar with two bandaged hands? Meanwhile, the emotionally challenged boys on the ward seem thrilled with my bandages, like I've just come from a street fight. Usually, they're reluctant and squirrelly when we begin, but now they're witch doctors who want to heal *me*. They pound the drums with purpose. I start to dance, and they play even louder. So loud, the supervisor comes rushing to see. She pokes her head in while I'm dancing with tribal abandon. Startled by the intense focus of the boys, she turns all shades of purple. Music therapy is new on the ward, and this rhythmic chaos seems dangerous to her. Yet she sees how responsive the boys are, how attentive to their playing. She can't quarrel with this and nods with tentative approval. Once she's gone, the boys squeal like they've slayed the dragon. They whoop and holler and slap each other high fives, and I quickly get them drumming again so we don't lose the momentum.

Each day I fall more in love with the patients who seem to have rejected reality, or rather live in another dimension, and they in turn love me more. Maybe because I *see* them and understand their suffering, their courage. They burst into smiles as soon as I arrive with my bandaged fingers, guitar, and sack of instruments. If only the doctors didn't medicate them so much. The sessions before the round of meds are animated, but right after they're like zombies. I mention this to the head nurse.

"Better they sleep," the nurse says, "than have a fit and destroy your instruments."

Is there no middle ground?

*** 

Despite my wounds, each time I sit at the piano, with all the yearning for Luca, a new song comes. I'm totally inspired as the music and words cascade around me. I don't sing very well, and I'm hoping that soon I can be with him again and that my magic voice will return. Can't help but think I've made the whole thing up. At the travel agency, when I'm selling the cruise, there's this other me that does the talking; otherwise, I'd be sobbing.

Today, on the way home, I pick up the developed pictures from the cruise (no, I didn't toss my camera overboard). There he is, in living color—Luca! One picture after the other of him and those amazing beaches. It's real; it's all real. *Luca, please write me! Otherwise, I'll feel sure I'm crazy.*

With my hands shaking, I can hardly get the key in the door. Amy, the neighbor from upstairs who I adore—she's mad as a hatter and makes me feel normal—is just coming and helps open it. She sees the photos in my hands and grabs them.

"Wow!" she says. "He's gorgeous."

"But he hasn't written. Maybe it really was just a shipboard romance."

"No!" Amy says, like she's the grand mistress of truth. "I can see in his eyes that he really loves you. You are going to see him again. I'm one-hundred-percent sure."

I hug her and tell her how much I love her and then scamper into my room. I have so much homework but can't do any of it. Instead, I take the photos of Luca and me and spread them out on my bed. Then I fall asleep dreaming of him, only of him.

# 11.

## CINQUE TERRE, 2002

JOANNA TRIES TO nap so she'll be rested for the dinner party. Not a chance. Her thoughts are scattered: the lingering dream, the possible war, Gino, and the silly worry of what to wear that would be remotely stylish. She shudders at the memory of Luca's reaction when she wore that foolish red Juliet dress. She can get it right this time. *Buy something here. This is Italy, for goodness sake.* With compulsive energy, she rushes for the second time that day for the train, this time to Levanto, the biggest of the nearby towns.

Once there, she's about to ask directions for a clothing shop when she hears someone call her name. It's Grace. Thrilled for this chance meeting, Joanna runs over.

"Hey, nice to see you. What brings you here? Time for a cup of tea?"

Joanna glances at her watch. "I'd love to, but I was invited to a dinner party tonight and need to get something—"

"More elegant, *Italian*?"

"Is it that obvious?"

"Hey, look at me." Grace laughs. "With my hair covered in dust and my clothes brown with mud. Come, I know just the place."

Grace leads them through the streets to a small shop and straight to a rack of clothing in the back. "It's still here," she says. "This should fit you." She holds it up to Joanna. "What do you think?" Joanna looks at Grace, wondering if it had been hers. "They sell it on consignment, and the money goes to a charity. I may have worn it once."

Joanna loves the feel of the silky peach dress, reminiscent of the sultry wraparound she'd worn when she met Luca on the *Leonardo*. She can't help twirling in front of the mirror, enjoying the swish and turn of fabric, her tan calves seductive below the scalloped hem.

"Fits like a charm. You should take it," Grace says. "And still time for tea."

They head to a café with a terrace under a shading palm. Grace orders in Italian and Joanna hears her strong English accent puncture the beautiful language.

"Have you been following the news?" Grace asks when their tea arrives. Joanna, unable to hold back, can tell how upset the warmongering has made her. "I watched Tony Blair," Grace adds, "and wonder what drug they've put him on. He has a weird Cheshire cat smile these days and a monkey-walk like he's in a special club with the boys. I try to not think of that world, to not be in that world, yet if we leave those naughty boys on their own, God knows what they'll do."

"Hard to know what to pay attention to and what to ignore."

"It is," Grace says, "and why I need the solace of gardening. Just look at my hands."

"I'm sorry I haven't come again to help you. It's just that—"

"No worries. You didn't come to Italy to pick my tomatoes."

Joanna wants to tell her about Gino and all she's discovering in herself, but she can't, not yet.

"I see gardening as a chance of going undercover, of being *inside*. There's a lot of noise in the world, a lot of nonsense. Can be hopelessly confusing."

"You don't seem confused," Joanna says.

"I work hard at it, believe me. I've never worked so hard at anything in my life."

"To not be confused?"

"To change how I think, to be more accepting, not fleeing from or fixing things. Like with gardening. You can't know how the vegetables will turn out when you plant the seeds . . . you literally can't know. You plant them, pray for rain and sun, and all that must happen while you continue to tend the garden. It's a ton of work. You've had a taste yourself the other day. When the harvest finally comes with things ready to eat, you're a bundle of gratitude."

Joanna can only listen. As attached to wild nature as Stuart was, they never did any gardening living in New York.

"Speaking of which, I must get back."

"I'm so glad I ran into you," Joanna says. "And thanks for the dress."

"Remember, come by anytime."

***

It's a beautiful evening to dine outside. Gino has made the table special with a shimmering gray tablecloth and candles. The balmy breeze on Joanna's naked arms enlivens her as her wineglass is filled again and again by her charming host until it no longer matters how many times the linguini slips from her fork before reaching her mouth. Gino serves the *pesce alla griglia* on a glazed ocher platter, the aroma so splendid. Thoughts of the coming war slip away as Gino expertly fillets the fish and presents each of them with a perfect portion garnished with grilled asparagus, slivers of carrots and zucchini, and pungent slices of lemon. The fish melts in her mouth. She's never tasted anything so exquisite. For the couple, though, this seems to be standard fare, and they go on chatting and asking questions as if she, Joanna, is the main course and the only item of interest. Joanna does her best to keep them entertained with New York jokes, like how a wife calls her husband to the terrace in NY: "Hurry, dear, before the soup gets dirty."

At the end of the meal, the wife, slightly older than Joanna but younger than her octogenarian husband, grabs hold of her arm. "Shall we make my husband very angry?" Without waiting, the woman calls for Gino, and when he arrives, she says to Joanna, "I'm ordering an ice cream cone! It is shocking and never done in Italy, not at the table. You will join me?"

Joanna, who really is too full and doesn't want to add to the *faux pas*, shakes her head no.

"Oh, what a pity," the woman says, and then smiling to Gino, adds, "then just bring me one, a chocolate cone."

Gino returns, grinning at Joanna approvingly that she's not ordered this crass item, and hands the woman her cone. She is just about to have a lick when her phone rings. She fumbles, with the cone in hand, through her purse to find the source of the ringing. With the phone clamoring, she snaps her purse shut (without finding her phone) and presses the ice cream cone to her ear and shouts, "*Pronto, pronto*." But the phone keeps ringing. Joanna can hardly contain her laughter. At last, the ringing stops, and the woman, still not realizing the cone isn't her phone, goes to put it in her purse. Joanna reaches a hand to stop her. The wife, in a snap, notices what she's about to do and bursts out laughing. Her husband seems less amused as he calls for the check.

"You must dine with us again," the wife says more times than necessary, and they leave. Joanna lingers a bit more, enjoying the last of her wine, the soft evening air.

Gino slips over in his dolphin way. "Stay," he says. "I won't need the table. Wait for me to finish." He refills her glass before clearing the rest of the table. She smiles at him, happy to continue sitting there.

The evening is delightfully warm, the stars overhead twinkling, and the moon is almost full, and she feels surprisingly calm and content. She thinks of the dinner conversation, of how this couple travels incessantly between their many homes, one here, one in Milan, one on Sardinia, and still they're bored. Though Joanna enjoyed the meal, she's relieved to not have to live like this every night. The simple healthy food she's eaten with Grace and the meals she prepares, or eats at the *osteria*, are more than satisfying.

Maybe it's the wine, or the dress she's wearing, or the elegance of the evening; she can't help reminiscing about her time on the *Leonardo*, the fanciest lifestyle she'd ever experienced. She wonders about Luca, if he ever moved to Rome and if he lives like this. He had plenty of money then, or so he would tell her; maybe now he has even more. If it had all gone differently, would she and Luca be as bored as this rich couple?

***

Gino is ready to go, and once she stands, realizes how much she's had to drink. He takes her hand to steady her, but it's she who steers them to the cliffs behind the restaurant, her favorite evening perch. They reach the top and sit on the bench. Gino lights a cigarette. She leans against his shoulder, with her eyes closed, drifting away in the night air and the hypnotic sound of the crashing waves.

"Joanna?" he says softly. "Are you sleeping?" It is dark; she barely sees his face, only the red spark of his cigarette. She opens her eyes fully. Just then, a shooting star flashes by. She thinks of the years it took for that light to be seen in the night sky. She closes her eyes again and feels his hand caressing her cheek, brushing her hair from her face. Every touch sends ripples through her like a pebble on the water. She feels him folding himself around her and then he kisses her. She reciprocates with hunger and urgency. She tastes the familiar cigarette on his tongue. So good to kiss him, really kiss him; her body melts. He pulls her tighter, closer. His hand comes to her breast, and she holds it there, pressing her hand against his. So long she's waited to feel this again. Just as he promised all those years ago when they'd carved their names in the sand.

"Joanna," he whispers, singing her name. "You're so beautiful."

Tears splash down her cheeks. She doesn't care. He licks away her tears.

"Oh Luca," she murmurs.

Gino jerks himself away. "*Luca?* Who the hell is Luca?"

"Wait. Gino, I was dreaming. Please don't go."

But he's already up. "You are crazy! What am I doing with you?"

## LUCA OF THE SEA, 1976

I practice Italian, saying over and over *ti amo, ti voglio, e tu mi ami.* I love you, I want you, and you love me.

The ship will be back in New York later today, and still no letter. What shall I do? If I don't take the chance and go to the harbor, I'll never see him, never play music with him, never kiss him ever again. Even if I'm being the biggest fool and missing a very important class, I still head straight for the harbor.

The subway takes forever to come. At Forty-Second Street, on the shuttle crosstown, I panic, when the train stalls, that we'll be stuck for hours. That I'll miss the chance to meet Luca, if by chance he's waiting. I never gave him my phone number since he said he couldn't phone from the ship anyway . . . that he would write.

At last the train moves. I transfer on the west side, rush for the local, get off at Fifty-First Street, and run like lightning through the slushy streets to Fifty-Fourth. Around the corner, I see the *Leonardo da Vinci,* sleek and mighty, like a goddess. And like a mirage, waiting by the gangplank, his dark wool cape pulled to his ears, his hair blowing every which way, his shoulders huddled against the cold, and a bag over his shoulder, is Luca. My voice heaves a broken

"Luu . . . caa," but he can't possibly hear; I'm too far away. I run like mad, and when I'm nearly there, he feels me and turns. We freeze; then he runs toward me. He gathers me in his arms. No words, only kisses, unbearably tender kisses. He holds me and says over and over how sorry he is for what happened the last time. I'm so relieved he's holding me in his arms that I instantly forget all the miserable days of waiting.

He links his arm through mine, and we hail a taxi, exactly how it was supposed to have gone eleven days ago. He still has my address on the paper I wrote for him and shows it to the driver. He reaches for my hands and sees the other bandaged finger. "Did you marry someone else?" He laughs.

"I was thinking too hard about you, and it got squeezed in a door."

"Then I am dangerous!"

"You are. I didn't know if I'd ever see you again. You promised you would write, but you didn't!"

"You didn't get my letters?" he asks, alarmed. I shake my head. He turns his body in the taxi, his fingers pinching in and circling to emphasis his devastation. "I wrote you a letter every day! You must believe me. *Mia piccola bambina.* I couldn't stop thinking of you!"

The sweetest words I've ever heard! Yet I'm still afraid to trust him. He sees my hesitation, the tightness between my eyebrows, and gathers me even tighter in his arms. "I am here now. We are together, and I will never leave you again!"

Once in my room, we fall onto my bed. I can hardly believe he is here with me. I touch his cheeks, ruffle my hands through his hair, breathe in his scent of cigarettes and sea. His skin so brown while mine faded to pale. His hands sweep down my cheeks, and he cups my chin and kisses me deep and hard, so hungry we are for each other.

My room has two doors, one to the kitchen and the other through the hallway bedroom that leads to the living room. Luca makes sure all the doors are closed. He goes to the window that's blocked by the metal fire escape. Hardly a view, just a square bit of concrete landing and a tiny garden before another brick apartment house, and another and another. He makes a face, saying it's not quite the Caribbean. Then he goes to his bag and takes out an already chilled bottle of Taittinger champagne and delicious snacks from the ship.

"I bring the Caribbean to you!" Our apartment is poorly stocked, so I get the best glasses I can find. He makes a face at that too. "This isn't the *Leonardo*?" We both laugh, and it feels so good and right to be together. We drink our champagne with all kinds of kissing, and then we make love again and again. We do not leave our little bubble, falling asleep in each other's arms. The morning greets us like a psalm, and we kiss and hug and make love again.

"Can we play some music?" I ask when we've come up for air. I point to my piano.

He shakes his head no. "I must go now. There's no time for music. But we are woven together. You can feel this now, right? So even if no letter arrives because it doesn't work so good to mail a letter from the ship, you must know that I write you and think of you and count the minutes until we are together again. You promise you will be there again in eleven days?"

"I promise," I say, trying to forget my heartache from eleven days prior. I want so to believe him. I think he sees my doubt and takes me once again in his arms. He covers my pale skin with kisses. "I shall be your sun."

# 12.

## CINQUE TERRE, 2002

JOANNA SLEEPS UNTIL noon and still can't get out of bed, can't move. The fish dinner and all the wine last night, on top of the intense day, was too much. The taste of Gino, the cigarettes on his tongue, and the new dress slumped over her chair like Cleopatra . . . it was because of the dress. So like the one she was wearing when she met Luca. All so familiar.

Gino called her crazy last night, and perhaps she was. But the world is crazy. The woman talking to the ice-cream cone, the incredibly bored couple with everything they could want. Craziest of all—the time that slips through your hands, the time you can never get back.

*Is there anyone not slightly nuts?* Joanna wonders. The ones with loving parents do get a better chance. Would she have been less anxious if she'd known her real father, a father who loved her? That's all you need, a loving person at the starting gate. *Oh God, how can I ever explain this? Gino will never forgive me.* All at once, she longs something fierce for her New York apartment, her predictable life, for Stuart. Even for her craziest-of-all mother.

She must steady herself, clear the muddle in her head. She

hasn't yet made coffee in her room but has all the fixings. Like a meditation, she opens the fresh package of espresso, with its rich aroma, unscrews the silver percolator, fills the bottom part with water, presses in the coffee, and lights the stove. Hypnotized by the flame, a calm overcomes her. As moisture gathers on the sides of the silver pot and steam begins to rise, she feels a twinge of desire, a longing for Gino, the same as she had last night when she'd let herself go. And see what trouble that caused! That wild abandonment, that complete giving over, only causes trouble.

Stuart always had his feet planted firmly on the ground. They were tender with each other, but not passionate. Being with Stuart protected her from that feral cat in herself, that hidden side. The one who crawled the city streets late at night, sniffing for raw sensation. Looking for what the eccentric therapist William Reich (one of the books she remembered reading in college) called the *liberation* of self. The release, a guttural, visceral, deep-in-the-belly sensation, where her voice, imprisoned like Rapunzel, was set free for a moment. She tasted a piece of that with Gino but ruined it by calling out Luca.

The coffee bubbles noisily. She pours milk in, drinks it down, then crawls back to bed.

*\*\*\**

When she next awakes, the room is shrouded in darkness. An entire day gone. Still in her nightgown, she walks into the garden and looks at the silent harbor, all the restaurants shut. It all looks so magical, so promising. She closes her eyes with longing, wishing Gino was on his way up to see her. That he's forgiven her. *Maybe he's somewhere having a cigarette.* Throwing on clothes, she grabs her fleece and keys and flies down the stairs. The streets are empty, only the sound of a stray cat scampering by. She climbs the slippery path to the cliff, shivering. Everything seems to have vanished: The warmth of summer, the balmy wind, even the waves lie weak and dismissive.

She heads back down, each slippery step a challenge. Gino is leaning against the wall behind the restaurant, smoking. His entire self seems to be fuming. She moves slowly toward him, sorting the words she will say. When she's close enough, it's he who leaps into speech.

"Just because you come from America, you think you know it here, that you know Italy. But you know *nothing*. *Niente*."

She tries to calm her beating heart. She's never seen him like this. "Gino, I—"

He puts his hand up to stop her. "I loved you last night. Did you know that? I don't think so. Last night, I feel love from a heart that's vanished from the world. Like my father, only in bathrobe and slippers talking to his parakeet, that was my heart." He clutches his crotch. "I can put *this* anywhere, in many women who come here with that look in their eyes. Gino makes them laugh and they feel good to be in Italy. But it's nothing. *Niente*! Me, Gino, he was dead until you. You and the way you look at me."

"Oh God, Gino, it's so easy to get it wrong."

"*Shh.* Now you listen to me. I listen to you, many times. You come to Italy, and you think you find paradise, but what do you know? You think I like working like a slave for my aunt. My mother, you have no idea my mother, working away in the supermarket. She comes only to sleep in the house. My father is finished, useless, funny when he tries to sing, but useless. They don't even fight anymore."

His hand moves sharply, cutting through the air. "You know nothing. Of me. The big dream I once had, so stupid in love, five years ago. The most beautiful girl in Cinque Terre! We were supposed to marry and have children. She was too pretty. I know that, now. You learn many things when you're a fool; maybe that's when you learn the most. I gave everything for this girl, for our life together. I moved to Milan, for *her*, and I worked all day, all night fixing our house. Everything so she could become a big model, a world-class model. For the beautiful illusion. Is that the right word, *illusion*?"

"Yes. I'm so—"

"*Per favore.* Don't feel sorry for Gino. It was a long time ago."

"Did you love her very much?"

"Heh! What is very much? I thought I did, but what do I know? Only that since then I've been in the darkness, like my father. But then you. Don't you see? You are different. You make me want to feel again, to live! It's good, it's good, Joanna."

She reaches her hand out. He looks at her with his eyes softening but doesn't take her hand. Not yet.

"This name you called out last night. He was Italian?"

"From a long time ago." She sees his face opening a little, his anger easing.

"He hurt you?"

"Very much."

"So we are the same, broken in the heart, the same never again." He takes her hand, and they stay locked in a pause. She gently touches his face, his dark eyes so honest, so wounded, and she kisses him. Can only kiss him and kiss him again.

"*Gino,*" she says, pronouncing it as if learning a new word. She doesn't want him to go, but he pulls himself away.

"I miss your music," he says before leaving.

## LUCA OF THE SEA, 1976

That I didn't give up believing we'd meet again, or he'd be *there* waiting for me, has filled me with new confidence. Luca loves me, and I love him, and we will continue to meet each time the ship returns to New York.

My confidence is still riding high when, later, in my music class, the professor asks us to come to the piano and improvise on the spot. When it's my turn—me, the quietest in class—I surprise everyone with what pours out. I can't stop thinking of Luca, and that inspires the music. Like a magic carpet ride of passion, until I panic at how much I've exposed in front of the class. My expansive expressiveness must have been insane. I'm desperate for reassurance from the professor, who says nothing. The point of the exercise was to learn to improvise and ride the wave of our own inspiration without depending on another person's approval. Still, my eyes beg for validation as I sink into the quicksand of insecurity.

Outside on the concrete, frozen with blackened snow, desperate for confirmation, I watch my classmates slink past without a word, like I'm contaminated. I'm an animal, exposed on an open field to the predator. Or like the confused souls locked up in the mental ward where I'm doing my internship. Maybe they're just like me, only more afraid.

I rush to a phone booth, call my mother, and moan about how brutally alone I feel after baring my soul in class. I hear the clink of ice, my mother refreshing her drink. Lillian loves these conversations. "I've warned you about being an artist," she says, taking a deep inhale of her cigarette and a sip of her drink. "It's a wicked life, Joanna. Think of Jack Kerouac and his pathetic last days. What good did all his fancy words bring him? Misery. He couldn't even drink in peace. Better to be a teacher or a music therapist and earn steady money. You aren't strong enough to survive the fickle world of art."

I exit the subway at Seventy-Seventh and Lexington and brace myself against the cold and wind. Why do I bother phoning my mother? Her words don't help. I wish she could believe in me, give some support. Then it hits me that my mother mostly talks to herself, convincing herself she was right to have given up *her* art, *her* acting—even if she never did it long enough to give it up; it was more the dream she gave up. I bet she secretly wants me to give up my dreams so we can sit on some mythical porch with drinks in hand, laughing into the sunset, like we've tricked the universe at its own game.

But I can't give up; I'd rather die. I need my music even if I'm no good at performing.

# 13.

## CINQUE TERRE, 2002

LINGERING ON THE empty street after Gino leaves, feeling the balmy breeze of the night air, she thinks of what Gino told her, of his heartache. Joanna can't help but wonder what her life would have been like if, forgetting about age, she'd met Gino instead of Luca. The children they might have had. So incredibly different, these two Italian men. Gino seems kinder, more playful, even if he's been heartbroken. And he's older than Luca was. Gosh, they were so young, Luca twenty-four and she twenty-one, how hopelessly young that seems now. They were so serious, so terribly serious and confused.

Heading back home, she lets her thoughts flow. *I'm falling in love with Gino, or a kind of love.* She's awkward and clumsy and by now frigid. It's been that long, but maybe she can thaw. And it was good to see Grace. She must go there again, to the farm, to help in the garden. Nothing more wholesome than that.

She climbs the five flights, enters her apartment, and walks out to the garden. A full moon glows, and the sea shimmers in the distance. She picks a fig from the tree; how sweet it is. She couldn't do *this* in New York. She can't leave Vernazza, not yet. Can't leave all this. Though Stuart's unfinished manuscript is in New York, and she owes the publisher an email, she'll figure something out. Maybe do some research online and find a good editor. She'll let her boss know she's staying longer. *Yes,* she thinks with a deep sigh, *I must stay longer.* Her decision made, she falls into a deep and restful sleep.

***

The next morning, she takes her time getting up. Just that, taking time to get up, feels wonderful. No train to catch, no job to get to, no meeting she's late for. How urgently she rushed from thing to thing in New York—swimming, yoga, all the activities keeping her glued to life. She's discovering a new way of being. Like the *slow food* movement they invite here in Italy, she's learning to do life unhurried.

She leisurely makes coffee, enjoying the aroma as it fills the room, then ambles out to watch Gino at work. It's been two days since she's had dinner there with the wealthy couple. Perhaps she'll surprise him and have lunch. Just her, alone. Finally, she's ready to sit on her own. Excited with this plan, she showers and dresses in the pretty wraparound, her one nice outfit. She does her hair up, puts in her prettiest earrings, even some makeup she's not worn in months. She fills her knapsack with a bathing suit, towel, change of clothing, and bottle of water, in case she decides to hike after lunch, and packs a book. Admiring herself in the mirror, at her cheeks aglow with confidence and her posture lifted, she heads out.

"*Buongiorno, bella!*" Gino says when she arrives. "You look happy today."

"I am. Can I have lunch?" Joanna asks.

"Just you?"

"Just me."

"Something special?"

Before Joanna replies, his aunt starts screeching; the restaurant is very busy.

"Tell me after," Gino says. "Come back in ten minutes. There'll be a table ready."

Joanna walks to one of the window bars to have an aperitif to awaken the appetite. How sweet the taste of the Martini Rosso with a slice of orange. How good life can be when one is free of the grip of fear. So good, she has another.

She feels a sweet buzz, promising herself not to drink too much today. When she returns, Gino has prepared a table for her with a single rose in a slender vase. Without asking for her order, he brings out a steaming plate of *risotto ai frutti di mare*.

She eats slowly, enjoying every bite. She didn't want to drink much, yet with each sip of wine, a little bit of heaven opens in her. She signals to him, raising her glass.

"Don't drink too much," he says. "The sea is still warm enough for a swim later."

"Just one more. It tastes so good."

The restaurant is empty now; she's the last table. "Let's go have a coffee," he says.

They walk to the kiosk by the harbor. It's the beginning of September, and the tourist season is winding down. Fewer boats and less people coming and going. Just the two of them.

"So." He smiles. "Tell me, what makes you so happy."

"You. The way you make me feel." There, she said it. His eyes pierce through her. She wants to meet his gaze, but her eyes shift down.

"You're still afraid?" Gino asks.

"Aren't you?"

Gino nods. "That name you called me the other night. *Luca*. Maybe you want to see him again?"

"No, no. I don't know where he is, or if he's even alive. I met him a million years ago. I used to work as a travel agent in New York, and one time I had to go on a cruise on the *Leonardo da Vinci* to represent the agency when it sailed from New York to the

Caribbean. A big adventure for me, as I grew up rather poor. Fancier than anything I'd ever known. Something about the dinner the other night reminded me. And this dress . . . I had a dress like this then. Luca worked on that ship, and we fell in love." She can't tell him the rest; it would come out all wrong.

"What was the name of that ship?"

"The *Leonardo da Vinci*."

Gino stops a moment. He looks over her shoulder out to the sea. "That ship sunk. It's in the water, near here, at the bottom of the sea."

"Here?" Joanna takes a step back, almost falling. "In the sea, where we've been swimming?"

"Not that close. There was a fire, and it sank far out."

"Are you sure it was the same ship?"

"I'm sure," Gino says. "It was a famous ship."

Joanna gasps. Her *Leonardo da Vinci* at the bottom of the sea. Her Luca—

"Nobody was onboard when it sunk. A strange story. I don't remember exactly, only that it was an old ship. Ah, my country . . . you never really know. But your Luca, he wasn't there. You still love him; I see it on your face."

How foolish she's been all these years. The ridiculous story that's kept her captive. Longing for that magic time. She has no idea what she must look like, her eyes beseeching his, her hand reaching to feel his hand, a life raft to save her as she sinks down . . . down . . . down.

Time stops. Nothing makes sense anymore. Hot tears burn down her cheeks.

"You know I hate to walk," Gino says. "But I will walk with you. Up in the hills to a place where no one goes. Where you can cry it out. Where you can also cry for me."

Gino keeps a fast pace. She recognizes the path, the one leading to the monastery. They walk in silence. With each step, she feels something loosening. When they arrive, the musty air from the ancient walls mixed with the scent of pine and lavender welcomes her.

"Joanna," he whispers. "How do you feel now?"

"I don't know," she says. "I'm glad you're here."

She's kept a steady vigil for Luca all her life. Who will she become without that? After all the years with Stuart, she still couldn't let it go. Can she let it go now? She comes down to the dusty ground. Gino, too, comes down.

More tears, cleansing, healing tears.

"Gino," she says. And again, she says his name.

## LUCA OF THE SEA, 1976

It's been a few days since Luca sailed away, and today, miracle of miracles, there's a blue airmail envelope in my mailbox! With my breath jumping wild in my chest, I hear his voice in my head as I read it. I see the date; it's from the last day we were together on the cruise. Luca told the truth!

*My dear love,*

*A few hours ago I was with you and I was very happy. Now I am alone. I have your shadow near to me, but I want you. Excuse me if I say this, but you must know that never have I been so unhappy. Maybe that tomorrow I change, but for now I feel it so. Joanna, maybe you do not know, but I have fear of the love and yet I want love. In my life, always I have given and sometimes I have received, but never in the same as my way. Until you.*

*Thank you for these days, for your eyes, for your love. Thank you for the tears (my drops and yours). Thank you for being you. Maybe all this will finish. I do not want it, but I know the life.*

*Maybe that when we meet again in New York, you have changed, and in that case, I want you to know that a patch of my heart has become you.*

Over and over I read the letter until each word is engraved in my mind. I'm about to explode, unable to contain all this love, this joy, in one body. Kathy and my other roommates are out, and so is my upstairs neighbor Amy. I change into my jogging clothes and go for a run in the park, even if it's about to rain. I don't care if I get soaked. Like Gene Kelly singing in the rain. Bursting with happiness, I leap and skip and hop around the reservoir, not caring if the people think I'm mad. I'm alive and in love, and nothing else matters.

Why do we learn to *not* wear our hearts on our sleeves? What if we all start showing more? Then we wouldn't be so ashamed and lonely, wouldn't need to overeat or get drunk or be medicated or escape into TV shows. I know Luca feels the same, that deflating our feelings makes us become estranged as we merely play roles for each other. Running laps around the reservoir, I imagine this kind of world, this loving world. Maybe it isn't true what they say, that we humans are mainly aggressive and violent. Maybe we become so because we're frustrated from not being able to love, *to be in the love*. I'm in love now, and it's the best feeling in the world. Maybe it's just a release of good hormones in the brain, but who cares. They teach us at school and at the hospital that medication is about balancing the brain's disturbed chemistry. What if we could find this balance with love?

I do two more rounds in the pouring rain, feeling amazing, but on the way home, the other side kicks in. How to keep this amazing feeling going and not give in to my usual self-doubts, self-sabotage. If I don't catch up with a mountain of homework and my thesis, I'll never graduate. And if I don't graduate, I can't leave in June to be with Luca in Rome.

Oh, sweet angel of love, please keep a watch over me.

# 14.

## CINQUE TERRE, 2002

THEY WALK DOWN from the monastery and go to the harbor, to the rocks that feel the most like home. Joanna doesn't know who she is, only that she has to keep moving. Despite her fear of swimming from the rocks, she wants to challenge everything, every single thing. Maybe all of it has been a lie. Longing for that big pathetic love she couldn't live without. *You can break that pattern now*, she tells herself.

She strips to her bathing suit and, not waiting to be helped, jumps straight into the deep water and starts swimming with manic power. She will challenge everything that's stopped her in her life. She swims back and forth until her chest pangs and she must stop to rest.

Her body trembles as she dares herself to get out of the water without his help. To climb onto the warm rocks. How good to lay her body down.

"You swam great," Gino says, lying beside her. He puts an arm around her, and she, who never naps, falls asleep.

When she wakes, she is all alone. The sun has disappeared behind the clouds, and the air is chilled. Disoriented, as from a strange dream, she has no idea where she is. Then it comes back. Gino is gone, probably at work. She remembers what he told her, about the sinking of the *Leonardo da Vinci*. Shivering, she puts on the walking clothes she'd packed earlier, folds her dress carefully away. She feels strange, so very strange. In a wobbly fog, she passes the corner kiosk and hears a wall of sound, a blast of Italian from the radio, loud and shrill like something terrible is happening. She hears *Presidente Bush* and *la Guerra*. The war must have started. She begs the waiter to translate. "Impossible," he says, waving his hands. "It's too complicated." She hurries to Gino's restaurant, but he's much too busy and his aunt is on the warpath.

Joanna has to talk with someone who speaks English and knows what's going on. She can't stop the roaring in her head, her pounding heart, the terror building. Too late to reach Grace's farm, she thinks of Pieter, the Dutchman she'd met the other day. She rushes for the café along the trail. Thank God, he's there, paying up at the bar.

"Hey!" he says with a grin. "Was hoping to run into you." His dirty-blond hair is disheveled, his grayish eyes bloodshot.

"I heard the news in Italian but had no idea what they were saying."

"I've been glued here all afternoon listening to CNN. It's making my head spin. But I'm starving. Come back with me to my place. I've some food in my fridge. I'll fill you in." Her need to know what's happening in the world overrides any hesitation to follow him. She can't be alone.

His studio is larger than hers, with a bed against one wall, a kitchenette against the other, and a large round table in the middle, where he clears away his papers and magazines. He sets out a few plates and knives and gets some bread, cheese, and a bottle of wine. When he offers her a glass, she lifts her bottle of water but smiles hungrily at the food. Eager for conversation, to leave her silly self and bewildering longings, she takes several forced breaths to restore her functional self. All this vulnerability she's been dabbling with, with Gino. All this singing and opening to love.

"There's no war yet," Pieter says, preparing sandwiches, "but the Americans seem to be gearing up for one. He's clever, that Cheney. Simplify the problem, create a bogeyman, then convince the masses that if only we get him, all will be well. The thing is," Pieter says, biting into his sandwich, "there's no money in peace. Someone will earn a whole lot more with a war, no matter who wins, so of course they want war! I get so angry."

"I'm so glad I found you," Joanna says.

Pieter takes a swallow of wine. "These guys sure want one, and with everyone jumpy after September eleventh, they'll get it. America calls itself a democracy, but you need a well-informed public for that, and your leaders are more interested in creating consumers who don't think. Those of us who challenge this are considered freaks and a danger to society!"

Joanna stares at him in awe. He's like a younger Stuart. The way he speaks and what he says is so familiar.

Pieter returns her gaze quizzically as if curious what she's thinking, but he doesn't ask, and she doesn't offer. He goes on. "Until people really wake up, there's always going to be a war."

Joanna resents the world. She wants to be vulnerable, to be with Gino and explore these new feelings. To let her voice open and feel love again. But the world has to be safe so she can. Why must the world be so restless and evil? Why always another war?

"Are you okay?" Pieter asks.

She looks out the window at the dwindling light. "I should get going before it's too dark."

He abruptly rises and starts clearing the plates. "I'm sorry if I talked too much. It's a lot of information to get through, to make sense of. Also, for my own writing." He points to the stack of papers on the table and by his bed. "You can drown in it." He seems suddenly nervous, shuffling his papers to organize them.

Joanna prepares to leave, except she can't. She's in a time warp, a suspended state of not knowing. She moves closer to his papers, smells them, feels their familiarity. Pieter lifts a handful of loose sheets. "I have deadlines to write these articles. I'm paid to be wise, but you get yourself in loops."

"I know that from my husband." The words come out so fast. "That chaos of papers."

He looks at her. "Is your husband here with you?"

"No, he died a few months ago, with an unfinished manuscript on his desk." There's a strong silence between them. "I used to help him."

Pieter eyes her. "How?"

"I'd read his drafts, make comments, edit them."

"Seriously?" He stares at her sideways, his hand cupping his chin. "If you had any time to spare, I sure could use some help. But I can't really pay—"

"It's okay," she says. "I don't need the money. But I need to be useful and do something I'm good at." After saying this, she feels stronger. Though powerless to stop a war, she isn't without power.

"Great." he says. "I'll prepare a few articles for you."

***

It's dark when she heads back. She walks slowly, carefully, paying extra attention. The full moon provides just enough light for her to negotiate each step. When the twinkling lights of Vernazza finally appear around the bend, she's giddy with accomplishment. Walking alone in the dark is no small thing, infusing her with raw courage. And distance, which gives perspective. For her, the sinking of the *Leonardo da Vinci* symbolizes the end of civilization. Not just a chapter of her own life sunk to the ocean's floor—the only passionate love she's ever known was onboard that ship—but of the entire world and the wrong direction it takes again and again. And in that liminal space between brilliance and insanity, she knows the sinking of her beloved ship is a metaphor alerting mankind that the lure of the luxurious life, the capitalistic model, the standard we're all meant to aspire to, is killing us. An illusion fueling an insatiable thirst for more and more. That *more* needs energy, thus more oil, the real impetus behind the looming war in Iraq. There's a reason she met Pieter. A connection to Stuart, a shared concern for the future of humanity, and maybe the purpose of her being. A powerful shiver passes through her. Her foolish love story isn't important—never was. Once and for all, that is what must sink to the bottom of the sea: her reckless and fantastical dream of love.

 Safely home, she makes a cup of tea and takes it out to the garden beneath the twinkling stars. She thinks of how Stuart knew so long ago about the threat of our climate changing. How we were on a wrong road. And that was in the early seventies. But it broke him, it finally broke him, her beloved Stuart. In all the years, all his articles and teaching and lecturing on the encroaching climate change, he hadn't been able to convince enough people to take preventive actions, each year making it harder. She felt that same burn in Pieter.

 Pieter was younger, still had years of fire in him. She has to help him. Again, she feels a shiver. How rare to be here on this specific dot of the globe at this specific moment in time and to have met the people she's met—Grace, Gino, Pieter. Staring into the night sky, she finds the seven stars shaping a ladle, and then Orion. She hears music wafting up from the restaurant below, a jazz tune she knows well, Cole Porter's "Begin the Beguine." With the soft evening air and shimmering starlight, she dances an impromptu foxtrot around the garden.

✳✳✳

Lost in this mesmerizing state, she doesn't hear the knock or notice his entrance. She hadn't locked the door, and Gino, who must have let himself in, reaches for her and joins the dance—a clumsy, peculiar dance. It is sweet and funny, and they cavort happily around the garden.

Gino whispers, "You're like a child, my little child." He holds her tight and lifts her up by the waist like a comic ballerina, then brings her safely down. He slows the dance, and they begin to kiss. Lifting her into his arms once again, he carries her across the threshold into the room, and they tumble down onto the bed.

"*Ti amo!*" he whispers. She, who has at last learned to swim, doesn't stop herself as she usually does. At first, she monitors her reactions as he peels off her clothing, as he kisses her arms and belly and breasts. *Stop thinking,* she begs herself. *You're not better or worse than any other person. You don't have to save the world. This feels good. Let it feel good. Leave Luca. Let him be dead. Maybe he's dead. But you're here, and Gino is here, and he's kissing you, and it feels wonderful.*

She closes her eyes and falls into his arms.

He finds her with his mouth, and she feels herself wanting him, opening for him. With a thousand hands, he soothes and strokes her, kissing her everywhere, whispering he loves her in every language he knows. She watches his undulating form like a wave, meeting hers. Not holding back, his hands hungry for her, and hers for him. There is no later or after or ever again as he enters her, as she lets him in. He moans in Italian, his voice like velvet. He reaches the place no one has touched for the longest time, the place she swore had vanished. It never vanished; it has always been there like the sun beyond the clouds. In the grace of a thousand miracles, she plunges from the world. Yet it's soft where she lands; his arms spread everywhere to catch her, to hold her, and she, to hold him.

Three lifetimes pass before she hears his voice. "I will go now," he says. "Please no thinking. *Fino a domani.*"

## LUCA OF THE SEA, 1976

I'm at the hospital, about to do a music therapy session. They wheel in some patients; others wobble in dazed and confused. It kills me to see them like captives strapped down, tied up, immobilized by medication. Tiny slits for eyes and pained faces that seem to cry out for help, though they hardly make a sound.

My supervisor, who stands observing by the entrance, expects me to waltz in like Houdini, unlock these people for the half-hour session. Her favorite expression? "Don't overexcite them!" What is she afraid of, a revolt? The patients are so drugged, they can barely hold, let alone play, the light percussive instruments I hand out to some of them, the ones who can still move.

A few of the more attentive ones, who probably trick the nurses by not swallowing their medication, grab hold of my hand at the end of the session and don't want to let me go. They're like starved children begging for more. It breaks my heart. But I must move on to the next session in the next ward.

Carrying my guitar and bag of instruments through the depressing halls that reek of vomit and misery, I can't stop thinking that all of us in our secret hearts are starved for real attention, to be alive and seen and loved, the way I feel with Luca. Even my supervisor who talks of dieting yet is always nibbling a donut or candy bar. Perhaps she aches for someone to hold her. Maybe someone once did, but that person went away, and she's shoveling down her feelings with food. Or maybe she also takes those multicolored pills.

\*\*\*

I finish the intense afternoon, then rush to the subway to join the masses. Everyone with their heads down, reluctant to be there yet crammed in like sardines for the harsh rumble and shriek back to the city. We're all crushed by the nonstop mantra *keep moving, keep moving.*

Once out of the subway, I catch a glimpse of sky between buildings, and it makes me long for the big open sky and beautiful beaches of Martinique and Antigua. Feels like a mean trick to be so far away from nature—our real nature. I want to live in a softer, more beautiful place. Luca promised we will.

I think of the eyes of the patients, their sad eyes like gorillas at the zoo. *Please unlock the cage and let me run free in the trees and the green.* No green at the hospital and barely a scratch of sky beyond the barred and narrow windows. Their eyes tell me they are locked up because they couldn't live in the real world, couldn't keep the charade going. I'm secretly terrified I'm not that different from them, that my deep thinking and questioning is going to one day get me into big trouble.

# 15.

## CINQUE TERRE, 2002

JOANNA WAKES TO the percussive sound of branches hitting the outside wall. She makes a coffee and steps out into the garden. A fierce, cold wind blows, so she nestles behind the fig tree. She thinks of Gino, longs for him. *It was a wonderful night, but where will it go from here?*

The changing weather seems like a warning, that what they have is just a summer fling. Maybe Gino will leave Vernazza soon. Maybe he only lives here for the season. She has no idea, really, who he is and what his life is like. Perhaps it's missing her mother, a war coming, doubts about what she's doing here with her life, that leave her unsettled. Why does her grieving state feel more genuine, that being in love is an illusion, a dangerous illusion? *I didn't come here to fall in love,* she reminds herself. She's here to heal and find peace. And with that thought, she decides to visit Grace on the farm and lend a hand. She'll be back in time to see Gino later, when hopefully she'll be more grounded.

She packs her things for the day and stops for a coffee before catching the train. Gino runs over, looks around to see who may be watching, then kisses her.

"I won't be here to meet you this afternoon," Joanna says, "but I'll be back before you finish the dinner shift. I promise." Gino's hangdog look nearly weakens her resolve. "You have your work," she says. "I need to have something as well. I'm"—she hesitates to mention Grace—"taking a long hike today. Will be even sweeter when we meet later."

"Don't you have your writing?"

"I'm going to write in my diary all about you when I take a break along the trail. I'll be back before you know it." She kisses him and leaves.

***

When she arrives at the farm, Grace is too busy to chat. Joanna is disappointed; she's bursting to tell her new friend about Gino and the sunken *Leonardo*. Grace seems frantic, and after quickly showing Joanna what vegetables to pick, she leaves.

Later, she comes around for a quick chat. "Sorry, I've been like a mad cow, but it's all sorted now. We're starting something new," Grace says with giddy pleasure, "so it's great you're here. A dance evening once a week, and it's tonight! It's freestyle, with music that helps you attune to underlying emotions. I did it years ago and loved it. Even if you're tired, once you give over to the music, it's amazing how good you can feel."

"I just have what I'm wearing," Joanna says.

"No worries. I have clothes you can borrow. Someone will get you to the train after it ends, which won't be too late. Please stay!"

How can Joanna refuse such a welcoming offer? Gino has to work the dinner shift anyway, and she'll be back in time.

While Joanna picks succulent tomatoes and plump ripened beans, she feels waves of undulating desire. She's moist from a longing not felt for years. Her thoughts jump to Luca and their lovemaking on the *Leonardo da Vinci*. She tries to picture the ship now, rusting away at the bottom of the sea. Later, after a simple meal, Joanna follows the others to the hall for the dance. As she changes into the clothing Grace lent her, she thinks with a sense of wonder about meeting Grace. *If not for the rainstorm . . .* The thought of unleashing her feelings on the dance floor makes her both uneasy and excited.

The hall is huge, with a pine floor and walls painted an earthy yellow. A diverse collection of pastel weavings and tribal masks line the walls. The leader of the dance is about forty, his body strong and compact like a wrestler. With an irresistible smile and sense of purpose, he speaks in Italian first, then English. "Just let the music take you, move you. Whatever comes up in you, be it sadness, anger, or even laughter, let it enter the movement. No way you have to be!"

There's a central sound system with speakers set around the room. The music starts, and the leader invites everyone to sway side to side, not to think of dancing, but just see what happens. He moves with ease and an infectious joy. Joanna watches in awe. She's never danced in a group without the structure of steps, as in ballroom dancing. One thing to swirl like Isadora Duncan alone in her garden, another to be in the middle of a large group. She feels self-conscious and can't stop thinking of Gino, which seems somehow wrong here; she should be more spiritual, ethereal.

Grace, who Joanna is convinced can read her mind, dances over and whispers, "Don't worry. This isn't an ashram. There aren't any rules. You don't have to dance in any set way. Think of air moving through the fronds of the palm tree. The tree has no set requirements on how it must move." *A tree.* Joanna smiles, thinking of the windy morning in her garden. *I can do that. I can move as stiffly as a tree.* She closes her eyes, spreads her arms like branches, and widens her toes like roots. She tries to sway like a tree in the wind.

The ambient music quickens, more passionate—with haunting voices. She opens her eyes, and the leader is before her, encouraging her. Not thinking, she follows him across the threshold of uncertainty and lets the music dance her. *This is fine, this is good.* But then it changes to the thumping house music she hates. The brutal tones rip through her as a dark, eerie light fills the room. The warrior masks, as if springing to life, seem to roar with threatening glee. This triggers a violent reaction inside her. Hating this, she heads for the door.

The leader rushes over. "Stay in the dance," he encourages. "There's nothing that cannot be danced."

"This music doesn't make me want to dance. It makes me want to scream."

"So dance *that*. You don't have to like the music. It brings up more feelings when we don't." She doesn't want more feelings. The leader stays with her, and though she has huge resistance, she somehow keeps moving.

The music gets louder, more chaotic, like a tornado pummeling through, threatening to trigger a firework of impulses. She wonders about Gino. *What would he think of all this?* And her mother, all the unsaid thoughts about her mother, not just an unknown father she'll never meet, but all of it. A life of excuses, of being ashamed, of adjusting herself to please others, guessing, always guessing, what is allowed. Hardly knowing what she really feels.

The music surges yet again with thundering rage. Joanna dances away from the leader to the wall, seeking comfort. Another angry song starts, and she erupts. Others in the room are shouting, barking, so it seems. She barks too. An angry, vicious dog. She loathes the feeling but can't stop herself. The poison in her leaks all over. She feels evil and cruel and flings her arms violently. Furious at Bush and Cheney, at all those destroying the beautiful world she loves. She swings her arms through the air, imagining her hands around their throats, shaking them, begging them to see that they've killed Stuart and have made many, like her, afraid of being sensitive, vulnerable, *and* different. That old fear of being locked up persists. *Why do the greedy leaders get power, while the meek remain powerless?* Like a sheet pulled away, she sees everything clearly.

As she dances around the room, a scene from her childhood arises of when the kids on her block in Queens came to her backyard to make a pretend circus. An annoying three-year-old girl had also come. One kid got so angry that he took hold of her feet and held her upside down. The child was screaming. Instead of comforting her or letting her down, each kid had a go at holding her like that, by her ankles, upside down, tormenting her, like they were in *Lord of the Flies*. Even Joanna. She remembers now, with a bolt of shame, the surge of sickening pleasure she felt holding the tiny creature by her feet—a child at her mercy, torturing her, before empathy returned and she let her down, cradling the hysterical child in her arms. That episode never left Joanna's consciousness; she's been obsessed with this potential evil, distorted pleasure in all of us, including herself. The rage and sorrow burn out of her as the music gets sweeter. Tranquility fills the void. She feels rich with love, *the love*. She thinks of Luca and their unfinished story but dances away from that into a fresh wave of longing for Gino. *Gino is here; he is now.* She looks forward to seeing him. All at once, Joanna hears herself sing, another kind of singing, as if an angelic form has entered her. Effortlessly, her voice weaves in and between the music. She slides about the room, singing or sounding, not knowing what to call it, checking if she's disturbing anyone, but everyone seems to be in their own private reverie.

The music stops, and the room grows quiet. The lights are turned off, and only flickering candles remain. Joanna joins the others as they lie down. She gives over to the cool wooden floor, her limbs empty and languid, completely spent. Ah, to float in the warm bath of a spent self. The leader begins to chant in Sanskrit. Though she doesn't understand the text, it seems to express the bittersweet transience of life, for no matter what, everything is temporary, everything passes. More real since Stuart's death. It stings afresh, how absolutely gone Stuart is. Once so vivid and sturdy, his absence like a crater, a desperate hole. In her quiet moment on the floor, cathartic tears fall down her cheeks.

*** 

On the train back, she can't take her eyes off a loving family sitting across from her. Four small children asleep in the arms of the parents. With all she's danced out of her this evening, she's able to watch the family without her usual envy. Can even feel happy for these lucky children to have parents who really love them, something she's never experienced and never will. Or the chance to hold her own child in her arms. The parents notice her looking and seem to sigh. *It's wonderful when they're asleep!*

Joanna also doesn't feel her usual tug at not having had children, that she's missed something vital. Watching the children sleep, she thinks of her own experience, that by not having children, she's had *more* to give others. That served her well at work, lavishing the old folks with love and attention they desperately needed. For once, Joanna feels content with her own life. For once, a release from the wrench of guilt, or whatever it is that convinced her melancholy is the only true emotion.

She notices an old woman sitting behind the family, a widow in black, and wonders if black is a code of suffering that gives the widow justification for her existence, or a measure of her worth. *But for how long is one required to suffer?* And when does suffering itself become a habit?

She closes her eyes to recapture the glorious peace she experienced at the end of the dance, and when they arrive at Vernazza, she steps off the train feeling like she's been gone for a century. It's just been a day, a long, long day. Excited to see Gino, she heads straight to the restaurant. She passes a darkened window and catches her reflection, her hair a wild mess. She fixes herself a bit and smiles at her face, glowing with life.

Gino is nearly finished, and when he comes out, he lifts his hands in a mix of surprise and distrust. "Where have you been?"

"To a—" She stops herself, remembering she hasn't yet mentioned Grace or the farm. "I told you, on a long hike."

"What kind of hike makes you look like that? Were you with a man?"

"No, Gino. There wasn't a man. But I . . . I rushed straight here, wanting so badly to see you."

"You want so badly to see me, but the whole day you're not here? That's a funny way to want so badly to see someone. You look too good, too happy. Who is making you so—"

"You."

"*Me?*"

"Yes, only you." Joanna reaches for his arm. "If I'm going to stay longer, I can't be a tourist all the time. I have to do something. I met a woman today who has a farm, and I helped her. There was a lot of work."

He flicks her arm away. "But why are you so late?"

"There was dinner, and a dance."

"A dance? What kind of dance?"

"A freestyle dance. I know I look wild, but—"

"I don't know what to do with you," Gino says. "You're not like any of the others. You're too independent. Maybe it's the American way, but this is Italy. Can you give me some days, *per favore*, days that I know you will be here, only for me? Days that you will sing for me in the afternoon? I miss hearing you sing."

"I can try," she says, smiling. It sounds very old-fashioned what he's asking, yet a part of her also likes it, this slipping back in time. She's happy he wants to be with her and hear her sing but is concerned with how jealous he can get. She needs other activities and will have to be careful to compartmentalize. She can't tell him about her plans to help Pieter; he'd never understand.

"Can we have the same day over and over, with no changes?" he asks. "The weather will be great the next days."

"Okay," she says, feeling that swoon in the belly. "I can do that. I won't go to the farm until next week."

"Good." He sighs, then strokes her cheek. "Go home and relax. I'll come find you when I'm finished."

## LUCA OF THE SEA, 1976

This is too exhausting! I'm on a merry-go-round that never stops—all my classes, the work at the travel agency, and at the mental hospital with the patients like zombies, their feelings like laundry that will never get clean. I can barely keep my own soul clean; it's too much. Plus, my looming thesis that I haven't even started. What do they think I am, a machine? I just want to be with Luca, living the life I'm meant to live, writing songs and singing them.

Lost in thought, I arrive hopelessly late and out of breath for my therapy session. I fall into the chair across the tiny room from *Mrs. Perfect*, my therapist. She sits there all prim and proper, well organized with her impeccably pressed clothing, while I'm a rumpled mess. She doesn't say anything about me being late again but leans sternly over to get her papers. I see the bulge in her stomach; she's definitely pregnant. She looks at me to begin, and my words rattle out like Morse code.

"Stop racing," she says. "Calm down and talk to me. One thing at a time."

"Except it isn't one thing at a time," I scream. "It's everything at once, and it's too much. They send me to a room of forty patients, scary, out-of-control patients, tied to their chairs. The music soothes them a little, enlivens them a little, but it's just a tease, a terrible tease. When they sing with me, it's horrible. Like a haunting plea to get out of there. It's supposed to be an internship, but I'm like an unpaid slave in a system bursting at the seams."

Once again, I'm scared I've said too much. Why can't she let me dance around the room making sounds, like we're *doing* music therapy, not all this having to sit calmly and talk? Why doesn't she have a drum? I need drumbeats; I need ritual. I'm at the edge of my seat, pummeling my hands on my thighs. There's still fifteen minutes to go. My breath is choppy and shallow, and if I don't move, I'm going to scream. Too afraid of what she'll think of me if I leap around the room, I burst out crying.

I've gotten it wrong again, I know it, as she hands me the box of tissues with her forced smile. "You just have to do one thing at a time. It's not too much. You'll manage."

What I really feel she's telling me with her icy-blue eyes is to give up my foolish romantic ideas of how the world could be. To plan wisely ahead and be just like her. No! I yearn to sing of my love and longing, to communicate the desperate pain of being alive. I can't live in her world, her practical, functional world. It's not only me but an entire hospital full of sad, misplaced people. But there's no way to get her to understand, and she holds the cards. It's up to her if I graduate. So I must learn to keep my big mouth shut and play the game until I can get out of here and be with Luca in Rome. That's it. That's all I can do.

# 16.

## CINQUE TERRE, 2002

*GINO, GINO, GINO!* The week is alive with Gino, like a montage in a romantic movie. Day after day, the weather perfect, stunning, they swim and kiss and love on their honeymoon away from the world. She thinks of her husband, of her healing grief, and feels it is okay, that he wants her to be alive and well.

It's only at the grocery shop, with Gino's mother behind the counter shooting scowls and grunts of disapproval, that she senses a dark cloud looming. When Joanna mentions this to Gino, he gestures with his hand. "Of course," he says. "She wants me to get married and give her grandchildren. But I'm a free man, and I do what I wish, and I wish to be with you!"

He's been in such a good mood, not jealous of anything, that Joanna dares not mention that while he works the dinner shift, she drops by Pieter's to help him with his articles. She needs this balance between being useful and being in love. She grows fonder of Gino each day. To sing for him, get to know him, hear his stories and tales. Lately, he spends the nights with her, sneaking home before his mother wakes. How lovely to share a bed, to snuggle up close, to feel safe and sleep soundly and deeply.

This morning, after he leaves, she's unable to fall back to sleep. The wind howls, and with it the beautiful weather they've had all week vanishes. She goes out to the garden and notices the view is lost in a murky sky. Nagging feelings rush at her. She hasn't once checked her email and suddenly remembers it's her mother's birthday. Must send her mother something. And Stuart's publisher, she'd promised him a letter.

At the internet café, she clicks anxiously through her inbox. And there it is, a glaring email from her mother, the subject, WHERE ARE YOU? in capital letters, as is the entire letter, like a screech: DO YOU EVEN CARE THAT TOMORROW'S MY BIRTHDAY! DO YOU EVEN CARE HOW DANGEROUS THE WORLD HAS BECOME, THAT I'M ALONE HERE, ALL ALONE.

A line cuts Joanna to the quick. IT IS TIME TO COME HOME AND LOOK AFTER YOUR FAMILY.

Her *family*? They have no family. Joanna reads on. Nothing, absolutely nothing about how Joanna is doing. Not a word about her real father, the reason they broke communication in the first place! *Has my mother already forgotten? Is the story even true?*

A seething anger consumes Joanna. In rapid fire, she writes back, *I didn't forget. I came today to write and wish you happy birthday. But you—you didn't ask once how I am. Not a word about my* real *father or how I feel about that. All the years taking care of you, all the years I did the mothering. ALWAYS YOU. And you call ME selfish. I'm not coming home. Not this time.*

Right before pressing the send key, she chokes, and in a swift movement, she deletes the whole letter. But the poison has soaked in. All the recent joy with Gino, her singing, her new life, washes away like a watercolor in the rain. She doesn't want to go back to New York, but it yanks her like a rope around the neck. She pays for the internet and slips out like a fugitive, heading for the path to Corniglia. On the empty trail, she picks up stones and throws them as far as she can, heavy stones of guilt and shame and who knows what she still carries about her mother.

"I hate this," she shouts. "I was happy, finally happy. Why do you take this from me?" Joanna stops short and chokes out the next part. *Why do I let you take this from me?* She's furious, like at the dance. Angry and open and vulnerable. She walks hard and fast, and without realizing, she's walked straight to Pieter's guesthouse. Much earlier than usual, but she takes a chance and knocks.

He opens the door with a surprised look. "Are you okay?"

She feels strangely awkward that she's come to Pieter, not Gino. But with Pieter, who's slowly becoming a friend, she can speak about the upsetting email from her mother. She hasn't yet told Gino about her unusual family.

"I'm happy you came early," he says. "I have a heap of deadlines and sure could use your help. Just made some fresh coffee." He brings over two cups of hot coffee and milk. "It's incredible the shit that's going down. They're so fucking clever. They get a journalist to release a leak that Cheney and gang have falsely planted, then all the papers react as if it's *real*, and soon everyone is reacting to *that*. Then Cheney and cohorts have a legal excuse to go forward with their sinister plans. It's incredible. Keep people shocked, and you can do anything, even steal the moon."

"That's true. My mother just sent a flaming email from New York begging me to come home. She's terrified."

"Are you going home?" Pieter asks with a noticeable tone of disappointment. They've known each other only a short time. That he reminds her so much of Stuart makes it seem longer.

"No." She shakes her head vehemently. "I don't want to go back."

"Mothers," Pieter exclaims sympathetically. "Then don't go. You seem to be doing well here, and besides, it's not a bad idea to be away from the States just now. I've managed to arrange more time. Would be great if you also stayed. You can't know how much you're helping me."

Hearing that lessens the guilt toward her mother; she has a clear reason to stay.

"I'm thrilled to have met you, to talk of these things." She stops her thoughts from worrying about betraying Gino. He doesn't have to know; she will keep these worlds apart. Pieter is just a friend. And with his stack of papers calling out, she's happy to dive into work—only work.

"What are you thinking?" Pieter asks.

She blushes. "Nothing. It's just so upsetting, what's happening."

"It is," Pieter says with an endearing smile. She notices that when his face relaxes, he's rather handsome, in a rustic way. He leans over and gently touches her shoulder. His touch is awkward yet comforting. Joanna looks at him, enjoying the warmth of his hand on her shoulder. But she's also relieved when he shyly moves away.

"It's so fucked up." He shuffles his papers with fierce determination.

Pieter doesn't know about Gino, and she intends to keep it that way. "I've had a break from the world, so catch me up. What was the leak you mentioned?"

"They're trying to convince everyone about the dangerous weapons Saddam Hussein has been stockpiling. WMDs, weapons of mass destruction, is their catch phrase. So they have an excuse to attack Iraq. What hardly anyone mentions is that Saddam Hussein is one of the monsters the West created. He's no longer of use, so off with his head. Everyone's life is just too busy to stay properly informed, and stories usually start further back than in the quick headlines of the news."

Joanna feels a bolt of electricity passing through her. Most everyone she knows back home, still reeling from the aftershocks of 9/11, has enough with their busy lives, or they feel powerless to get *too* involved. Whereas Pieter, like Stuart, has an urgency to help people understand the larger picture. Almost in confirmation, the late-afternoon light pours through the window and shines on

Pieter's face, making his gray-blue eyes sparkle.

"Can you have a quick look at this?" He hands her an article, which she reads through. She makes several small corrections, then gives it back.

"You're really great at this," Pieter says. "I can imagine how you helped your husband."

"I hope so. And, like him, you write really well, and it's interesting, so it's a pleasure. I need to get back to meet a friend, so give me some more and I'll bring it back tomorrow."

Pieter gathers his papers. "Can you check these two? You're sure it's not too much? You're on vacation, right?"

"It's okay. I'm enjoying it. See you tomorrow."

*** 

Curious on her way back, she peeks into the café and catches the end of a Tony Blair interview. When did he jump on that bandwagon and side with Bush and Cheney in their buildup of a war in Iraq? Grace had mentioned something had shifted in him, like a kid finally included on a team. His face seemed glazed, almost drugged, getting high on his own importance. Stuart worried that politics had become a show, with politicians the new rock stars. Power has always been intoxicating, but TV only made it more potent.

The café is empty now, and she's relieved the young cheering crowd has gone. The sure sign of the season ending. She notices a computer against the back wall. Focused and determined, she sends off a short email to her mother. A few lines to say she's sorry not to be there for her birthday but has found important work in Italy and needs to stay. Period. Doesn't matter if she has some guilt, she's sticking to this plan, and with a deep sigh, she hits the send key.

It's time she stops feeling guilty for every breath she takes, every choice she makes. It's not Pieter's business to know of her love affair with Gino, nor of Gino's concern that she's helping Pieter. Still, she feels that nagging unease, like she's being a sloth or a sneak. Is it even possible to be completely honest with anyone, especially new people you've just met?

She stops by the restaurant to blow a kiss to Gino. He seems happy to see her, and she signals, showing her hands strumming an air guitar, that she'll be up in her room practicing.

Not surprisingly, after such a day, she feels a tug, like a new song will emerge. Her fingers find dissonant chords, odd tonalities, and a new melody emerges in a gush of raw feelings and chaotic words. She can't change anything in the world, not her mother or politics, but she can pour her feelings into the music.

She's deep in this new song when Gino arrives. From his startled expression, it's clear he doesn't like the new edge in her voice, nor the dissonant tones. Not her usual sweet voice that relaxes him and eases him into sleep. He doesn't lie down but instead keeps standing nervously, his arms across his chest.

"I've written something new," she says.

"It sounds angry."

"I am angry. The world is going crazy."

"It doesn't sound like you." He kicks the soil awkwardly with his foot. "You don't need me anymore. You were singing full out before I came."

"Because I *knew* you were coming soon. You've been helping me to keep at it. I've sung every day this week."

She takes off her guitar and goes over to hug him, but he pulls back. "At least you have your music," he says. "I wish I had such a thing."

If only she could divide her music and give him half, like sharing a sandwich. "Surely you have something you love."

"No." He takes out a cigarette but doesn't light it. "I do what I'm supposed to do, and the days go by. I work in my aunt's restaurant, to make money and help my father, because that's what a son does when the father is too ill to work."

"You told me how you went to Milan. Do you have hopes to go somewhere else, away from here?"

"Hopes, plans, what does that even mean?" He looks distracted and weary and makes a vacant sound that hides more than it reveals.

The more time you spend with someone, the more you realize how much you don't know them, how most of their life has been lived without you. "Are you okay, Gino?"

He hesitates. There's something he isn't telling her—or can't. She feels his unsaid words like a punch to her gut, like some rug being pulled out from under her.

"Shall we meet later?"

"Not tonight. I have a lot of work with my aunt. There's a special party, and the restaurant will be full. Tomorrow. We'll meet tomorrow."

"I've promised to go to the farm again tomorrow." Joanna feels she's treading on fragile glass, but she really wants to go to the dance. "I'll be back in the evening. We could be together then."

"That's okay," he says sadly. "I may have to go away, so maybe I'm not here."

"Away? Where will you go?"

"I don't know," he says.

"Tell me, Gino." She's almost begging now. He shrugs, then comes over to kiss her. His lips seem to sag from his face, like he's no longer in his body. She feels that cringing sensation creep over her shoulders. She didn't tell him about Pieter. Who knows what he isn't telling her?

## LUCA OF THE SEA, 1976

Who'd think a geology lecture could be so moving? It's the only place where I hear the truth. Mr. Karpel fears for us as a civilization.

"And the danger," he says, "is that we keep adapting to the

wrong course, allowing it to become right. That's the gift and killer of our humanness, our imagination. But nature isn't fooled by our foolishness."

It seems Mr. Karpel talks just to me, as the other students doodle or sleep, not the least concerned that what he says affects them. I linger after class, listening to each and every word he speaks. He is the smartest, most enlightened person I've ever met.

I'm late again for therapy and charge through the consuming streets of New York like a madwoman. Completely out of breath when I arrive, I end up telling Mrs. Perfect, with her shiny navy-blue skirt and matching pumps, the foolish dare I made with Luca on his short visit a few days ago. It had been a half day turnaround, and our visit felt like a tease, which is why I burst out with the crazy idea of him getting me onto another cruise so we could spend more time together. Luca had thought it was a brilliant idea and even said he would try.

"What if he actually does get me a ticket?" I say in panic. "I couldn't possibly go. The last trip was perfect. It could never be that perfect again. I'll only be a huge disappointment for him."

"Is that why you're scared?"

I nod, stalling for time. "To be with Luca for so many days in a row, he'd finally, you know, see the real me. And besides," I say, trying to make it like this is the main reason, "I'd never be able to get away now. Too much work."

"Never mind the specific details," she says. "We've an interesting dilemma. How would *you* feel about being with him for an extended period? It's a great opportunity to explore what it means to have a committed relationship, to be willing to get to know each other deeper."

"If he got to know me more, there's no way he'd like me. And I can't be *that* close with anyone."

"Then maybe he's not the right one. Perhaps with someone else, more appropriate, you wouldn't feel like that." And there it is—bingo! Give up Luca, marry a lawyer, and you'll be as happy as I am. She doesn't say this, but I'm sure it's what she's thinking.

"I'm not saying to give him up," she says, with that therapeutic leaning-forward bullshit, like she really cares. "I'm challenging you not to build a castle in the sand but to investigate what you have."

"It's perfect now," I squeal. "We just meet for a few days every few weeks. Yesterday was too short, but mostly he stays overnight."

"That's not much time."

"It's very intense time!" I snap, yet I suspect she's right. I squirm in the chair, then slide halfway down, trying to disappear into the floor.

"I wonder," the therapist continues, "if you believe this is what makes you creative, this restless chaos. You think you need the drama to write your songs. What if you took a chance and lost? Isn't it better to know?"

"Hang on a second," I ask, scooping my body upright. "Are you suggesting that if Luca actually arranges passage for me, I should leave everything and go?"

"I'm *challenging* you," she says. "If you went on the cruise, you would discover if what you feel is something real or just a fantasy. That's how we find out, by going into an experience fully, not just dreaming about it. By taking the risk of possibly losing. It's the same when you speak of your singing. If you want to be a singer, then go for it, within reason. I'm talking sensible risk-taking here, not stupidity. And if you think you found the love of your life, then by all means find out if he *is* the one."

Without leaving me a second to respond, she announces the session is over.

***

When I arrive at the ship for our next visit and Luca isn't there, a piece of me is relieved. I won't have to decide anything in case he did get a ticket. But that's not how most of me feels. I wait a bit longer before heading home. I stare at the gray curl of cloud circling the *Leonardo*, feel the wind blowing out to the ocean. I think of never seeing him again and, in the next instant, miss him so much, I have to find him. At the gangway, Luca's mustached friend comes running. He grabs my hand and leads me onboard.

"He's in his room," he says. "Waiting."

# 17.

## CINQUE TERRE, 2002

JOANNA RUSHES OFF the train, returning from Grace's dance, and heads to the restaurant. There's another waiter working, the one she saw when she first arrived. She goes inside to ask where Gino might be. The aunt responds, with a sour face, "He is ill," shooing Joanna away. Not knowing what to do, she returns to her room and gets to work on Pieter's articles.

The next morning, with the articles finished and nothing more to distract her, she goes out to the garden to peek over the railing. Still no Gino. She has to find out where he lives, and if he's really sick.

At the restaurant, she pesters the aunt to tell her more about Gino. Her face glows red. "He isn't here. He went to Milan. You shouldn't be with him anyway. Go away, you." The aunt, with a sharp fling of her wrist, deletes her from the world.

How fast a place can change.

Again powerless, she gathers Pieter's articles and heads for the trail. While walking, she thinks of these last two days, of what may have caused Gino to change so drastically. He didn't like her new song, yet that's hardly reason to disappear.

*Is it really over, just like that?* She feared it would end, but not this fast. *I'm a fool, hoping to find love, big love once more in my life.*

***

Pieter clears a space for her at the other end of the table and sits to peruse the papers she's edited. "These are excellent suggestions." He points to a note she's written in the margin. "I hadn't thought of that. *Dank je wel*," he says, thanking her in Dutch. "If you have time now, there's a long article that could use a read-through." His voice holds a note of warmth, almost tenderness, she's not heard before.

"I do," she says. "Plenty."

He hands her a coffee and the article and goes to work on something else. How comfortable to work alongside him. It helps stifle obsessive thoughts about Gino.

"Hardly anything to fix in this one," she says, when finished. "Your English is excellent."

"I don't think so, but nice to hear." He goes to the computer to make the corrections and sends it off. He leans back in his chair and smiles at her. "I've been noticing how healthy you look, not like me, all ragged and pale. Must be all your walking."

"I don't think I look so well today."

"Next to me you do."

"All the walking's been great. I also help at a farm of an English woman I've met."

"What kind of farm? Is that where you were last week?"

She nods, feeling guilty with her white lie but glad for a way to mention Grace. She's been wanting to tell Pieter about her; these worlds should connect. "It's a sort of community."

Pieter makes a quizzical face. "Not a cult or anything"—Joanna laughs—"if that's what you're thinking."

"How do you know what I'm thinking?"

"By the look on your face."

"Sometimes those places aren't exactly what they set themselves up to be," he says, turning back to his papers. "But I do need some fresh air. I've been inside, day after day of great weather, and I'm as pale as in the Netherlands. Can we walk and I'll air out some ideas with you?"

She heads them away from Vernazza, just in case someone might see them. On the trail toward Corniglia, Pieter starts talking. "This whole September eleventh is very suspicious. Your government just spent a heap of money pretending to investigate, but they don't dig for the truth. The *owners* of America. I think you know what I mean—the billionaires and corporations who run things. They're too good at creating seductive half-truths. Enough to shock and distract the masses until the next disaster, the next enemy, the next war. Does the name Milton Friedman ring a bell?" She shakes her head. "He was an American economist, and he got this terrible ball rolling. Margaret Thatcher, who already loathed governments caring for the weak, read Friedman's book and got all jazzed up and convinced Ronald Reagan, and away they went, spreading this *turbo-capitalism,* preaching that too much government crushed the individual and how that would lead to totalitarian control like in the Soviet Union. Only a free market and individualism could prevent this disaster, and an unregulated market economy would make everyone richer, at least for the people they thought deserved it."

Pieter stops for a moment to take in the view. "I forget how lovely it is here. I get so riled up. Forgive me." They start walking again. "Take away all regulations, which they've done, and the economy booms," Pieter says, "like an endless cancer. More and more raw material and new markets are needed, and nations that resist most topple. In democratic countries of the West, governments are losing power to banks, corporations, and economic elites. The final goal is a happy, nonquestioning, and ever-consuming society. Not like us. We, people who think, *we're* the new enemy, and terrorism is the new uniting enemy that's leading us to war. But if you write about this, you meet a wall of resistance. Only half of my articles go through. I'm keeping them, though, for a book."

"You should," Joanna says. "Your stuff is great." All at once, her skin buzzes with a brilliant idea: *What if Pieter could be the one to edit Stuart's book?* She'll have to wait for the right moment to broach this subject.

"I read a rather sobering report this morning," Pieter excitedly continues, "about all the new security machines, monitoring cameras, and paraphernalia at airports and other public places. After the cold war, when the demand for weapons plummeted, the ailing defense industry jumped eagerly in and helped create this convenient new market that no one could object to, and once again they're earning a fortune. I'm not saying there aren't terrorists, but these corporate vultures surely benefit from the ever-increasing *fear* of terrorism." His eyes flicker with indignation. "Sorry," he says. "I can go on and on."

"And I can keep listening," Joanna says. "But I should get back." The time with Pieter has emboldened her, but she's anxious to find out about Gino. "Let's stop at your place so you can give me a good stack of articles to go through, and then I'll leave."

"It's not too much?" he asks, once back in his studio.

"Not at all," she says, putting his pages into her knapsack.

"Hey," Pieter says, following her out. "It feels so good to be outside. Why don't I walk you to Vernazza? Otherwise, I'll just keep working."

"Well, I—"

"What?" Pieter asks.

What can she say? She's afraid someone in town will see her with Pieter and tell Gino? It seems foolish, yet she's concerned. Or what if the aunt has lied and Gino is still in town? She quickly decides to walk with Pieter only until the turning, then do the rest on her own. They walk on, with the conversation opening to other things, not just politics.

Before the turning, she sees Gino coming. He never walks here.

She jerks to a stop, and Gino stops. His hands up in the air seem to shout, *Who is he? Why are you with him?* He slaps both hands on his chest, ape-like, and in a huff turns around.

"Wait," Joanna calls.

Pieter shoots her a puzzled look. "Do you know him?"

"It's complicated. Sorry, I'll explain later," she says. "I'll have the pages done as soon as I can."

"Sure," he says, stunned.

"Gino, wait!" She calls out, catching up.

He turns, slicing his hand through the air. "Why should I wait for you? Is that who you spend all your time with?"

"No. I'm helping him with his writing."

"You help everyone. Who are you, Mother Teresa?"

"He's writing articles, warning about a possible war."

"You and your war. You Americans love a war."

"No, I don't. You're unfair. I went to the restaurant when I got back from the farm yesterday. You weren't there, and your aunt said you were ill. I went again this morning, and she said you'd left town! I've missed you so much."

"You have a strange way to miss me."

"But I do. I want to go back to how we had it last week. I was just helping my friend, and he wanted to walk. Many people walk here." Gino rushes down the steps. She charges after him, grabbing his arm. He flicks it away. "Gino, *please,* you don't understand."

"I do," he says, his face on fire. "I finally understand. I understand everything. Nobody tells the truth. *Nobody.*" With a poisonous look, he runs off.

## LUCA OF THE SEA, 1976

So odd to enter the *Leonardo* alone with all the passengers gone, like walking into the mouth of a sleeping giant. Not sure if I remember the way to Luca's cabin, I run down one hallway and then another. Finally, I see his door and knock. Luca opens it, grabs me in his arms, and we kiss and kiss and fall onto the bed, the familiar bed where we've spent so many magical hours on the cruise.

We make love stronger than ever, spontaneous, passionate. He's well inside me when I remember I don't have my diaphragm in. Swept away with abandoned pleasure so intense, I can't stop; neither of us can.

We're soaked through with sweat. He gets a towel and dries me off while speaking tenderly of an old couple from Napoli, his hometown. How they sit together on a park bench every Sunday, their limitless love for each other.

"I want to grow old with you," he says. We hold each other tightly and drift off to sleep.

It's dark when we wake. Luca gathers me in his arms. "I couldn't get you a ticket to come on another cruise, but I want to be with you every moment I can."

As happy as his words make me, I worry about what might have happened during our wild abandoned lovemaking. I've always been so careful. I don't mention my concern, as Luca is in such a good mood. He even wants to explore the streets of New York, a thing we've never done, to see *my* New York.

Not in uniform, he wears an elegant suit with his dramatic woolen cape. He stands out like a prince. New York all at once seems shabby and ugly and dirty. I take him to the places I love, like McSorley's, the oldest bar in New York, with its ancient cobwebs hanging like chicken wings over the rafters. It seems crude and low-class, a bar that hasn't been swept for at least a hundred years, a thing we students love. Luca keeps picking bits of dust off his cape. I also stupidly take him to Chinatown for dinner, to the restaurant Lillian and I go to celebrate our birthdays. We know the waiter, and he always brings us things from the kitchen to taste. Luca won't touch the food, pushing his chair from the table, with its sticky plastic cover.

"It's a pigsty, this city," he says. "Let's go back to the ship." He takes out a cigarette and lights it. I can feel him thinking a mile a minute. "You'll never leave New York," he says so mean and cold, it shivers up my skin. "It is a big thing to leave your home. I don't think you know that."

"I do," I say as loud as I can, but my voice catches in my throat. "I hate being here."

"No, you don't."

I can't bear for him to be this angry, and I crumble in a thousand insecurities. What would happen if I got like this in Italy, on his home turf? Would he leave me all alone? I'm furious to be such a scaredy-cat, such a worrier. I want to be brave and strong, like him. He turns, daring me to follow him when he hails a taxi for the *Leonardo*. We arrive and walk silently through the empty corridors to his bed, where we make love again, ferociously, desperately, as if searching for something deep inside the other. We pound and smash each other like waves against a rock. When he falls asleep, I lie awake in a mix of worry and the erotic juice of danger. I imagine the egg in my womb embracing the start of life, the life he's ignited in me. Aroused, I wake Luca, and we make love again. I've never felt anything so strong. Nothing matters, as long as we're together.

"I'm not afraid to leave New York," I announce. "And I will, as soon as I graduate."

"That's good," he says. "You must have faith that I love you. The ship will be gone longer this time, but I will be back."

I come home and pour my love and longing out into yet another song. After I play myself raw, I fall in a heap in the middle of the room, overwhelmed. I'm still not able to take care of myself. How could I ever take care of a child?

# 18.

## CINQUE TERRE, 2002

JOANNA IS DESPERATE to speak to Gino, to explain Pieter is just a friend, nothing more. She comes down early that evening while Gino is setting up and tries in vain to get his attention.

The following morning is the same. It seems cruel and so unlike Gino, and there's no logical explanation. She can't go see Pieter *this* distraught; she needs a day as a breather. She's going crazy on her own. Feels jinxed, like Lillian has something to do with making her sweet life disintegrate. Grace will take her in any form or mood, so Joanna decides to escape there. She has Pieter's email and sends him a quick message to say she'll be a bit delayed with the current articles, and when he quickly replies that it's okay, she heads for the train to Levanto.

As always, there's a ton to do on the farm, and for two full days she works in the fields until exhausted. It helps. But the third morning, it's pouring, with no sign of letting up, making it impossible to work outside. And Grace, who she's barely seen, apologizes in what seems to be her normal unavailability. Joanna slips into the main hall to dance away her anxiety. As she leaps around the room, croaking out various sounds and yelping, she thinks of her mother. How they enabled each other through the years. She thinks also about this new rage that's awoken in her since the funeral, since hearing Lillian's confession. If it's true, is Joanna like her father? This ugly rage. Is that why she's buried so much of herself all these years?

The dance isn't helping. Too curious whether her mother has written back, Joanna runs through the pouring rain to the main house, to the common computer, and logs on. There's no reply from Lillian, but there is an email from Pieter. He doesn't need to know what happened, but he sure can use her help, and if she can, please come ASAP. She writes back that she'll be there in a few hours.

On the train to Vernazza, she stares at the window, mesmerized by the streaks of falling rain. She traces her finger along the rivulets of water forming on the outside of the window, curious how some repeat the same path while others get stuck or carve something new. Just like people. She thinks of Grace's presence and consistency, and although busy, she always makes Joanna feel welcome. Hoping the same with Pieter this day, she closes her eyes and settles into the soothing movement of the train.

"Can I sit here?" a voice calls out in accented English.

Joanna is startled. The train is empty. Why would someone ask if she can sit here? Standing there, towering over the seat, is a strikingly beautiful woman. Like a magazine cover, her chiseled cheekbones and sculpted brow, her spotless skin and hair so shiny black, as if each strand has been polished. With eyes like Elizabeth Taylor's, violet and piercing, she hardly seems real. But why, why insist on sitting *here* with plenty of vacant rows? Joanna hesitates before lifting her knapsack from the empty seat. The woman places her bag overhead, then settles into the seat.

"I think I know you," the woman says, like an actress building suspense.

"Me?" Joanna squeaks. "How . . . how could you possibly know me?"

"I'm sure it's you," she says, staring at Joanna intensely.

"I've never seen you before. I'd remember if we'd met."

"That doesn't mean I don't know *you*."

The woman turns her long legs, sealing Joanna against the window. She feels trapped, claustrophobic. "I'm getting off soon," Joanna says. "Please, let me out."

"I'm also getting out in Vernazza," the woman says, not moving.

Joanna leans forward to get air, for the woman has sucked up all the oxygen.

"I'm coming to see *Gino*," she says, watching for Joanna's reaction. "He works as a waiter. I think you know him."

"Who are you?" Joanna scrambles to put the pieces together.

"I'm Gino's friend, from Milan."

"His old girlfriend?"

"Yes." She smiles. "But I'm not old." *Not as old as you are*, her eyes seem to convey. Joanna's skin crawls. Gino must have known she was coming. That's why he's been acting so peculiar, and so quick to jump to a wrong conclusion with Pieter. Perhaps he was looking for an excuse to end it with her, to return to this beauty, the love of his life. Why had Gino come to find her on the walk? Was he coming to tell her, to end it with her anyway? Pieter being there just made it easier.

"He told you about me, didn't he?" She smiles, her brilliant white teeth in a perfect row. "I was supposed to marry him once."

"You live in Milan." Joanna gasps, fighting for breath.

"I do," she says. "But my mother's very ill, and there's only me."

"How do you know I know Gino?"

Another perfect smile. "You must have noticed that everyone knows everything, and they tell their family, even if they live in Milan. You're the first one he's spent so much time with, since me. And you're not so young, which gives everyone even more to talk about."

"How did you know it was *me*?"

"The color of your hair is quite striking, unusual. And the green of your eyes. You have beautiful eyes."

Joanna touches her hair as she looks at this woman, this beautiful woman who gives nothing away, yet when the train announces Vernazza, it's impossible not to notice an abrupt change. She seems to wilt, as if something is sapping her power. Joanna doesn't want anything in common with this stunning creature, yet she shudders to think of her own hesitation to return home and confront Lillian. What if she were dying and Joanna *had* to go back?

The woman grunts as if confirming what Joanna suspects. "I don't look forward to being in that suffocating town."

"Does Gino know you're coming back?" Joanna asks. She feels a click, like pieces of a puzzle fitting in place. It's all making sense, sad, terrible sense.

She nods. "I called him a few days ago, checking if he were still in town. He's not always around. My name is Eloise." The woman takes down her case. "And you are Joanna."

"So they told you my name," Joanna says, wondering what else they've told her.

Eloise nods. "I told you, everyone knows everything."

***

Joanna has not seen Eloise again, but the whole town is consumed with the recent death of her mother. Joanna stayed away these last days, alternating her time between assisting Pieter and working at Grace's. But this morning she's come to her stoop for a coffee and keeps a nervous eye on Gino. He looks terrible, his facial expression harsh and twisted, his eyes puffy and red. She's about to leave when Eloise, in a tank top and jeans, as if she can't be bothered with proper mourning attire, plows through like a truck.

"How long are you planning to stay?" she demands. "Gino won't tell me, so I'm asking you." Joanna turns away. "Okay, so you won't speak, but you can listen. I'm sure Gino never told you the whole story. He pretends he's a free man, with all his flirting, but he's not."

With forced laughter, she adds, "When the cat's away, the mice *will* play. And I," she says, extending her already long neck, "am the cat. You know how that goes."

"Look, I was just leaving."

"Ah, she speaks!" Eloise tosses her hair. "I suppose he told you that he came to Milan to marry me, and that *I* found someone else. Did he also tell you about *his* choice to come back to Vernazza to open his own restaurant? No, I didn't think so. Interesting, no? What a person tells and what they leave out. Now you are curious. I can see."

Eloise seems to enjoy catching Joanna in her web, stunned, paralyzed.

"I've heard he's been teaching you to swim. He's a good swimmer, no? He thinks he owns the sea. But it is not his sea." Eloise pauses to lick her lips, then looks toward the restaurant. Gino hasn't come out yet. "He is charming. A great card the Italian man plays, to seduce women. He found a convenient way to end with you now, didn't he? Blaming it on you. Oh, don't look so surprised. Everybody knows. There's nothing else to do here, don't you get it? You foreigners come here thinking you've found paradise. But it's a prison, a beautiful prison."

Joanna cringes to think that Gino already knew Eloise was coming back. He wasn't sick that day . . . or maybe he was. Maybe it was a shock for him, the thought of seeing her again. What does Joanna really know? Only that she's been a fool to think she loved him.

"You're quick, I see." Eloise flashes her glossy teeth. "Now, with my mother's death, there'll be plenty of money for his restaurant. That was our deal. Whoever got the money first would help the other. He's a smart man, not only charming. That is *his* game," Eloise says.

"What game?" Joanna bursts out. "What are you talking about?"

"You fell in love with him. I can see that. *That* makes him strong. *That* gives him power."

Is she right? Is Joanna wired to fall deeply in love only with wrong men, the ones that feed her illusion of passion? She feels disgusted to even think this and forces herself up; she has to get away.

"Don't go yet," Eloise says, her voice like glue. "Of course he didn't let you know I was coming back. He didn't know himself until last week. It all went so quickly with my mother. But we've both been waiting for a chance, a second chance, to have our children, our family. We're both thirty-six, so we better get started, don't you think?"

Joanna can't bear one more word. Her head is exploding. She rushes inside the bathroom, feeling sick, poisoned by Eloise's words. She rinses her mouth, then stares in the mirror, hating the deep rut between her brow. Her make-believe Italy, her perfect country that she's waltzed into, pretending to belong, doesn't exist. It never existed. Busying herself with Grace and Pieter to keep the illusion going that she's found home.

She turns to leave but stops at the exit of the bathroom, remembering the spot where Gino had dropped the glasses that fatal night. The longing she'd seen in his eyes. It wasn't just *her* longing he'd mirrored back; it was his own. She saw it, had felt it. *You can't pretend that.* Joanna may have been mistaken about Luca, but not this time; she isn't that blind. *There's more to the story with Gino.*

Eloise is no longer at the stoop but outside the restaurant with Gino. The two of them, wild at it, voices shrieking in Italian. Joanna can't help staring, intrigued. Eloise on her long, lecherous legs, tossing her hair like a whip through the sky. Whatever she's telling Gino is making him boil, his face flaming red, his arms chopping violently at the air.

The wind picks up as if the raging Eloise and Gino, with their churning body movements, have caused a human tsunami. Gino storms into the restaurant, and Eloise, in disgust, rushes off, completely ignoring Joanna as if she no longer exists.

## LUCA OF THE SEA, 1976

My workload is relentless. I plug myself with a sort of mental Novocain, to keep going. I don't look anyone in the eye, so they can't register how hopelessly behind I am. Except they do, and the warnings have started, from the head of the music therapy department to the supervisor at the hospital.

"Where are you?" they keep asking. "You seem to be in a trance. You need to be present and attentive, or you won't graduate."

If only I had the courage to quit it all and live the life I crave. To be a musician and songwriter. But I'm terrified to starve to death, that I don't have that extra pizzazz, that confidence, to withstand the impatient, judgmental world. I only want to be with Luca, to be in the world we create.

\*\*\*

About to explode, I cut the rest of the day of school and the hospital and take the subway to Penn Station, to catch the Long Island Railroad to visit my mother. The packed subway inflames my already dismal mood. A Vietnam vet without legs wheels his torso on a skateboard. He pushes his way through, begging for money. I wish I could hug him, give him back his legs. I hate the world of war. All the young men giving their bodies against their will, against their choice. For what? To satisfy rich old men. All the protests I've marched on, all the songs I still sing, as if they make a difference. There's never an end to war, and nothing ever changes. One generation to the next, we remain just as stupid, while the young get sent to war to be crippled, traumatized, or killed.

This stump of a man wants money, not a hug. I reach into my pocket and give him all I have, then fill with fury when the other passengers pretend he's not there. How can they not see him?

How can they not care?

I want to scream, "We are this Vietnam vet without legs. We are not separate. If we each only care about our own individual survival, we'll never be able to change this terrible world." But I say nothing, too scared to stand out.

At once, I understand that's exactly what the other passengers are doing, burying their heads in their newspapers and books. Trying to survive, to not stand out. I'm not able to convince them. I'm weak and powerless and can't even stop my mother from drinking.

Later, at the travel agency, it's yet another world. Of the rich, intimidating people who fly to Arabia to seal big oil contracts that Leo, my boss, keeps reminding me not only pay his rent but mine. "Stay in line, girl, I need that voice of yours."

Around it goes again—to classes, the hospital, the therapy, the travel agency, a visit to Lillian—all of it a blur.

Since they've raised our rent, we have a new housemate, Aaron, who's moved into the middle room, meant to be a dining room. He's becoming a gynecologist and is completely obsessed with vaginas. He's also taking an art class, or so he tells us, to learn more about vaginas. He makes them in clay from every possible angle, so now we have vaginas all over the apartment, like ashtrays.

*** 

It's been a few weeks since my last visit with Luca. He told me he'd be away longer, but it feels like forever. My belly has inflated, and I'm hungry all the time. Tomorrow, the ship arrives, and what the hell shall I do? Can't tell him what may be growing inside me.

I arrive early at the harbor to not miss him. I wait forever until finally he appears, taut and virile and handsome as ever. His skin a deep brown and his hair grown longer, waving in the wind. It stuns me, his beauty. He comes in close, wraps his arms around me, and all the stress and worry float away. *"Amore mio!"* he says in a swell of kisses.

He looks almost too good, and with a jolt, I suspect he's found someone new. Remarkably, he keeps hugging me like he can't believe it's *me* in his arms. "You can't know how much I've missed you. There's no one like you!" For once, we seem like a normal, happy couple reunited. And why not? Why must I always paint the room black? He leads me onboard and seems happier than ever to see me. He kisses my finger that's mostly healed, though it still aches when it rains. "Are we still married?" he teases. With his hands on my shoulders, he leans back, looks at me, and notices, so I assume, my weight gain, my fuller breasts. He smiles approvingly, though we don't mention the reason.

"Joanna, Joanna." He absorbs me in his arms, and it's impossible not to melt in his embrace. My skin grows rowdy with sensation. He pours cold champagne and toasts to our life in Rome. He miraculously has two full days this time before the ship sails again, and for two whole days, we never leave the boat, never brace the outside world. When the time is up for me to leave, he holds my head gently in his hands and begs me to remember how much he loves me. "You are *mia piccola bambina*."

# 19.

## CINQUE TERRE, 2002

AFTER HER UNNERVING confrontation with Eloise, Joanna lumbers restlessly up the path to the monastery, needing the comfort of that soothing place. She struggles up the steep climb that seems even steeper this day. She longs for Stuart, aches for him, he who always knew what to do. The irony, she thinks, smiling, that he never needed people, not as she does. He mostly kept to himself. Humans, with their fickleness, their inability to see the big picture or feel connection to the earth and nature, were what he thought caused many of our problems. This in contrast to the rocks he cherished, rocks that mostly stayed true and solid and permanent.

She spies a multicolored stone on the path and picks it up. It feels smooth and warm from the sun, yet when she reaches the top, the rock turns cold, as if to taunt and tease and remind her that she needs more than a rock. Betrayed, she flings it against one of the walls of the monastery, taking pleasure in the sound of its impact. She gathers more rocks and throws them, one after the other. In a flood of useless tears, her mind rages: *I am not a rock. I am human and vulnerable, and I want to know love.*

She thinks of Eloise and how her presence has destroyed the sweet bond she'd shared with Gino. Completely alone, she remembers Terry and her going off to a remote place to scream. Joanna does this now, not caring if she's shredding her vocal cords; she needs to express this rage, this powerlessness that's always in the mix no matter what. You open the door on one thing, and the rest spills out, whether you like it or not.

At last, completely spent, she slides down against the wall. The rocks she's thrown about at random look like broken pottery. Oddly satisfying, this destruction, this empowering display of violence, *her* violence. Probably, it does come from her real father, with his fierce and passionate nature. She thinks of her mother, young and beautiful and full of a million dreams, unable to resist this hot-blooded, inventive man who fathered her only child, who in the end she had to flee from. Yet, to have once experienced that degree of passion, you can hardly live without it. Was this part of Joanna's wiring as well, to seek that charge? Perhaps it was the same between Gino and Eloise? They needed that fire she'd witnessed between them. The fire that easily slips into rage, such a fine line between love and hate.

She gathers the pieces of the broken rocks, and one by one, as if befriending her broken self, she places them around her in a large circle. With her finger, she draws an inner circle in the malleable dirt, the dust of all the years. Her face covered in tears, she lies on her back within the circle and stares into the gusting sky, the swiftly moving clouds, trying to make sense of her feelings.

*\*\*\**

Much later, shivering in bed, she hears a knock. A loud knock and then another.

"Joanna, it's me, Gino. Are you there?"

She clutches her blanket. Slides further into the bed.

"Joanna, I know you're in there."

"Is it only you?"

"Just me. Please, let me in."

"Why?"

"I need to talk to you." She hears his voice crack. It wrenches her, the ache in his voice. She creeps out of bed to let him in, then hides behind the door, feeling too confused with her muddle of anger and longing. She doesn't want him to see her like this, her eyes bloodshot from crying, and doesn't switch on the light.

"I'm so sorry, Joanna." There's a heavy pause between them.

"What do you want?"

"Can I come in?" He enters, and she doesn't stop him. "Eloise makes me crazy."

Joanna shuts the door, then rushes back under her covers. "Is that why you reacted as you did when you saw me with my friend Pieter? Who is just a friend, by the way. And why you haven't spoken to me since?"

"I found out she was coming back, that her mother was dying. I wanted to tell you, but when I saw you with that other man, I don't know, everything exploded in me."

"What do you want from me now?" She tentatively looks at him in the soft light, his forehead creased like an old man. He leans against the kitchen sink with his shoulders caved in. His mournful look, like an arrow piercing her heart. Joanna still feels so much for him. He turns away to fill a glass with water, which he drinks down, then fills again.

"Can you pour me one?" she asks. She watches him from the back as a breath of relief seems to come into him. He gets another glass and fills it, then comes to the edge of the bed and hands it to her.

"We've known each other since we are children. She knew me when I fell down and cracked my tooth. She knew me when I jumped into the sea to save my old friend Roberto and almost drowned myself. There is a bond between us, too strong. I don't know what happens to me around her. My father had the same with her mother; it's why he fell apart. They had a brief affair ten years ago. They're witches, those two women. I don't know what Eloise told you."

"She said you were still together." He looks down, sheepishly. "If that's true, why aren't you with her now? She told me you still want to have a family together. Go be with her."

"No. You don't understand. It's impossible." Gino puts his face in his hands, his head shaking. "You can't believe what she's done."

"Eloise told me about the money from her mother," Joanna says coolly. "Now you can buy a restaurant. Surely that's good news."

"No! That's all a lie. I don't want a restaurant. But there's something else she wants. And I—"

His body seems to collapse. He forces himself up, restless like a caged bird, then goes to the French doors, moves aside the curtain, and peers out into the darkness. "It wasn't the man she left me for," Gino says. "There was another." He turns, his face distraught, frightened. "She plays with me, Eloise, and I let her. I could kill her, Joanna. I swear I could kill her."

"Gino, why are you telling me this? Do you have any idea how sad and hurt I've been? Eloise plays with you, but you . . . you play with me."

"I'm so sorry." He comes again to sit at the edge of her bed, and Joanna, despite her mind telling her she should be angry, is somehow pleased he's confiding in her.

"It wasn't enough to be a model; she had to be an actress too. She was in a movie with a famous director, someone stronger than her. And she got pregnant, with *him*. Has a child with him. A baby girl. What a liar she is. She didn't tell me until today."

Joanna sits up. "It's not your child?"

"Of course not. I haven't seen her in years." Gino goes on. "He's married, the man who made her pregnant. Eloise was sure he'd leave his wife. She, so sure of everything, was wrong this time. He won't leave his wife, not even for her. And now she's . . . I am not good with the words now."

"Gino, what are you saying?"

"I see who Eloise has become, like the mother she hated. Not the girl I loved when we were young. She doesn't want her baby to have the same as she did. And she knows she will be a terrible mother, like her mother." Gino turns to Joanna. "I wish you could speak Italian. This is too hard in English."

"Where's this child now?" Joanna asks.

"She's been living with her aunt in Milan, a crazy aunt who used to be a famous actress. That whole family is crazy. No one saw this aunt for many years, nobody knew what happened to her, and you know how hard that is here, to keep a secret. The aunt's been taking care of the child. This secret child no one knew about. A little girl with a funny name, not anything Italian. *Zoe*. What kind of name is that? And now she wants to—"

"To be with you again," Joanna says.

"No. Eloise doesn't care about me. She's going to try to get *him* back, the father, the famous director. She thinks, without Zoe, she can. She wants to bring the child *here*, to live here with her aunt. There's money now, from her mother. Not for the restaurant but for this child. It's too much for just her aunt alone, and Eloise will be mostly gone, so she asked . . ."

"What, Gino?"

"I've promised to help raise this child. Oh, Joanna, what have I done?"

"But what do you want from *me*?" Joanna sneezes, then sneezes again several times in a row. Gino becomes quiet, then sighs heavily.

He takes her glass and refills it and gives it to her. Then, with a new thought, or so it seems, he comes again to the edge of the bed. She sees that look in him, that look through the crack, the look you can't fake, that pierces her straight to the heart. "Do you love her?" Joanna asks. "Do you want her back? Is that why you agreed to help with her child?"

"I don't know anything anymore." His face distorts with sadness, and his eyes fill with tears. "Only that when I am with you, I can a little bit breathe."

## LUCA OF THE SEA, 1976

I return from my visit with Luca, and Kathy, my roommate, is blessedly there. I hand her the bottle of rum she had asked Luca to get. In seconds, she's in my room with frosty glasses of coke and plenty of rum, so strong my room smells like the tropics. I always cry after my time with Luca, but now, being with Kathy, who no longer says *cheers* but a weirdly accented *l'chaim* and asks for a *bisl* more rum, I'm okay. She and her funny Yiddish get me laughing, and I make it through the starting gate of transition. Like a spaceship leaving earth's atmosphere, I escape the intense gravitational pull of Luca.

"Admit it," Kathy says, taking big slurping sips, "you're having a wonderful time. It's hopelessly romantic all this."

"Yes." I smile as the punch of the rum knocks out any worries and concerns I should have. "Love is wonderful." I want to tell her that I'm probably pregnant, even though every pregnancy test has come out negative. I'm too busy pretending everything is fine.

When I wake the next morning with my head heavy and pounding, there's a new worry. That if I am indeed pregnant, did the rum and all the champagne I drank with Luca harm my baby? The baby I keep ping-ponging in my mind about having or not. No time to think in the endless repetition of my killer-busy days.

Day after day, week after week, to get my diploma, to do even more racing through time, living a life I don't want. It can't be good, this doing, doing, doing. But I have no choice. Despite my scholarship, I've had to borrow heaps of money for this degree.

That, too, terrifies me; if I don't stay the course and graduate and get a proper job, I'll never manage to pay back my loan. It's an evil labyrinth with no way out. Why can't I live on one of those pretty beaches Luca took me to? Like an ancient gatherer, eating fruit from the trees. Or maybe, just maybe, when we're happily married and living in Italy, Luca will help me pay it all off?

I rush home and change to go meet my mother for dinner. She comes into the city from Long Island once a week. She knows I live on the cheap and insists I eat at least one good meal a week with her. We meet at a snazzy new place as she's brought her new boyfriend who tells us to order the most expensive thing on the menu. He looks at me with suggestive eyes, and I can't believe my mother could fall for such a creep. He orders the most expensive wine on the menu and makes a whole drama of swirling it in his mouth, keeping the waiter longer than necessary before approving the bottle. Each minute in that bogus atmosphere, with muzak pumping out, is unbearable.

I'm starving, but when our food comes, I gag at the expensive steak. Literally. I'm about to puke and have to rush to the bathroom. I don't care how many pregnancy tests say I'm negative, there's something growing in me that's making me sick; I never get sick like this. Back to the table, I push the plate away. Lillian jokes about how she couldn't stand the smell of meat when she was pregnant with me. Yet she doesn't connect the dots, so goofy in love with her wealthy clown of a boyfriend.

I come home, starving, and find two more letters from Luca. I crawl into bed and gobble them up, along with two peanut butter sandwiches, five apples, and three bananas, reading the letters over and over. He can't live without me! *I am the moon and the sun and the stars.*

I adore his letters, though they also shoot bullets of fear into me. How could I tell him that I suspect I'm pregnant? I'm drowning in this fear of unknowing when Amy, my delightfully bonkers neighbor from upstairs, bangs on the door. "You gotta come up," she cries. "*The Sound of Music* is on. I know it's hokey, but I need a break from being cool. And you're the only one I know who won't mind."

I have a heap of pages to read and my thesis to begin, but without hesitation, I join her upstairs. She's made a bowl of popcorn, gives me a dirndl skirt with an Alpine apron to wear, and we yodel until the movie starts. I'm so enthralled by this story, this wonderful family and all the music, that I get excited about what's probably growing inside me. By the end of the film, with all the songs we've sung and tears we've shed, our souls are washed clean and ready for bed.

*** 

Because February this year has twenty-nine days, the schedule is askew, and there's a free day. I start questioning my roommate and soon-to-be gynecologist, Aaron, who already knows of my incessant testing.

"The body is a rare instrument," he says. "So if you feel you're pregnant, you probably are. Testing can be tricky."

"That's just it," I say. "How do I know by my feelings? Which feelings?"

"Well," he says, with an empathetic turn of the head, "for example, aching nipples and swollen breasts, a revulsion to certain foods like meat, and mood swings."

"Except for mood swings, as mine are always swinging, the other symptoms are new. And I have them all."

"There you go," he says. "You're probably pregnant."

"If the tests keep coming out negative, does that mean my body isn't sure?"

"It doesn't work quite like that," he says.

"But," I say, getting anxious, "if I don't know for sure, how can I proceed?"

"Ah, the devil's in the details."

"Ugh! They don't teach you to say *that* at medical school, I hope."

"No," Aaron says. "That's my creative input."

"Well it doesn't help!" I storm out and go to my piano.

There's no way he won't hear me as the walls are paper thin, but I have to play. I'm deep inside the cave of music when there's a knock on my door. It's Aaron, who is standing like a question mark. "Can I come in and listen? I really like your music."

"You do?"

"Are these your songs? I've never heard them before. They sound a bit Joni Mitchell-like, but not quite. Moody and depressing, how I like songs to be."

Aaron sits on the floor, listening. I don't feel at all afraid, and even if I'm not singing great, it feels good to play my songs, all these new songs I've been writing for Luca.

"Gosh, you're a real artist. No wonder you're so sensitive, that you can feel your pregnancy before the hormones are strong enough to affect the testers. That's cool."

*Cool?* I moan to myself. More like torture to be so sensitive.

I play a few more songs; then Aaron gets up. "I could listen all day, but I have a ton of work. Don't ever give up. You're great."

"Thanks," I say.

"I think you probably are pregnant, but you'll still need to get it confirmed so you know what to do."

*How will I know what to do?* I look at Aaron, his straggly brown, kinky hair, his pock-marked face, his small, skinny fingers, and his thumb that turns clumsily away from the rest of his fingers. I hate myself for judging him, but he's ugly and has this musty smell, like a closed-in room. He's friendly and kind, and I wish I could fall in love with him. He's going to be a doctor, so there would be plenty of money to pay off my school loans, and he'd probably let me stay home all day to do my music, and I wouldn't starve. But I could never love him like I do Luca, even if I wish Luca would ask to hear my songs. Oh, this life, this crazy life, that I fear is going to get even crazier.

*** 

I'm again at the doctor's, and again, it is negative. "It is strange," the doctor says. "You *do* have all the symptoms."

How shall I face Luca when he arrives later with this dreadful uncertainty? I want to scream—*it's unfair to make only the woman responsible*. When we're finally together, at my place this time, it's like hot chili peppers on my tongue to not say anything. I pretend, as we laugh and kiss and sip the expensive Taittinger champagne Luca always brings, that I haven't a care in the world. And somehow, I succeed.

After he's gone, I find love letters all over my room. He's hidden them in folds of my clothing, in between papers, under my pillow. His beautiful poetry, seared with longing, is everywhere. Maybe he'll want this baby, and everything will be okay. I let myself feel excited for my life ahead, for the children we will have, for the child I'm most probably carrying, for our happy soon-to-be *Sound of Music* family.

## 20.

### CINQUE TERRE, 2002

THIS MORNING THE air seems calmer and lighter, as if Joanna can feel that Eloise has left town. It's probably more of a hope, for she has no idea. She hasn't seen Gino since his surprise visit, or anyone. For two days, she's stayed in bed with a lousy cold, enjoying the excuse to retreat from the world. She woke ravenous and, with her cupboard bare, needs to venture out to replenish supplies.

Out on the main street on her way to the shop, she stops, completely stunned. Gino, as happy as a lamb, is sitting outside the internet café with a little girl on his lap. An older woman, presumably Eloise's aunt, the famous actress he'd mentioned, is at his side. She's completely unlike anyone Joanna has ever seen in Italy, a character straight from a novel, with long, crinkly hair streaked with gray blowing in every direction. Joanna heard she's in her early seventies, though she seems robust and fit. Her face is marvelously expressive, lined with story, like many a good actress. Sitting there, theatrically and noble, wearing a colorful tentlike African dress, a cigarette dangling in a black holder held away from the child, she belts out a raucous smoker's laugh. The little girl is as cute as a child can be: her face framed in black ringlets, her features already strikingly beautiful, with her mother's violet eyes. The three of them sit there like the most normal thing, as if Gino spends every morning relaxing with an espresso before work.

They haven't noticed her. She stays still and watches as Gino contorts his lips and tongue to the delight of the child. He seems almost too happy, considering how desperate he'd been the other night. Intrigued, she can't take her eyes off the playful child. And then the little girl looks straight at Joanna, her gaze intensifying.

Gino, noticing, turns around with a surprised smile. "Hey, Joanna, come join us."

For a second, she's frozen in place. There's no way to get to the shop without passing them. So, with tentative steps, Joanna walks over.

"Sit with us." Gino points to an extra chair. His old friendly self, like everything has started afresh this morning. "This is Zoe, the child I told you about."

The little girl jiggles to hear her name. Joanna is immediately seduced by her presence, the way her eyes dance with joy. She understands why Gino doesn't resent this lovechild from another man, he who can be so jealous. There he sits as cheerful as she's ever seen him. He leans back and shrugs in the typical Italian way, one hand leaning up to the sky. "It's Zoe!" he says. "She's won my heart."

The older woman smiles. "She does this with everyone. She's a wonder, this child." She reaches out a hand to introduce herself. "I'm Simone, with an *e*. Here in Italy, this name usually ends in *a* for a woman, but I prefer the French spelling. And you, I suppose, are Joanna."

She tries not to show her surprise that Simone already knows her name, but she can't not comment on her accent. "You speak with a wonderful lilt, like you're from an African country."

"I lived in Zanzibar, in Tanzania, for many years. It's where I learned English. Now Eloise wants me to speak only English with

Zoe, so she's going to sound Tanzanian as well! We're giving the town so much to talk about that they won't notice when winter comes." She gives the child a hug. That Simone already knew Joanna's name means she already knows about her and Gino, but why is she being so friendly? Zoe, the remarkable child, seems to thread them together by crawling from Simone's lap to Gino's and then to Joanna's.

"What a happy little girl you are," Joanna says. She hadn't planned to have anything to do with this odd arrangement, yet Joanna can't resist hugging Zoe.

"I've been with her since the moment she was born," Simone says. "I swear she came out like this. Not every child is so easy. God can, in his benevolent mercy, do a kind thing. And he has with this little one. I bet you were on your way somewhere," Simone says. "I suppose you've already forgotten to where you were heading. Truly, she does this with everyone."

Joanna laughs. "I was on my way to buy some food, which I do need to get." Not easy to resist Zoe's shrieks of joy, she hands the child back to Simone and gets up.

"Wait," Simone says. "Gino will go to work now, but I'd love it if you'd stay and have some lunch with us."

"Me? I have to—"

Simone reaches an arm around Joanna and pulls her tenderly in. "Whatever you have to do, I'm sure it can wait. You look surprised."

"Well, I, this isn't quite the reaction I've received from Gino's mother or his aunt. They're never happy to see me."

"They're never happy to see me either." Simone laughs. She looks intensely at Joanna, as if bonding with her on this shared experience. At the same moment, little Zoe, snuggling on Simone's lap, also stares up at her. Four eyes, sending out a bath of sweet energy. Joanna feels overwhelmed and moved.

"Sometimes it's good not to think too much," Simone says. "And you are, I assume, hungry."

\*\*\*

A green tie-dyed sheet drapes across the ceiling of Simone's apartment, turning the room into an Arabian tent. The furniture seems African or Arabian. Shelves are full of handmade ceramic bowls, plates, mugs, little statues, and dancing figurines of dark wood. Bark paintings cover the walls.

For lunch, Simone sets out hummus and grape leaves, stoned wheat crackers, and other delicacies Joanna hasn't seen in the local shops. She has so many questions about Eloise and Zoe and this strange arrangement, yet she doesn't know where to begin. Simone seems to enjoy Joanna's reaction to her eccentric apartment and the un-Italian lunch she's serving; her eyes twinkle with mischief. After Simone puts Zoe down for a nap, she makes coffee and they go out to the balcony. Lighting a cigarette in her elegant, Audrey Hepburn-style holder, Simone lets her words ride out on the smoke. "I see you are wondering."

"I do appreciate the lunch and your kindness but—"

"You're curious why I'm being *so* nice to you." Simone takes a few slow pulls of her cigarette. "The deal with Eloise is that I won't be alone with Zoe all the time. Gino will assist and do what he can, but it's not enough. You know he works many hours, even when the season is slowing down." Taking another drag, she stares fully at Joanna. "She likes you, you know."

"Zoe?"

"Yes, Zoe likes you, but she likes everyone. I mean Eloise. Eloise likes you, and she wondered if you'd have time to help us out. She can pay you, but it's important that you *want* to spend time with Zoe. You have to admit she's a special child."

"I don't understand how Eloise could leave her."

"Eh!" Simone returns to the more typical Italian swirl of the hands. "It's complicated. You will learn in time, just as I did. Eloise is unique. Gino said perhaps you might be staying longer," Simone says with an inviting smile. "You'll soon get used to me. If you can read my face, you'll know everything I'm thinking. And I, my dear, can easily read yours." She sighs impishly, playfully. "I haven't been in a movie for ages, not since going to Zanzibar. Yet isn't all the world a stage? Why don't you take time to see how the idea settles in you, and let me know tomorrow?"

That Joanna has the time to *feel* this new idea and how it settles already seems special. Most of her life, with urgent moments of decision-making, there was never time to take time.

"*Buongiorno*," Simone says the next day. Her voice is hushed. Zoe is asleep on her lap. "She's tired today. She was up part of last night. She does well, but it's still a big change moving here."

"She must miss Eloise."

"She misses the nanny more. Zoe rarely saw Eloise. She will be fine. With her mother's apartment now empty, it made sense to come back here. It's me who needs to get used to being in this little town again. It's small and confining." She pinches her fingers together and circles them for emphasis. "Now, with Zoe and my art, I hope to make it different this time. Did you see the pottery in the apartment? They're mine."

"You're very good."

"I only do things I'm good at."

Simone shifts the whimpering child in her lap and takes a bottle from a large Mary Poppins-like colorful bag to feed her. "My plan, with your help, is to continue my art in the afternoons. I see from your eager face that you are willing. Who can resist this darling child?" She cuddles Zoe closer.

"Hey!" Gino calls out, coming over with an espresso. Simone reaches out to include him in the conversation. Ever the actress, keeping the cast on script, her eyes on her various tasks, including Zoe. "I was just explaining to Joanna how our days will go. Gino will do what he can and maybe you—"

Joanna's heart beats rapidly; she feels an emotional pull, a gigantic yes forming inside her to be part of this new equation.

All at once excited, Gino speaks up. "Hey, Joanna, what if I brought Zoe to your place after I finish my lunch shift and you sing for us?" His smile, first sheepish, spreads to a warm grin. "I've missed your singing."

"I was hoping for something like this!" Simone cheers.

"We can try it for a few days," Joanna says. "Let's see how it goes."

As if in response, Gino lifts Zoe in his arms and waltzes her around the table. "We will sing and dance when Joanna practices." Zoe squeals happily. "You see," Gino says. "She loves the idea."

## LUCA OF THE SEA, 1976

At my next session, I see my therapist's belly is visibly growing, and so is mine. I've gained a noticeable amount of weight. It pisses me off that she gets to have her baby without problems, whereas, for me, there'll be only problems. Luca is far away, I hardly have money, and my mother, not to mention Luca's parents, will pop a cork. Yet I can't help wanting this baby. The first time in my life, there's a bundle of love inside that needs me no matter what. I won't ever be alone again.

I step outside and breathe the fresh spring air. Glorious spring! The sun is bright and full, the sky is a burning blue, and the cherry blossoms are blooming. Instead of going to my next class, I take the subway uptown, walk to Central Park, and, with no one around, start singing.

I lose track of time and arrive way too late at the hospital. The supervisor storms in.

"This is unacceptable! You must be here at the start of your session, not ten minutes late. This is not good." Terrified I won't graduate, I end up telling her about Luca.

"Why haven't you told me this before?" she says, smiling. "I'm a sucker for a love story. I'll give you one more chance. But don't come late again." I blubber out thanks before I tell her about maybe being pregnant.

Until now, I've not mentioned it to my mother, knowing how she'd react. Yet, I'm bursting to tell someone, and once I phone her, she stays surprisingly calm and sensible. At first. Just before we hang up, she makes one of her huffing sounds and slips it in.

"Love is hard to resist. Believe me, I know. But if you truly want to be a musician, I'd get rid of lover boy and all that comes with him."

I want to insist it could work—Luca, the child, *and* my music. I hear her light a cigarette, a clear sign, sober or not, the conversation is over.

Later, with my roommates, I try to act normal. It's only Aaron who knows. They've all met Luca and love to tease me. They call him Prince Charming, with his expensive clothing from Italy and that cloak of his like he's in some nineteenth-century drama. They keep it up until my cheeks burn, and I crawl back to my room lonelier than ever.

I lie in bed, my eyes pried open. I don't want to sleep. I try to feel this baby inside me, who I know, from my roommate Aaron, is just a tiny form surrounded by water, yet I swear I can feel the soul growing inside my womb. A place I'd like to crawl into myself and get a chance to start it all again.

*** 

I am terrified the whole way to the doctor's office the next day. This time it comes out positive. I am pregnant. Despite the negative tests, I've been pregnant all along.

"Seven weeks," the doctor says.

"How long do I have before—" I can't even say the words.

"You mean if you want to terminate the pregnancy? Not long."

Once outside in the spring sunshine, I realize how badly I want this child. All these weeks, I knew it. I felt it! No longer lonely but connected to the sweeping cycle of life! I fantasize about this child, this daughter, or so I imagine. I sit on the subway, in a cloud of specialness—me and my baby. I love her so much.

Later, when my mother phones and I tell her that I want to have the baby, she's livid. "You can't," she yells. "You just can't. It's much harder than you think to raise a child on your own. I have no money to give you, and you have no money. Where are you going to live with this child? Not with me. You can't live with me."

"I won't need to. Luca will help. He'll be with me."

"No, he won't. I promise you, he won't. You can't have this child," she says with such conviction, like she sees into the future.

"Mom, I really want this!"

"No, you don't. You're a barrel of hormones and can't think clearly. I'm making an appointment for you, for next week. Tell lover boy. He's also responsible and seems to have loads of cash."

My roommate, Kathy, sees me in the kitchen, my eyes red from crying. She sits with me in my room, hears my sorry tale.

"Oh man, welcome to the club. I had one last year. It sucks, but you'll get over it. You're too young to give up your whole life."

Alone in my room, I want to feel my baby. I want to love her.

*** 

At the harbor, for the last visit of the *Leonardo* before she sails back to Italy, I feel like an old hag, fat, with red blotches all over my face. No worries about how to tell him; he'll see it immediately. The contrast between my bloated belly and breasts and the beautiful girl Luca fell in love with on the cruise is devastating. I squint to see him, all radiant, without a care in the world. The moment he's close enough, he sends stolen looks at my belly. He sees it; he must see it.

No longer able to hide the fact, I bend my head down, broken and ashamed, forgetting he was a big part of making this baby. I can't bear to look him in the eyes and see his reaction. The pavement shudders and seems to crack under my weight.

"This visit will be very short," he says. "All hands are needed on deck to prepare for the rough Atlantic crossing. I've decided to come back sooner. I will only stay one month in Italy. I think you will need something from me. Tell me what you need."

I can't name it, and he won't either, but the way he looks, I know that he knows I can't afford a child. He's seen how basic I live.

There's relief to not say the words. And I don't stop him when he reaches into his pocket and pulls out a wad of bills. "Here, take this," he says, handing me a few hundred dollars. "I'm sure you'll need it."

If only I could time-shift us back to that windy night on the bridge, to my thin and lithe body.

"How can I reach you?" I ask.

"I'll be staying with my family, and my father is very strict, so I can't use the phone. But here's my address. We can write." I take the paper and tuck it safely into my pocket.

"It is only days," he says, though it will be more like a month, "days that we will get through because our love is that strong. You will remember. Promise me, please." He hugs me and says he loves me, and he will write the date of his return.

When he's gone, I feel a cold draft around my limbs and force my body to move in the opposite direction.

## 21.

### CINQUE TERRE, 2002

EVERY MORNING NOW, Joanna sits with Simone and little Zoe at the café. It feels odd to not start her day on her own, writing in her diary. Yet she enjoys being around Simone—her intensity makes Joanna feel lighter—and little Zoe, who's changing by the second. Gino pops by for a quick espresso and some friendly exchange, and then Joanna goes off to Pieter's for editing and lofty conversation, keeping her well-informed about the state of the world. On her way back, she adds in a hike to the monastery, her favorite place now, and if it's warm enough in these pretty fall days, she goes for a swim off the rocks. She can do this on her own now if the waves aren't too high.

Like clockwork, Gino carries Zoe up to her place a bit after three. He's set up an extra playpen in the garden to contain her. The child bounces happily, holding onto the rail, while Joanna sings and Gino naps. When he wakes, he sweeps the child into his arms and dances her around. Joanna feels him, from time to time, steal a curious glance at her, and she enjoys the soft whisper that maybe their love story could begin again, just not yet.

After the first week, this new scheme feels so natural that they hardly need to exchange words. "It's all okay?" Simone asks. Joanna spontaneously smiles. Extracting little Zoe from her life would be like removing a limb.

So in love with the child, she hardly speaks of anything else. That very morning, Zoe, about a year old, starting walking, and later, with Pieter, Joanna couldn't stop gushing.

"You'd think she was yours," Pieter laughs, "the way you carry on."

"You can get lost in each tiny change. It's incredible."

"Well, well," Pieter says with a smirk. "I'm happy you're still finding time for my articles on the depressing world."

"It's also important for me," Joanna says. "You know that."

"And I thank you for your help. I just wonder if you won't find it tedious, bogged down with childcare?" He, like Joanna, hadn't the idyllic childhood. He's briefly mentioned his brothers and sisters but never spoke of wanting a family of his own.

"A long time ago, I once thought of having a child," Joanna says. "But never did. Not having any siblings, no nieces or nephews, raising a child seemed a mountain of work. The way we've divided it up, with the child's aunt, Simone, and some others is great. I get to play grandmother."

"Who can give the child back."

"Exactly." Joanna laughs, feeling a weird pull. She knows this whole setup with Zoe is temporary, but she's awfully attached to the child.

"So when am I going to meet this wunderkind?" Pieter asks.

"You're kidding, right?"

"Actually no. This unusual constellation you've described is appealing, with this eccentric actress and your friend—"

"Gino," Joanna adds.

"I like that it breaks the normal family nucleus. I have more faith in family when love and care come from various sources."

They work on in silence until they stop to make fresh coffee.

"You're quite remarkable," Pieter says to her. "I've been to Italy I don't know how many times, but never have I met so many people as you have."

"You met me," Joanna says. "That was your doing."

"True, but still."

"I'm not entirely sure," Joanna says, "except I suppose I ... wanted this, to build a sort of life here. Not just be a tourist. You have to meet my friend Grace. You'd like her. Why don't you come with me next time?"

"Maybe," he says. "If I don't have to dance!"

She smiles to imagine Pieter and Grace meeting. Pieter meeting Zoe, however, means Pieter meeting Gino again, and she's not ready for that.

Walking back to Vernazza, Joanna thinks of Pieter's comment about her meeting people so easily. Has it been curiosity and neediness or just coincidence? She arrived in Vernazza a blank and lonely canvas, a widow hungry for a new life. Yet she's found something she's always wanted: to be part of a creative community. She never found that in New York. The harsh competition always intimidated her. Here in Vernazza, with the odd characters she's met, she doesn't feel this competition. Instead, there's a sense of belonging, that it isn't too late to find purpose and connection.

The sharp, autumnal light sparkles on the sea, and for once she's not afraid to feel happy. How she longs to see Zoe, to notice each new change in her. What joy to see a child grow. Tears spring to her eyes as she gasps for a moment, not wanting to lose any of this amazing tapestry. She feels a pull, remembering an old quote: *"We don't inherit the land from our ancestors, we borrow it from our children."* More than ever, she wants the world to be beautiful and to *be* there for this child.

She jumps when her new cell phone rings, not yet used to carrying the phone Simone gave her in case of emergencies. Simone's voice is urgent. "You must come back immediately. Eloise is here. She wants to see you, and she doesn't have much time."

Joanna's chest caves, her heart stammering. This is the bad news she's been fearing.

"Come have lunch with us."

"Does she want Zoe back?"

"Just come back. You will see."

Joanna is totally out of breath when she arrives. Eloise sits at the kitchen table. Her hair cut short, and she's hopelessly thin, her long neck like an exquisite yet awkward giraffe. Simone has laid out two plates of colorful salad and her special crackerbread. "You two can have lunch here. I'll be with Zoe in the other room."

"Hello," Eloise says. Her voice is almost a whisper. "I'm happy you could come. And thank you. Zoe is doing so well."

"She's special, this little girl of yours," Joanna says, her body tense and alert.

"She's more Simone's than mine. I came to bring the rest of her things."

"Not to take her back?"

"No. No, I can't. I'm working too much now. It's better if she stays here."

"But this arrangement is temporary, right?"

"Everything in life *is* temporary. But no, she will stay here."

"How can you leave her?" Joanna can't stop herself. "She will hate you for it when she grows up."

Eloise twists her mouth in a sad smile. "Not to the degree of hate she would feel if I stayed. I'd resent her for ruining my life, just as my mother resented me. I can at least spare her that."

"How could you resent her? She's the sweetest thing."

"Have you any idea the kind of life I lead? The pressure, the expectation, the traveling? I've already lost a mountain of work with all this," she says, her hands on her stomach. "God, the weight I gained."

Joanna is shocked, as she's never seen anyone so thin. "Are you eating at all?"

"I eat plenty. This is Italy. There's food everywhere." Joanna doesn't believe her. The plate in front of her is untouched. "Not everyone is meant to be a mother. God knows my mother shouldn't have been. I don't hate my daughter now. That's the rightness of the plan, that I can love her, like this."

Joanna feels a punch to her own gut that she never became a mother. She swallows hard, refusing to cry.

"She's a special girl, my Zoe. She'll understand one day that this was the only way her mother could love her, by leaving her."

"But surely there are all sorts of solutions. With the money you've been left, you could—"

"That money is for Zoe," Eloise says with conviction. "I know you don't like me, but somehow you aren't wired to hate, and that's good. You aren't going to make her hate me."

*Can it be,* Joanna thinks, *that she has a heart? This is Eloise loving her child.* The best she can do, and she knows it. Parents did this during wars and famines, sending their children off to a safer place. Loving them by leaving them, to give them life. Eloise gets up and takes the plates, both uneaten, to the counter.

"There never was a restaurant, was there?" Joanna slowly asks. "The story of Gino coming back to save money, that wasn't true."

"No, it wasn't," she says, sitting again. And then with a half-laugh, as if most of the sentence she says to herself, "I saw that in you, that you'd believe him no matter what I said, and you should."

Though painfully thin, Eloise's newfound vulnerability makes her even more beautiful. "What about the father?" Joanna asks. "Will he complicate things?"

"The father?" Eloise laughs. "He wants nothing to do with me or Zoe. He gave me a good chunk of money and has lined up work for me in Asia for what seems like years to come. Very clever to keep me as far away as possible. I'm taking a flight from Milan to Fiji tomorrow."

Joanna is speechless. She feels an odd desire to touch Eloise, to comfort her. And Eloise, perhaps sensing this, leans away. "God, I hate this place. I hate Italy. We've molded ourselves into the ceilings, painted ourselves into the walls of museums. This isn't a living place anymore; it's just to observe and photograph. But you," Eloise says, coming slightly forward again, "you aren't from here. You won't let her become too Italian. And she'll learn proper English. That's all I ask."

"But I . . . I've never had any experience with—"

"I know," Eloise says, cutting in. "You never had your own child. But that doesn't mean you can't be good for her."

## LUCA OF THE SEA, 1976

Lillian phones to say she'll come into the city later, stay the night, and go with me to the clinic in the morning. "This is no time to think," she says. "It'll be over before you know it, and everything will be as good as new."

I don't believe a word of it. Will never be as good as new ever again. That afternoon at the mental hospital, I nearly ask the more lucid patients if I'm doing the right thing; there's still time to change my mind. They must sense my uncertainty, for the group gets fidgety, and one patient starts smashing things. Before I have a chance to gain control, the aides rush in, put him in a straitjacket, and stick a needle in his arm to squelch his screams. In the next second, to prevent a riot, they break up the session and take everyone back to their rooms. It happens so fast, with me standing like a moron, my guitar strapped across my shoulders. Completely useless in this hysteria, the answer hits me. *No way to add a child into the chaos of your life.*

\*\*\*

"Lie down," a voice says with an accent I can't place. Was he sent here to clean out the uteruses of foolish young girls who mistook an illusion for true love? It's terribly painful. Incredible that the same part that felt like magic with Luca can hurt this much. With all the dollars Luca gave me, there wasn't enough for total anesthesia. I have to be awake for the whole vile thing. It feels like the doctor is sucking out my innards and ripping out my soul, and the noise, this horrific noise.

"Close your eyes," the doctor says with a bland voice, like he's vacuuming a hallway. "Just removing air and water, no form yet, no baby." Then why does it hurt so much?

The nurse wheels me out, and I can't stop crying. She gives me pills I recognize from the hospital. If this is anything like giving birth, there won't be another pregnancy, not on my watch.

"Try not to think," Lillian says, doing it the best she can. "You've done the right thing. No point ruining your life." She takes me back to my apartment, prepares some soup and toast, and tucks me in.

"Why didn't you get rid of me?" I ask, in my pajamas, under the covers. "Wouldn't that have been better?"

"What," she says in her best nightclub voice, "and miss all this?"

When I wake, Lillian is gone. She must have told my roommates, who bring in tea and oranges and sing Leonard Cohen's "Suzanne." Kathy sings out of tune, yet with such compassion, she makes me smile. She's phoned my supervisor to say I'm raging with a fever and gets me the grace of two sick days. Still sore, my mind, at least, is quiet. Looking at this circle of friends, I feel huge gratitude.

Yet when they've left for work, it's Luca I crave, Luca I miss. I had felt so angry at him during the procedure, but the pain has left, and I miss him so much. Inside my private cave of insanity, I wonder if it's all a test to see if I really love him.

By evening, I can sit at the piano. I touch the keys, ripple out chords of sadness, and tears come, healing tears; I miss my wild redheaded daughter. I will miss her presence growing inside me and how much I would've loved her. She wouldn't have had my fears. I would've helped her laugh on the movable stage of life, helped her tame those vicious lions of fear that trip me up. She would have leaped far and wide because of the wings I'd have given her, wings I can never give myself.

In the next breath, I hate Luca for causing this loss. I pound hard on the piano and play out the deadly passion. I must vacuum it out just as the doctor vacuumed me out. If I can rid myself of that, I'll be cured. Will become realistic, as Kathy suggests. "It's no big deal whether it works out with Luca or not. You'll meet someone else. When it's the right time, you'll have a child."

But they know nothing; I will never let this happen again. There will never be another child.

## 22.

### CINQUE TERRE, 2002

NEW CREASES HAVE appeared on Gino's brow. Joanna can't help but wonder if all this being around Zoe—a constant reminder of the betrayal of Eloise—has gotten to him. Today, after he settles Zoe into the playpen in Joanna's garden, he lies down like an old man on the grass and falls directly asleep. The joy has gone out of him. He isn't playful with the child, no dancing around with her.

Joanna isn't sure how to communicate with him and dares not upset him further or disturb the fragile balance between them. Joanna keeps singing like everything is okay, but her voice feels tight and tense. She wishes she could comfort him, be closer to him. After a few more songs, she's unable to continue.

Zoe grows still in her playpen, with her head cocked to the side, as if waiting for the next song. Joanna forces a smile, her arms tight around her guitar, trying to extract courage from the instrument. The sudden silence seems to disturb Gino's sleep. He opens his eyes and leans up on his elbows. Zoe turns toward him, her voice whining, her arms reaching out. He drags his body up, like an elephant rising, lifts Zoe out of the playpen, and takes her down with him onto the grass. He doesn't look at Joanna, but she longs to be with them, to cuddle with them. Gino wraps his arms tenderly around the child, the way he used to with Joanna.

"Please keep singing," he says without looking at her. His voice sounds as broken as she feels. She begins a mournful lullaby, surprised she remembers the words.

*Hush-a-bye, don't you cry, go to sleep you little baby*
*When you wake, you will have cake and all the pretty little horses*

She doesn't want Zoe to hear her cry, but the mournful melody touches her, touches her deeply. She strums the last minor chord, wishing to hold the time fast and not break this spell, this subtle vibrating thread that connects her to Gino and Zoe. When the tone has vanished to nothing, the child reaches her hand out with her fingers spread open. Their eyes meet. No words, just this tender yearning. Joanna puts the guitar down and slides to the ground beside Zoe. She wraps her arms around the child, making a sandwich with little Zoe in the middle of herself and Gino. She feels the warmth of the child's body, the excursion of breath through arms and legs and fingers and toes. Gino remains on the other side. Joanna carefully touches his hand, and he doesn't move it. What feels like an exquisite eternity, they all breathe as one, again and again and again.

For this endless moment, they remain in a peaceful reverie. The sun begins to sink below the palm fronds, and the air grows cooler. Zoe suddenly wiggles free and crawls around them. Without a word, Gino gets up and prepares to leave. He lifts Zoe into his arms. Joanna stands and dusts herself off. She walks them to the hallway. All in silence. Even the little girl remains still.

Gino carries Zoe in one arm and briefly hugs Joanna with his other, still not looking at her. When he says his habitual *ciao*, his eyes flash into hers with yearning, and for a moment, she feels a surge of love.

\*\*\*

The next morning, Joanna finds herself fussing over her appearance. She decides to have a coffee at the familiar brick steps, to repeat the ritual from the beginning of her stay when Gino looked forward to seeing her.

She knows Gino can't possibly be expecting her, as she hasn't been there for a while. Yet she feels terribly disappointed that he doesn't glance even *once* in her direction. But she sees him standing there, with all the time in the world, flirting with two young blonds. Never an end to new arrivals of young and pretty tourists. Joanna knows it's part of his job, attracting people to the restaurant, just as he'd done with her and Terry, but does he have to enjoy it so much?

She slips away before he can see her and heads straight for Simone's flat, as they're not at the café.

"You must have read my mind," Simone says, opening the door quickly. "I was just going to call you. Something came up, and I won't be able to take care of Zoe this morning. Could you maybe take her with you to that friend of yours?"

Joanna looks aghast. "I couldn't possibly. We work the whole time. I . . . could stay here instead." Joanna looks over at Zoe, who is happily involved with a picture book. "She seems quite content."

"If you wouldn't mind, I'd love to be alone this morning to work on my art. And it's a beautiful day to try this new gadget Eloise brought on her last visit. Zoe will love it." Without waiting for an answer, Simone lifts Zoe and urgently leads them to the other room, where a baby carrier is on the floor. "Can you try it?"

Joanna, going along with this, as she can't get a word in edgewise, slips the carrier onto her shoulders, and in a snap, Simone places the little girl in. "Do you want to go with Joanna on an adventure?"

Zoe can't possibly understand, yet she picks up Simone's enthusiasm and bounces with glee. "*Sima, Sima!*" she cries.

It feels a bit fun to have Zoe on her back, the gleeful sounds the child makes lightening Joanna's mood and distracting the circling thoughts of Gino. Besides, she has quite a few articles to return to

Pieter, and one that she hopes can inspire a segue into the subject of Stuart's book. Pieter had expressed interest in meeting Zoe, so hopefully he won't mind.

"It's not too heavy, is it?" Simone asks.

"Not yet."

"If you get tired on the way back, just leave the pack hidden in the bushes, carry Zoe home, and we can get it tomorrow. I'll walk with you up the steps to carry Zoe; then it shouldn't be too heavy to go the rest." Simone fills the pack with extra diapers, a bottle, snacks, and a few light toys, and off they go.

After Simone leaves, she hears Zoe whimper. Joanna jiggles her body and reaches a hand over the pack to touch the child. Joanna starts singing one of the songs Zoe likes. *"The wheels on the bus go round and round . . ."* And she hears happier sounds, with the child babbling along. As they walk on, the pack gets heavier and heavier. When they reach the bench outside the café, she carefully lifts the pack off, sets it down with Zoe in it, and rubs her sore shoulders. She then lifts Zoe out and onto her lap on the bench.

A few moments later, Pieter happens to walk out of the café. Seeing Joanna and Zoe, his face lights up. "Hey, look what we have here!" He scoots over and bends down to greet the child. "What a pretty little girl you are."

"Bit of an odd story this morning," Joanna says. "I was coerced into trying this pack, and Simone's a tough one to say no to. You wanted to meet her, so here she is."

"Perfect," Pieter says, smiling at Zoe. "Let me get some drinks. Juice for Zoe? I'll be right back."

"Thanks," Joanna says. She rolls and massages her shoulders. Zoe turns to her and wiggles her little body, trying to imitate Joanna's movements. The gesture is so endearing, Joanna hugs the little girl in a bundle to her chest.

Just as Pieter comes out with the drinks, a young man stops him. "How much longer are you staying?" he asks. "I'd like to talk with you again."

"Just a few more days," Pieter replies. "I have to get back to Holland."

"Let's make sure to meet before that."

"Sure thing," Pieter says.

*Just a few more days?* Joanna had assumed he was going to stay much longer. When he hands her the drinks, she says, "I didn't know you were leaving so soon."

"If I can squeeze it, a bit longer," he says, sitting on the bench, making playful faces at Zoe. "But not by much." Pieter takes a long sip of beer. "Why?"

"I just . . . thought you'd stay." Why hasn't he told her? She busies herself, pouring juice into Zoe's sippy cup, but she can't stop her mood from sinking. Pieter has become a sort of Stuart for her; he can't leave. Plus, she still hasn't found the right moment to mention his book.

"Hey, hey, what's going on?" Pieter asks.

"It's just that, I wish you could stay."

"I wish I could too. Still haven't that money tree. You'll be fine. You seem quite smitten with this little girl, and—"

"Zoe is great. But I'll miss you."

Pieter turns away, like he's embarrassed for her to see he's touched by her reaction. Just then, with an eerie timing, Zoe motions for Pieter to lift her. Flattered, he acquiesces. "That's unusual," he says to Joanna. And to Zoe, he adds, "You are a special one."

"She is," Joanna says. "Like a wise old soul."

After a short stay in his arms, she wiggles to come down. While Pieter lets Zoe down, his hand accidentally brushes across Joanna's thigh. She feels a shiver, a pleasurable jolt. Her surprise reaction seems to register on Pieter, or maybe he, too, is feeling something surprising. They both turn their eyes away and push aside the moment.

"Come, let's go," he says. "It's good you're here earlier today.

There's a ton to get through." Pieter lifts the carrier while Joanna picks up Zoe. "Can I try it?" he says, smiling. He slips it over his shoulders. "This fits me perfectly," he says, adjusting the straps. "Why don't I carry her the rest of the way?"

With Zoe snug in the pack, Pieter bends and sways his body. He takes little hops, not too much, just enough to bring out squeals of delight in the child. "This is fun!" he says.

"I've never seen you like this!" Joanna says. "You're in such a good mood."

"Well, it's not from the news, I can tell you." He flashes her a brilliant smile that shows undoubtedly how happy he is with their company. He turns forward with another few skips that bring out more shrieks of laughter from Zoe. It's a lovely moment of respite and pleasure, and Joanna gobbles it up.

"It's nice to see you this happy," she says.

"Ah, well. It will soon pass once we get back to work and remember the mess the world is in." Pieter's mood shines so bright, he begins whistling as he takes the keys from his pocket to open the outer door and the one to his private room. He continues whistling as he and Joanna work easily together, arranging a blanket and pillow as a makeshift crib for Zoe. He prepares a lunch of cheese and bread and fruit. Once the child is settled in and asleep, they get down to work.

"You're really good with her," Joanna says. "You sure you have no kids?"

"Always an interesting question for a man," Pieter says, smiling. "I don't think so, but you never know."

## LUCA OF THE SEA, 1976

Little by little, my bloated stomach returns to normal, but not my vigilance. If anything, I've become even more cautious and weary of passionate feelings. Amy, my upstairs neighbor, who's decided I'm still moving to Rome so she can visit, is on a mission to keep me from getting too functional. She brings me novels by Henry Miller and Anaïs Nin. "They found their art in Paris, and you will find your voice in Rome." When I'm with her, I hope against hope this will come true.

I take the happy feeling Amy's inspired, and as it's a spectacular spring day with everything in bloom, I walk through Central Park, singing the whole way. Suddenly, I get a lurch in my belly, my empty belly, that it's just me. No longer do I have my wild redheaded daughter (or so I always imagine) growing inside. God, how I miss her. As if the sky registers my sadness, clouds gather and completely hide the sun.

When I turn the key to my apartment much later, I'm hit by an aggressive wall of noise. There's a party going on, a party I had no idea about. The place is packed with Kathy's new friends from her snazzy new job at the advertising agency. I rarely see her these days; all she does is spend hours perfecting copy to sell a thing nobody needs. She's changed so much; we hardly hang out. She no longer has any interest in my artistic life or tragic love story. I rush upstairs to find refuge with Amy, but she's out. I slink back down to my room and force myself to take out my books, get my typewriter ready, and begin my thesis. I'm crying so much that the few words I'm able to type turn into a river of gray mush. Like driftwood that's lost contact with the bigger stream, I'm never going to graduate.

***

Strangely, these days, I feel the most peaceful at the music therapy sessions at the hospital. The rooms are horrid, but the music that comes through me is from another world. The stray moments between sessions, when the more lucid mobile patients stop to touch my hand like I'm a bit of sunshine for those starved for light, feel magical. It's those moments when I sense Luca all around me, the beautiful world we created and the stars we saw in each other's eyes.

Today, I ask my supervisor if I can do more sessions. Not just for the added grace of my sometimes being late, but I actually *need* these sessions. "Yes!" she says. "You can do another one now. I'll get the aides to gather everyone."

With my guitar across my shoulders, prancing around like an eager leprechaun, I notice that in minutes the patients are laughing and swaying to the music. Even the aides clap and sing, and before we know it, we've got a real hootenanny going. I hear the music still echoing on the concrete walls as I head to the drum session, where the young boys pick up on my good mood. They hoot and holler with percussive precision. They pound fingers to the root of their rage, and their sweaty muscles glisten in the tiny shards of light through the vaulted windows. I play along with them, in a trance, until the session ends, and the boys fist each other's shoulders and slam high fives like proud warriors. At least they've had an hour's reprieve from the madhouse. It's something, all this, a profound forgetting of one's troubled existence, even my own.

The minute I'm away from the hospital, it all grows precarious, and I once again have that dreadful sinking in my belly. The punishment for the terrible thing I've done is this dreadful loneliness. That I'll never ever get to see her, get to know her. And there'll never be another one. It was a once-in-a-lifetime letting go that created that child. I'll never be that free again, never get past the words of the doctor: "Just close your eyes, and you'll hardly feel a thing."

# 23.

## CINQUE TERRE, 2002

Z OE WAKES IN Pieter's room, whimpering for *Sima*. Joanna comforts her, bouncing her on her lap, then changes her diaper and gives her a bottle. "I'd better get going," Joanna says to Pieter. "She usually spends the morning with Simone, and I think she's missing her."

"Can I help you carry her back?" Pieter offers. "You've been rubbing your shoulders a lot while we've been working."

"No, I'll manage."

"C'mon, let me do it. The pack is heavy. Are you worried about running into . . . what's his name?"

Joanna shrugs, not wanting to investigate how she really feels. It's all so muddled with Gino. "I should just go." She lifts the pack to her shoulders, then holds the straps as Pieter places Zoe in. She takes a few steps, with Pieter watching, then cringes with pain. It's not just her shoulders that ache; her lower back is numb. Pieter helps her get the pack off.

"Come on, you've helped me so much with the articles, and you don't take a penny. This is the least I can do."

"I should be able to do this," Joanna says.

"Why?" Pieter says. "You didn't come to Italy to be a child-minder."

"I know. It's just, I've been enjoying her and Simone and feeling, you know, a part of something. It's been harder than I thought, losing my husband. And my mother, I never told you the full story. She threw me a doozy at the funeral, telling me about my *real* father. Something she withheld all my life. There's so much, and I—" Joanna stops herself from getting emotional. She'd finally got comfortable showing her vulnerability around Gino, but with Pieter it's different. All at once, little Zoe, who goodness knows must have felt something, lifts her arms to Pieter, asking him to carry her.

"There you have it!" Pieter says, grinning. "This wise soul has spoken. Gino doesn't own the trails. If we run into him and he gets angry, let him get angry."

"You're right," Joanna says, gesturing for Pieter to carry the pack. Once on the way, Joanna feels nervous and annoyed with how much she misses Gino, longs for him; she has absolutely no idea how to get things going again.

Lost in thought, she smiles to see Pieter up ahead, bouncing as he walks. "You're a natural with her," Joanna says, catching up. Zoe's face is a bundle of joy, her giggles and gurgles contagious. "I can't imagine you not having children."

"I never think about it," Pieter says with a laugh. "But I am enjoying this."

"We've hardly spoken about our lives."

"Besides the warring, angry outside world."

"Did you ever, I mean, do you have someone waiting for you in Holland?"

"Not that I know of," Pieter says with a wry twist. "Once upon a time, I was terribly in love. Who knows, if we'd stayed together, we'd probably have had some. It tends to happen."

"What was she like?"

"Oh, my oh my. She was spectacular. We were spectacular, like Simone de Beauvoir and Sartre." Pieter seems to stand taller, even with the heavy pack. "Both of us writing away with an inspired thrust to change the world. Goodness, how spectacular we thought we were. Ha! It's a shock when you learn the world couldn't care less. When no one would publish our remarkable writing, she needed someone to blame. Just didn't think it would be me." He slows as if coming to the edge of a cliff, though the path continues straight on.

"Was this a long time ago?" Joanna asks.

"It was, but it still feels like yesterday. I haven't been able to get close to anyone since. Too busy working. Another drug, I guess. At least my work is something I can control." Pieter took a few crooked steps to entertain the child again and perhaps give himself a breather. His face contorts. "There's nothing worse than believing you have to be everything for the other, which we were for about a year. But perfection eventually devours itself, and we couldn't keep it up. We were starving, literally starving, and one of us had to get a real job to buy food. You'd think I'd committed treason by getting normal work, the way she raged at me, that I destroyed our bubble, *her* bubble. She wasn't able to finish her book, and then she left me."

"I'm sorry," Joanna says, feeling closer to him.

"I completely broke down. That, too, was unbearable, reminding me of my mother. I felt exactly like my mother."

"Your mother? What do you mean?"

"Maybe a Dutch thing, more common in the south of the Netherlands where I grew up, with this *breaking down*." Pieter hesitates as if he's already revealed too much. Yet he continues. "When I grew up, many families were large. We were eight children. I was the youngest. Hardly time for a mother to catch her breath. If you couldn't manage the household, you became *ill* and went to a hospital to *rest*. It terrified me as a kid, never knowing when this could happen again or if she'd come back. Later, I learned it was mental exhaustion, *burn out*, we call it now. If you must carry a heavy rock, you have to allow yourself to put it down once and a while. We didn't know that back then. No one can carry a rock all the time, not even a mother." Pieter sighs. "And not someone like me, who had to be the absolute best."

Joanna's touched that he's sharing his story with her, knowing how private a person he is. Maybe this explains his stubbornness in wanting to help her with the pack. As she walks on, listening, she keeps discreetly checking the trail to see who may be heading their way.

"Maybe the biggest problem was that we were too much alike. She also grew up in a large family, where no one spoke about anything. You resent your parents, and you think you can be stronger, can manage it better." Pieter makes a few grunting sounds. "In the end, you can't. You're human, flawed and impotent. And she blamed me. Then she met someone else, a *wise superior soul*, so she thought, a yoga teacher passing through, and left with him for Colorado. Who knows if she's still with him. I think she needed to be in a continuous spiritual orgasm. Hey, I just made that up, *spiritual orgasm*. Sounds good, doesn't it?"

"You're great with words," Joanna says. "I keep telling you."

"Luckily, I am," Pieter replies, biting his bottom lip. "Because I sure am not in relationships. The work helps, and being here in Italy." Pieter smiles a tender, vulnerable smile. Not knowing if he's referring to her and their time together, she takes this awkward moment to check on Zoe. She absolutely doesn't want Pieter to leave Italy and wants so badly to broach the subject of helping with Stuart's book, yet she also fears insulting him.

Pieter slows again, which he seems to do when deep in thought. He looks out to the sea. The wind is calming down, the air getting warmer. "My mother died last year. I still wonder why she couldn't allow herself to be tired or feel exhausted, to get us kids to do more." He doesn't say more and starts walking on.

As the two continue on in silence, Joanna wonders if it is just luck who people meet and fall in love with. *Or is the pull of unfinished business in our lives, the things we never got in our childhood and still crave, the strongest factor in attraction?* The latter has certainly been true in Joanna's case. Was it possible to have both a caring relationship, as she had with Stuart, and the big passionate love, as with Luca? *Is there just one soulmate, or do we need different people at different times in our lives?*

So lost in her thinking that when she sees how far they've come, she stops short, with a twitch of warning.

"You're worrying about him, aren't you? You're afraid he's going to have another fit when he sees me walking with you, carrying Zoe."

"I'm being stupid," Joanna says. "We just had a fling a few weeks ago. We're not together anymore. Just this morning, he was busy *flirting* with some new girls." Joanna was surprised and ashamed of how angry she sounded.

"That doesn't mean anything," Pieter says. "This is Italy. All the men flirt."

"Let's just keep going. I couldn't carry that pack now."

It's well before three when they arrive at Simone's apartment, but Gino is there pacing outside her door. Pieter calmly takes off the pack and places it on the ground. In a flash, Gino pushes past and lifts Zoe out. The difference between the two men couldn't have been more striking. Zoe feels the sudden tension and starts crying.

"It's not what you think," Joanna says to Gino. "It was Simone's idea that I went to Pieter's with Zoe. The pack was much too heavy, so Pieter carried her back. Nothing more."

Gino won't turn; he won't listen. He bangs on Simone's door, holding Zoe and muttering something in Italian.

Simone sees the three adults and a crying child and quickly surmises the situation. "Oh, God." She sighs. She takes Zoe from Gino and lets loose a flood of Italian at him. Joanna understands enough to get that she's reiterating what Joanna has said. Somehow hearing it from Simone, in Italian, gets through to him, and he sulks away. Joanna starts after him, but Simone pulls her back. "Leave him," she says. "I feared this would be too much. He wants to help, he wants Eloise back, he also wants you . . . he doesn't know what he wants."

"I better go," Pieter says, folding his body in awkwardly.

Joanna turns to him, realizing the impact of what's just happened, but before she can say anything, Simone asks, "Is this the guy you've been working with?"

"Yes," Joanna says, introducing them. "My shoulders hurt, so Pieter offered to carry Zoe back."

"That was good of you. Come in," Simone says, also inviting Pieter. "The coast is clear. The mad Italian has gone."

"Thanks," Pieter says, holding up his hands as if to push the drama away. "But I better get going. Need to get back to work. Bye, Zoe." Pieter waves to the little girl and turns.

"Wait," Joanna says.

He turns coldly to her. "I really do need to go. See you." And then he's gone. All of it so fast. Still in shock, Joanna follows Simone in, completely unsure how to proceed. Zoe won't stop crying.

"She had a nap," Joanna says apologetically. "It went fine at Pieter's."

"That may be," Simone says, "but she isn't fine now. The change of schedule must have upset her, but I had to take care of some important things this morning. Look"—Simone turns her attention fully onto Zoe—"just come back tomorrow."

The door closes fast and loud. Joanna stands there in shock. How hard to get things right. How easy to create a mess. She takes the new cell phone Simone gave her and finds Pieter's number. Not used to writing messages on this little flip phone, it takes forever to explain how sorry she is.

Back in her apartment, she goes out to the garden that feels hopelessly empty without Zoe or Gino, without the music. She walks anxiously around in circles, not knowing what to do with herself. Then she remembers, with a huge sigh, that it's the day of the dance at Grace's farm. *Boy, do I need to dance today.* Her darling mother trained her to be symbiotic and codependent, and she still is. Impossible for her to detach from the things of the world and the reactions of people, to not torture herself with every mistake. *To wear the world as a loose garment,* a phrase she's heard enough times over the years, yet it's still so difficult.

With a rush of momentum, she gathers her things for the dance. Taking her guitar, she'll stop and do a few songs with Zoe before she leaves. If the change in routine was unsettling for the child, perhaps a few familiar songs will bring comfort. She'll find Gino and explain.

When she gets close to the harbor, he's there, without a care in the world, flirting away to those two young blonds she saw that morning. All to feel better about himself, the handsome Italian gigolo. Furious, she takes a few deep breaths, then walks over.

"I'm taking the guitar to Simone's to sing for Zoe this afternoon. In case you want to come by."

Joanna turns away before she can see his reaction.

## LUCA OF THE SEA, 1976

Today in music class, due to my bottomless pit of longing, I belt out that rare voice in me. The singing teacher leaps into applause, then asks me why I keep my striking voice mostly hidden. As if I have a choice.

"You're very sensitive," she says, placing a large imposing hand on my shoulder, her voice rising in operatic dynamic. "Good to be sensitive, to interpret the music, but you must also be *tough*, not let the world affect you so much. You need *courage* to sing, and you had courage today. Don't hide that courage. You must dare expose yourself to the world."

"I was lucky today," I say.

"No!" she sings out so loud, I go nearly deaf. "You were *courageous* today!"

I thus conclude I'll always have to be in a desperate place in order to sing like this. In any case, for a rare moment, I believe her and decide to go later to the Village to the open mic at the Other End, the musical café I sometimes haunt on Tuesdays to listen, but I never dare sing myself. I cut my afternoon class, go straight home, and practice one of my songs on the guitar, which I bring to work so I can go straight from the agency to the club. Leo makes all kinds of comments when he sees my guitar. "Come on, give us a song," he begs, but just the idea of spontaneously doing a song without even a mic to hide behind brings on panic. Luckily, it's crazy busy with the phones ringing, so there's no time.

I manage the courage to put my name on the list for the open mic but then go to the bathroom so often, I use up all the toilet paper. I'm completely dehydrated and about to faint when they call my name. The all-or-nothing moment. My hands shake so badly, I can hardly get the capo on, and my knees knock together like a percussive instrument. In such a state, instead of doing the song of mine, I play Joni Mitchell's "Big Yellow Taxi." Everyone's heard that song a million times, and instead of singing along as I'd hoped, they all get up and order a drink or talk to their friends. It's miserable trying to sing in that atmosphere, and I make the song shorter just to get off the stage. I feel small and ashamed. I'll never have the courage to sing my own songs or be a real performer. Once back in the busy, heartless streets, it roars in my head. *What good is talent if you don't have the courage to access it when you need it? Better to know your limits than pretend you can do something—and crash.*

What came out of me in voice class today was an accident, just like what happened when I sang on the ship with Luca. Only once in a blue moon, when I can really sing.

I end up walking the whole way home to East Eighty-First Street, furious God made me so sensitive while the world gets noisier and noisier. I jump at the screech of the subway, the ambulance, the police cars, the boom boxes with disco music burning holes in my ears. I long to live where it is civilized and quiet, like how I imagine Italy, quiet and peaceful and loving.

I turn onto Second Avenue when a gush of warm, balmy air, almost tropical, hits me. I suddenly feel Luca there, his larger-than-lifeness. *Oh Luca, if you could have been with me for the audition, if you were playing the drums behind me, I would have dared to sing one of my songs. I would have dared let that voice out.* As I walk on, the balmy air wafts off the East River and follows me. I start to calm down, even begin to have the hope that when I'm finally with Luca in Rome, I will sing. People won't be rude there as they were tonight, and bathed in the love from Luca, I won't be so afraid. When I get home, even if my shoulders are sore from carrying my guitar, my mood is high because I know my life will work out. Instead of going to the other entrance, the one leading to the kitchen and my bedroom, I come through the living room. Kathy and Aaron are there watching TV. They invite me to join them for the large pizza and ice cream they've ordered.

"Sure!" I say, like I'm a retired person with all the time in the world. It's a great movie they're watching, and they quickly catch me up. In minutes, I'm completely sucked in. After it's done, and we finish both containers of the rum raisin Häagen Dazs, talking about the movie over and over, I go to my room happily bloated and spent. It's eleven at night, and I look at the heap of books and the tiny start—not even one full typed page—of my thesis sticking out of my typewriter. I know I've blown it. I'll never graduate by June. Will need the summer to finish. I calm myself. At least with no hospital internship in July and August, the courses will be easier to finish, and I'll be able to work more at the agency to save up for my great escape to Italy. I go to sleep and must have dreamed about golden hills and bougainvillea and sweet kisses from Luca, because I sail through the next day on a soft cloud.

There's a thick letter in my mailbox from Luca. Amy arrives just as I'm opening the blue airmail envelope, and she snuggles in beside me so she can also read the letter, as if it's also for her.

"Oh my God," she says, grabbing the letter to reads some of it aloud. "*I am waiting for you, but I need you to be strong. It will be a long, long walk up to our mountain, and your feet will ache, and you will ache for home. But you must know, your home will be with me. No one can ever love you as I do.*" Amy starts to cry. "He's amazing. Who writes like this? So what if he has stormy moods. He's magnificent. A real poet."

After she leaves, I allow the impact of Luca's words to settle. There's also a package he's sent, a Riccardo Cocciante record Luca wrote about in his long letter, "*hoping I will feel his love through the music.*" I run up to my room, strip off the plastic seal, and place the record on my little player. My hand trembles as I lower the needle and when the music starts it's as if Luca is right there. I can't understand the Italian words Cocciante sings, yet his ragged voice, his thrashing visceral cry, cuts straight to my heart.

With my eyes closed, I dance madly around my room, feeling the pure throb of the music. His voice inspires courage to never give up. He doesn't seek the numbing comfort of the couch, the banal TV. Rather, he burns at the stake of life, runs barefoot over hot coals. This is the roughest, most amazing music I've ever heard, and I play the record over and over. His melodies dip and dive, and while I dance like Isadora Duncan, I get so aroused, it scares me. I take the sleeve cover and kiss it, then roll with it in my arms onto my rug, as if I have my arms around an invisible Luca. I haven't felt this raw passion since way before the abortion. I thought I was dead. But I'm not. I'm so not dead. It's both wonderful and terrifying, and I can't stop listening. Cocciante is my new God. My soul cries out that someone somewhere sings what I feel. What I didn't even know I felt. Oh, to have the courage to sing like he does.

In the next breath, I realize how terrified I am of falling over the edge, of going mad. That they'll lock me up in a hospital, and before

I know it, I'll be wheeled in with that dazed look all the patients have. Oh God no.

## 24.

### CINQUE TERRE, 2002

JOANNA STANDS OUTSIDE Simone's door, the guitar on her shoulders, waiting to be let in. The longer she waits, the more her confidence wanes. When Simone finally comes, she opens the door just a crack.

"I thought I'd sing for Zoe as we've been doing in the afternoons. She loves it. It might help settle her."

"Not now. I finally got her to sleep. Thank you for taking her this morning. I'm glad I met your friend. He seems a levelheaded person, and it's good to know people like that." Simone speaks hastily, as if she has something in the oven, clearly not going to invite Joanna in. "See you tomorrow."

"Could you let Gino know I came by?"

"Why?"

"Just tell him, please?"

"I thought you planned to go to your friend at the farm this evening, for a dance."

"Yes, but—"

"Go, enjoy. Don't worry about Gino. *Ciao!*"

In an instant, the door again slams shut. Joanna suspects it was the wind; still, it hurt to be dismissed so abruptly. Deflated and unable to move from the door, Joanna suddenly feels how small Vernazza is, suffocatingly small. Like Eloise said, *"It's a beautiful prison."*

*** 

It's a small group of five dancers this evening, and they begin slowly. Joanna hankers to start, to dance through her mountain of feelings; it's not only the child who suffered the change in routine. When the music grows stronger, Joanna charges like a warrior around the room, until her heart pounds. To catch her breath, she goes to the corner of the room, which is set up as an altar with candles and quotes. The creator of this dance style, Gabrielle Roth, had many inspiring lines.

Joanna reads one: *Sometimes you have to accept that certain things will never go back to how they used to be. We need to be here now, to dance our present reality.*

What is her present reality that she isn't accepting? Impossible to be lovers again with Gino, never seeing Pieter again, or getting help with Stuart's book? Simone realizing she doesn't need Joanna after all? Most of her life, she felt okay about not having her own child, yet after these last weeks with Zoe, she can hardly imagine a life without one. Conflicting feelings boomerang. She circles the room a few more times, then swoops in to read the next quote.

*The feelings I have for you, I cannot explain. You are everything I need.* Whose feelings and for whom? The words, *you are everything I need* hit like an arrow. She'll lose Zoe, just like she lost her wild redheaded daughter long ago. Like a shot, a sob comes, and she collapses to the ground. Was she *really* okay with not having a child? Stuart's kids were so far away and rarely part of their life; *I won't ever be a grandmother.* Which is what she feels with Zoe, this grandparent connection. Or has Zoe awakened deeper feelings or regret?

Grace dances by and, seeing Joanna in a heap on the ground,

kneels beside her. Without words, Grace takes Joanna's hand. It feels soothing, comforting, and when Grace slowly gets up and starts dancing, Joanna mirrors Grace's movements. When the music changes, Joanna takes that moment to bow a soft thanks to Grace and to dance away. She feels a deep vibration coming through her, and without thinking, that deep voice, the elusive voice that feels better than anything, pours out. So much rising up that only the voice can express. Had she gotten it wrong with Stuart all those years? Had he wanted more, yet didn't ask because she'd so thoroughly closed herself off? So complicated to be a person. She keeps singing or sounding or whatever this vocal release is. In a sudden flash, she realizes it was *she*, herself, who threw away the music after losing her child. The infamous baby and the bath water. Unable to bear the pain, she'd discarded that whole side of herself.

The music changes again, bringing them into the still part of the dance. The music is soothing, African style, cradling her, or so it feels, back into the fold. She isn't alone, even if she feels alone. And if she gets it hopelessly wrong, she can find forgiveness. She can come home.

* * *

Later, getting dressed, looking out for a ride back, Grace slides over on the bench. "Is the guitar yours?"

"Oh right," Joanna says. "I was so into the dance, I forgot I'd brought it."

"You sang beautifully at the end."

"I hope it didn't disturb the group."

"Not at all. I know you already think I'm rather intuitive, but you can't know how happy I am to see this guitar, and that you sing." Grace hardly stops to take a breath. "We had a voice workshop recently. An amazing woman brought out the best in us, including me, who's the world's worst singer. We've continued to meet, to sort of keep it going. Someone came last week to our session, a dance director from around here who has a troupe from Milan that does improvised dance. She so loved our group that she asked if we could supply the soundtrack for the upcoming performance, inspiring them while they dance. And stupid me, who can't even keep up with what's already going on, said yes."

Joanna bursts with curiosity. "Where?"

"Believe it or not, in the church in Vernazza. To have a real singer and guitar player in the group would be amazing, as I've not been able to sleep since I said yes. We're going to meet tomorrow evening, so if you could stay," Grace says with a sigh, "I'd be, I don't know how grateful. We're calling it a *healing* group so none of us get spooked that it's a *singing* group. Oh Joanna, you're the one we need!"

## LUCA OF THE SEA, 1976

At last, the final day at the hospital, and I oversleep. *Shit!* Three alarms set and none wake me. I rush through the streets, push past people to leap onto the subway, the closing doors almost catching my arm, but I make it. I run the whole way to the hospital, arriving in a pool of sweat. I do my last group, get a stamp of approval from the supervisor, who says they will miss me, that the patients *are* easier to handle after the sessions, and then I'm done.

Amazed that I've managed it, that my internship is over, I realize I will miss the patients but not the tedious trip to the Bronx three days a week. I can't stop humming the song from "Fiddler on the Roof", *Wonder of wonders, miracle of miracles . . .*

Now, the only thing I care about is leaving for Rome in September. Even if I'll miss Mr. Karpel, I have to get out of here, have to be with Luca; he's my life. Just have to graduate and earn enough money to leave. I take on extra hours at the travel agency, work as a waitress, and sell my piano, hoping to pay off a big chunk of my school loan.

I've given away most of my clothing, for Luca has promised when I arrive to take me shopping for a completely new Italian wardrobe. On a freak impulse, I buy a beautiful Juliet-style red dress for when we meet in Rome. It's a little tight, but I'll slim my way into it and surprise Luca, show him that I'm the girl he met on the ship, the one he fell in love with. I conjugate Italian verbs diligently and watch Italian movies. There's a nearby Italian restaurant where they let me peek into the kitchen and watch the chef, to learn how to cook proper Italian food—no ready-made spaghetti sauce for my new life.

With the end in sight, I sail on a cloud of adrenaline-charged activity. I don't even mind that Luca's letters are short, perfunctory, for he too is working like mad to prepare for my arrival. He writes that he's sorry there's no time for poetic letters, but *la vita*, is asking too much of him. He can't come to New York now because the ship is sailing the Mediterranean but reminds me that soon we'll be together in Rome.

Those words pump me up through the final marathon weeks. With no time to practice music, I dream of the songs I'll write in Rome, in our inspired house filled with light and love. I dream of Luca *wanting* to hear my songs because he's playing music too. We'll be living the life we're meant to live. Finally!

# 25.

## CINQUE TERRE, 2002

G RACE'S WORDS—*"You're the one we need"*—circle Joanna's head, keeping her awake. Should she have gone straight back to Vernazza after the dance, to be there in the morning to confront Gino? He doesn't have a cell phone or email; the only way to talk with him is in person. And she wants to check in with Simone, that everything is okay, and to apologize to Pieter, neither of whom have answered the sent messages. Grace had begged her to stay so they could practice with the guitar before the group in the evening. And Joanna, nervous with this new responsibility of leading a group, needs all the practice she can get.

She gets up to find something to read. The selection on the shelf is always changing, as people take a book and leave another. She sees the exact book Stuart was reading the night before he died: *The Book of Life* by Krishnamurti. She randomly opens it and reads. "Behind all our actions lurks this desire for certainty. It is only when there is freedom from fear that there is an inward quality of understanding, an aloneness." She sits on the edge of the bed and stares at the photo of Krishnamurti on the cover. His face, open and endearing. His eyes, vivid and clear and so caring, similar to how intense her husband's gaze could be.

"Stuart," she whispers, "this aloneness is still so hard."

*It is scary,* she hears or wants to hear. *I didn't always get it right. The best of me went into my writing.*

Joanna presses the book tightly into her chest. She feels a distinct shiver. *Pieter.* Pieter has to be the one to help finish Stuart's book. When she finally asked if he'd take on the task, he brushed the idea away, saying his English wasn't good enough. Joanna knows that isn't true. Was his negative response more about his need to develop his own work, to not be influenced by Stuart? Their styles are very different. She must convince Pieter to have a look at Stuart's manuscript. And the only way he'll do that is to hire him.

In an instant, a letter to Stuart's publisher charges through her head. With a rush of inspiration, she creeps through the silent halls to the computer room. Like a sleuth, she finds links to Pieter's published essays and articles and includes them in a proposal to the publisher. Her thoughts on fire, her fingers tapping fast as she composes a compelling letter, she sends it off with a shudder of daring. Feeling bold, she sends a message to Pieter that it's urgent they meet before he leaves. With these wild actions completed, she slips back to bed.

\*\*\*

Grace begins the singing group by reading a passage from Lao Tzu. "If you want to awaken all of humanity, then awaken all of yourself. If you want to eliminate the suffering in the world, then eliminate all that is dark and negative in yourself. Truly, the greatest gift you have to give is that of your own self-transformation."

Joanna recognizes a few faces from the dance and others she's not seen before. They began on their backs, on the floor, with their eyes closed. Unlike the dance, this healing group has no set leader or music to inspire and initiate. It's all improvised. After a long silence, with only the sound of breathing, she hears a soft hum. At first wavering, it gets stronger with more voices joining in, including hers. Little by little, it expands into other tones with more dynamic expression. Then, one by one, they rise and begin to move. Joanna has never experienced anything quite like this; it isn't a song, not an improvisation yet, more a resonance of energy.

She sways with the others, at first uncertain, and then, with conviction, the vibration takes over. The growing sound seems to emanate from the room itself. She pushes against the wall for support as a hypnotic chant rises in her. This fresh melody encourages the others, who start to sound stronger. The more the group dares, so does she, until the room is rich with melodic and rhythmic variation. Impossible to tell who initiates the shifts, the various tones held and those that release, but it keeps changing. Sometimes Joanna backs off and others sing louder; sometimes her voice leaps forward. Like multicolored strands, their voices weave in and around each other.

In a hushed moment, Grace points for Joanna to get her guitar to add the tonal patterns the two women had practiced during the day. Joanna is warmed up from playing all day, so the good voice pours out, the angel singing through her. New words spring to her lips, easy, repeatable words, that fit perfectly into the infectious melody. Grace's face lights up as she and the others join in, as if they already know this song. With each round growing in intensity and invention, they sing it over and over. After what feels like forever, the momentum diminishes softly, like a swan landing on a still lake.

Joanna is floating in a hypnotic state when Grace rushes over. "Will you remember the words you sang tonight? It would be perfect for the end of the performance. Never have we sung this well, not even in the workshop. You have to stay. Please say you will."

There's no question Joanna wants to be in this group, but she is uncertain whether she can continue being this open.

She feels ecstatic on the train heading for Vernazza, like she's passed through a baptism of fire. *Things will work out!* She turns her phone back on; at last, a message from Simone. Zoe is better, everything back to normal, and Simone hopes Joanna will meet them tomorrow. Glowing with hope that she'll also make things right with Gino, and with Pieter, she jumps off the train like an eager schoolgirl.

Instantly, a mighty gust nearly knocks her over. She can hardly reach the harbor. The noise is overwhelming with the wind and waves crashing high onto the concrete landing, spray flying. She sees the lights on in Gino's restaurant and rushes in, hoping for a chance to speak with him. The place is empty, except for the two young blonds chirping hysterically in a corner. In an awkward twist, Joanna accidentally knocks over a chair that falls noisily to the ground. Gino rushes out of the kitchen. He throws her a surprised and hostile glare.

"Gino, please, can we talk? Maybe I can order something to eat?" The young women look at Joanna like she's some old hag, like what the heck does she want with their man?

"It's too late," Gino says. "We're closing." He disappears into the kitchen. With no recourse, she heads back into the brutal wind. Starving and cold, she makes her way to the osteria. They're also empty and about to close, but she's able to order a bowl of minestrone. She eats it quickly, pays her bill, and leaves.

Back in the wind, the howling wind, wild and dangerous and thrilling, her guitar jerks about, so she takes it off her shoulders and wraps it in her arms. She thinks she sees him in the corner of her eye but doesn't stop. She pushes through the relentless wind, trying to climb to the top of the cliff, to the thundering roar of waves crashing below.

"Joanna!" Gino cries out. "Don't go higher. It's dangerous when the wind is this strong."

Something destructive in her wants to push on. He comes after her and grabs her arm, like she's under arrest. The wind blows ruthlessly, infecting them both. There's too much noise to say anything. Back down and further away from the sea, Joanna wants to speak; there is so much she longs to say but doesn't know where to begin. He, too, seems stunned.

"All this wind," he finally says. "It can't be good for your guitar."

"No, it isn't." Joanna hesitates, looking at him. Their hair wild, their faces stretched and distorted in the streetlight, it makes them laugh, a shy, twisted laugh.

"Would it be easier for you if I was no longer here?"

"Yes." He nods. "It would. But I'd miss you. I'd miss you a lot."

"You'll keep busy with the girls passing through."

"Busy," Gino says, "is not the same as love. No one like you. But you're too strange and too free, and you will never be just mine. You only confuse me, like Eloise." He leans against the wall. "I went yesterday to Simone's, but you weren't there. Why weren't you? Where did you go?"

"Didn't she tell you?" Joanna is aghast. "She asked me to leave because Zoe wasn't doing well. I wanted to be with you, to sing for Zoe and have it nice like we did all those afternoons. It hurt me to see you with those girls."

"They're nothing, those girls." He gives her a look: *Don't you know how we Italian men are?*

"When Simone wouldn't let me in. I went to the farm. I left a message with her to tell you."

"Well, she didn't." Gino moves his hands in the air. "Anyway, you have many friends. You don't need me."

"That's not true. I wish we—"

"I have to go away," he says, tossing his hands up in a hopeless gesture. "I'm so tired. It's too much, every day working here. You can help Simone. She needs you to help her, but me, I will leave for some days."

Joanna watches him move his hand restlessly through his hair, which looks like he hasn't washed it in days. She doesn't want him to leave. Maybe they both need this; Gino needs this, a chance to get clear what he wants with Eloise, and with her. And she could devote time to Grace and the healing group, and hopefully the work with Pieter.

"I hope we can meet when you come back," Joanna says. She goes to hug him, and he doesn't resist. They hold each other for a poignant moment, and then he lets her go with his *ciao*, a faint whisper.

## LUCA OF THE SEA, 1976

I blink, and it's already September. I miraculously finished everything in a good way—the therapy sessions, my thesis, and the remaining courses. I have graduated! Leo gave me a farewell gift of a one-way ticket to Rome, so everything is set to be with Luca. My mother is aghast I'm really going, yet she doesn't try to stop me. Instead, she gloats, "You'll be back soon enough. These things never work out." Only Amy, who can't wait to visit me in Italy, is my ally.

\*\*\*

I don't sleep a wink on the plane, and when we land, I can hardly believe it. I phone Luca, who sounds rushed and somehow annoyed, like he wasn't expecting me. He tells me to meet him at the central train station in Rome, that I must wait as it will take several hours to drive from Naples. It's boiling hot and I arrive drenched in sweat. I go to a restroom and change into my new red dress, my Juliet dress. It fits perfectly, the red highlighting my cheeks. I splash water on my face and feel almost too excited. My new life about to begin!

Every time I think it's him, I get hopelessly disappointed. One hour, then two, then three. My neck strains from twisting every which way. It's getting later and later, the station packed with people. I'm cramped in a corner with my guitar and canvas bag. I didn't dare travel with a knapsack; Luca would have cringed. I notice how sophisticatedly the Italians dress, especially the women. In comparison, I'm like a windup doll with my hair pinned behind my ears and my Juliet dress, with the sash bowed in the back, so girlish. I undo the clips and shake my hair free, but it's wilted from the flight and the heat and the exhaustion of waiting. I cringe at my reflection. It's too late to buy something new, as Luca may arrive any minute, and this is the nicest thing I've brought. In an angry second, I realize I've made a mistake, a terrible mistake. This is not how it was supposed to be.

I'm wondering if he'll ever show up when all at once he's there and not at all happy to see me. Not a kiss, not a hug. Like he's meeting an annoying relative, not his long-lost lover. He grabs my bag. "Come," he commands. "We have to rush." His voice is hard, brittle. "Walk faster. I parked in a bad place."

We're at his car, halfway parked on the sidewalk. He slams my canvas bag in the trunk, eyeing it with disdain. He throws my guitar like a naughty child on the back seat. He is so tense and angry. I have no idea why. The air is thick with heat, making it hard to breathe. I struggle into the low seat of his sport's car, a snazzy Dino Spyder, while the sash of my dress gets stuck and rips. He makes another ugly face and speeds off so fast that I grab the strap above the window and hold on tightly.

The scenery rushes by like in a movie, except he is no Rock Hudson and I'm no Doris Day. This is more like a Hitchcock film. Luca drives recklessly, like he's trying to kill us. I hang on for dear life at each hairpin turn. *Please stop,* I pray, too afraid to speak. He hasn't said a word, doesn't look at me. I study his cropped short hair, the crisply ironed shirt; he's so serious, so miserable, that I don't recognize him. This man is not my Luca from the *Leonardo*. Something has happened, maybe with his father, something he can't tell me. But he's furious. After each curve, he shakes his watch loose on his wrist, as if to shake off something foul. The radio is on full blast, loud, aggressive heavy-metal music, the kind he knows I hate.

Nothing like Cocciante. This music is vulgar and so crushingly loud that it's impossible to speak. It blocks any path that might connect us. Why? Why is he like this? What have I done?

# 26.

## CINQUE TERRE, 2002

JOANNA IS GETTING ready to go down to Simone's place, thinking about how she can tell her about the decision to join Grace's healing group, when the phone rings. It's Simone, out of breath. "We're coming up to you today. We're almost there. I've brought some fruit. Can you make coffee?"

"You're coming here?"

"Yes." Simone is panting so hard, she can hardly continue. "We're at the bottom of the stairs."

"Wait! I'll come help you." Joanna hangs up and rushes down the stairs.

"Why did you come here?" Joanna asks, taking Zoe from her. "You hate these steps."

"I know, I know," Simone says, huffing. "But today I saw myself in the mirror, bloated, like an Italian grandmother, a *nonna*. I don't want to look like that. I have to start moving. Like you, you stay so slim. I'm going to do what you do, eat what you eat, even if it kills me."

"I hope not," Joanna says, laughing, opening the door of the apartment. "It's bad enough Gino's leaving town because of me."

"It's good he goes away," Simone says, sitting down with a heavy sigh. The five flights have worn her out. "He came by before he left this morning. I let him blow off steam. He's going to stay with some friends up the coast. They'll go fishing. They'll get drunk. Will do him good."

"I think he'd prefer for me to leave," Joanna says, lighting the stove and setting up the coffee.

"Well, I don't." Simone waves her hand into the air. "So let him be."

"But—"

"*Basta!*" she says with a laugh. "I have much to teach you about life here, not the least our men."

\*\*\*

Joanna can't believe Simone's determination to mimic her diet and exercise. She's decided to stop her pottery for a while, blaming the weight gain on all the sitting. Only when Joanna prepares a simple meal of fruit and nothing more does Simone complain. "This is food for a monkey! A person can die eating just this!"

"You'll get used to it." Joanna laughs.

"Never!" Simone says, reaching for Zoe. "I'm going to have to eat you!" She nibbles Zoe's arms and legs, making the child giggle. "Now I understand why slim women smoke," she says, going outside for a cigarette once the meager meal is finished.

Joanna is anxious to get to Pieter's this morning, as he still hasn't answered her messages.

"I'll be right back," Joanna says. "I just have to check my email at the café in town. You're okay here for a bit?"

"Yes, yes," Simone says. "I couldn't move just now for all the gold in Africa."

Though still nothing from Pieter, Joanna is thrilled to see a quick response from Stuart's publisher. A positive go-ahead to hire Pieter, that he'll allocate the funds.

She's back in her room and prepares to leave for Pieter. "I won't stay long," she tells Simone, "but I have to go see Pieter today. It's urgent. Just stay here."

"Oh no!" Simone cries. "You're not leaving me alone that long. Without you, I'll go straight to the bakery, or smoke myself to death! I'm coming."

"With Zoe?"

"Why not? We can nap while you work with Pieter. Please. We can pick up the pack at my place."

"You never walk," Joanna exclaims. "And remember how heavy the pack was."

"We can take turns carrying Zoe. I sent you away, the other day, because I'm getting depressed, and that's not like me."

*\*\*\**

Midway, they stop to rest on one of the benches along the path. Simone munches on the last of Zoe's carrot slices and, a cigarette in the other hand, cries, "*Mamma mia*! What man will ever have me now? To think how beautiful and slim I once was."

"You're still beautiful," Joanna says, meaning it.

"Not like how I was," Simone says, huffing to keep up. "Do you know the movie *Swept Away*? Can you believe I almost got the lead?"

"Really?" Joanna exclaims. She's shocked to hear the name of *that* movie, that stunning Italian movie she'd seen at least five times years ago. The erotic scenes on the deserted island, the secluded beaches, like watching herself and Luca. Joanna had wished to live in that movie; a part of her still does.

"I was that beautiful and that thin and that good."

They walk steadily on, with Joanna deep in remembrance,

thinking of that first beach Luca took her to.

"Hey, hey," Simone says. "I didn't mean to make you sad. It was *just* a movie."

"Was it?" Joanna asks. No movie had ever portrayed raw love so vividly, a love like she had with Luca.

"I'll carry Zoe so you can rest your shoulders." Simone lifts Zoe out of the pack and gives her the last of the carrot sticks. "I'm sorry I mentioned that movie. I didn't mean to upset you."

"No, no, it's just—"

"It's just what?" Simone asks with deep inquiry. Maybe hunger was making her more attentive, curious. Joanna hasn't told her about Luca. It all pours out, the story itself like a movie. "I never knew what happened with him, why he changed into a monster," Joanna says.

"Ah," Simone says. "Life, love . . . all too complicated."

They walk on in silence to the brush of their steps on the dry dirt. Just then, the child begins to whimper. "We're almost there," Joanna says. "I can carry the pack for the rest." With Zoe back on her shoulders, Joanna begins to hum unconsciously.

"What a nice voice you have," Simone says. "Don't stop."

Embarrassed to be caught off guard, Joanna hadn't realized she was singing. But she's also relieved that Simone has finally heard her. "I've been scared to sing for you. That you wouldn't like my voice."

"Why?" Simone says. "Even if Italy is famous for opera, we can't all sing. I can tell you, I sure can't."

"How do you know?"

"I know." Simone makes little circles with her hands, emphasizing the fact.

"Try it with me," Joanna suggests. "I'm just going to hum, not sing. You don't have to match my note. Just think you're yawning inside, that you're not responsible for the sound that comes out."

"That's good to know."

"It is, by the way," Joanna adds with a smile, "the secret to losing weight. If you sing, even terribly, the fat jiggles and falls off more easily."

Simone rattles off a jumble of Italian words, her hands swirling through the air, but she turns to Joanna, curious and willing.

"We'll start with a humming sound like you're eating delicious food."

"I can do that. *Mmm.*" Simone makes a full sound. "I'm enjoying a large bowl of *penne al pesto.*"

Joanna laughs. "That's it. Let's just keep making sounds and follow my lead." Simone's voice is husky and resonant, an actor's voice. She looks startled at what's coming out of her, yet she seems pleased and lets go with gusto. By the time they turn the corner, their improvisation isn't half bad.

"Wow!" Simone says, collapsing onto the bench by the café that's now closed for the season. "How did you get me to do that?"

"I don't know." Joanna smiles. "I just learned this last night at a gathering at the farm with Grace. Amazing, isn't it? It's like heating water over the stove. The fire does it. It cooks us."

"Do you think I could come?" Simone asks. "Can you ask Grace if I could join?"

"Sure," Joanna says, more than thrilled.

Close to Pieter's place, she's getting anxious. She tries again to phone him, but still no answer. "I'm not even sure he's still here."

"Let's find out," Simone says.

"I'm sorry to barge in on you," Joanna says when Pieter opens the door. "You haven't answered my messages. I had to see you before you left. You remember Simone?"

He nods, rubbing his face. He looks tired, with bags under his eyes, and thinner than when she'd last seen him. He stands in the doorway, stalling for time.

Simone jumps in to salvage the situation. With her warmest voice that could seduce anyone, she says, "Don't be mad at Joanna.

It was my idea to come and bring Zoe." She peeks over Pieter's shoulder to the common room of the guesthouse with a couch and a few chairs. "It's the end of the season. No one will mind if we nap here. We'll stay out of your way, I promise."

Pieter hesitates but opens the door fully and ushers them in. Simone flutters her hand, showing she'll manage just fine. "Zoe and I will rest while you two work." She heads for the couch and gets her and Zoe set up. She waves for Joanna to do what she needs to with Pieter.

Joanna follows Pieter into his room. She can't wait, it's bursting from her, and with a gulp, she tells him about the offer from the publisher to hire him.

"You want to *hire* me?" Pieter's voice has a ragged edge.

"Remember when I asked you," she says, hurriedly, "you feared your English wasn't good enough. It's not true. You write great. The manuscript is mostly done, and I can help."

Pieter goes to his desk. She's never seen him this unfriendly. Usually, he offers her a seat, but today he makes no effort.

"Pieter tell me, what is it?" she says, standing behind the chair she usually sits in. "I've tried so many times to reach you. I'm really sorry the way things ended the other day."

"Ah, what people do and what they don't do. It's all a mystery, is it not?"

"You told me how you can't get some of your pieces published. It won't be too much work for you to finish my husband's book, and then his publisher might be interested in yours." She takes a deep breath, then adds, "You've told me how important your work is." She notices a row of empty bottles along the wall, a thing she'd not seen before. "You've been drinking a lot."

"It helps when there are deadlines."

"You're mad at me. I know you are."

"I poured my heart out the other day, and then I don't see you, don't hear from you."

"Are you serious? I tried so many times to call you, left a zillion messages."

"I switch off my phone when I work."

She glares at him. "Yes, I know, but I've seen you switch it back on."

"I get too many messages," Pieter says, fetching a new bottle from the fridge. "Plus, you've gotten yourself embroiled here with Zoe and what's his name. Do you have any idea what you're getting yourself into? Italy is complicated. The Netherlands may be boring, but we think things out first, *before* we act."

"Well, I have. At least the part concerning you. You said you didn't want to go back to Holland, and now there'll be money, so you won't have to. You told me how well you write here. I think you're brilliant. You could do your own book *and* Stuart's. They're both urgent. The publisher sent a contract today for you. It's for real."

"How does the publisher even know about me? Did you send him my stuff?"

"Just links that are online. Anyone can read them. Please don't be angry. Even before I met you, it was hanging over me to find someone. The publisher has offered to pay a good amount. I can give you something today." Joanna knows she's sounding desperate, but she can't stop. "Don't you know how important you are?"

"Well that's just it, isn't it? *Important*, not more." He takes the corkscrew and hastily uncorks the wine.

"Pieter, please, this is so much bigger than us. It was you who told me that."

"Did I? Well, people say all kinds of things." He goes to the door, his whole body asking her to leave. His face is a cascade of anguish, revealing that he knows that sending her away is a cruel thing, a thing that will also hurt him, but he has no choice. Joanna, not sure what to say to change his mind, stands there for an awkward moment.

"You can let them sleep," Pieter mumbles, pointing to Simone and Zoe napping on the couch. "You won't bother me if you stay a bit more. But I really need to work." He firmly closes the door behind him.

Joanna remains there, frozen. Gino is gone and now Pieter has dismissed her. She hadn't realized quite the extent of the feelings he had for her. How confusingly different every culture is. She sees the sleeping Simone and Zoe and knows to wake them would be unwise; they'd both be cranky for the trek back. Joanna goes outside, making sure the latch of the door is unlocked. She needs to walk, to think, to understand if there's any way to convince Pieter. She can't squander this opportunity.

Pacing, she thinks of her childhood, that early rejection by her supposed father, the man in all the photos, the one that left them when she was three. Always assuming if she'd been worth loving, he would have returned. Except it was never her father! She feels a fresh rage that her mother never told her the truth. During these weeks in Italy, she's tricked herself into believing she's moved past this. It burns in her that she'll never get to meet him. Was her mother in denial all her life?

Was she also in denial? Busy with her need for Pieter to be a substitute Stuart that she'd been blind to his feelings? Has he wanted more all along?

She thinks of her commitment to Simone and Zoe, of Grace and the healing group. Her nature would be to flee these painful confrontations, but for once she will stay the course, as painful and confusing as it feels.

Just then, Pieter emerges. He stands sheepishly with one arm holding onto the doorframe. "I'm glad you're still here."

"We'll leave soon," Joanna says, brushing away her tears.

"Your husband," Pieter asks. "You really think he'd have wanted me to finish his work?"

"I've never been surer of anything."

"Well." Pieter sighs, with a genuine smile. "That's good to know."

"So you'll do it?"

"I need to return to the Netherlands for a few weeks, but I'll definitely be back."

She couldn't help but hug him. "Oh Pieter, that's the best news. I'll have to go back to New York for a short time myself to arrange things to stay here longer. And to get the manuscript. You still haven't met Grace. There are some vacant rooms at her farm where you could live and write. And you won't have to pay rent. If that sounds okay, I'll get it all arranged."

## LUCA OF THE SEA, 1976

The road to Sorrento is dazzling, with views of steep, lush hills and flowering terrain and quaint villages sweeping down to the Mediterranean. It should be the Italy of my dreams, but with Luca acting so strange and terrible, I instantly hate Sorrento. He pulls sharply into a parking lot of an elegant hotel landscaped with palm trees and bougainvillea. The sky is so bright and blue, it hurts to look at. But there's no time to look. He's in a big hurry. For what, I have no idea. Without a word, he takes my bag, and I follow, sheeplike, with my guitar. The room is large and airy, nearly a suite, with one big bed and a balcony facing the sea. A cruel irony. Of all the times on the ship we wished for a balcony. Now we have one that we will, I'm certain, never use.

"Luca?" My voice is broken. I know he hasn't heard me. Who is he, this impostor? What has he done with my Luca? The real Luca would have gathered me in his arms. The real Luca would have remembered the letters he wrote, of how much he loved me and missed me. Of how he longed for us to be together again.

I lean my guitar against the wall and am about to open my canvas suitcase when he charges over. "That stupid red dress," he says, as if it is the dress to blame for ruining everything. He unzips my bag and flings through my things: jeans and shorts and T-shirts, nothing with style.

"How could you?" he shouts. "How could you bring such ugly clothing?" He takes a pack of cigarettes from his pocket and grabs one with such force, it snaps in two. He takes out another and lights it. Of all his moods, I have never seen this one. Nothing has prepared me for this degree of madness.

I pray for this black cloud to lift, that he'll gather me any moment in his arms and laugh and explain and be Luca again. But he doesn't. Suddenly, America doesn't seem so terrible, and I want to go home. We are freer there; we can be silly. Here, with centuries of tradition, I have no idea how to behave; I'm devastated by cultural confusion. The Luca who pierced my finger in symbolic marriage, who I've bled for, is absolutely not here. Did I make him up?

"Let's get something to eat," Luca says, like a bad actor trying to play nice. "I'm hungry. I was just about to have lunch with my family when you called." He looks at me sharply when he says *lunch*, like I forced him to commit a crime to leave his house during the sacred lunchtime to come get me.

We sit in a restaurant, and here, at least I get cues from the other patrons on how to behave. I watch how they eat, when they drink. No help from Luca, who's abandoned me completely; he won't even look at me. Without asking, he orders in Italian. When the food arrives, I take delicate Italian bites, dabbing my lips with the linen napkin as the others do, and leave most of it untouched. In contrast, he gobbles his food down like he can't leave fast enough.

We walk home, and he automatically links his arm through mine. Not in a romantic or reassuring way, rather something he *has* to do, and he resents it.

"Luca, what have I done? What happened? Why are you like this?"

He stops and looks around. The street is empty, with everyone still in the restaurants. "I must work again on the *Leonardo*."

"What? I thought you were going to study music to be a

drummer." I watch his beautiful face crack into a thousand pieces, as if mirroring my broken heart.

"Luca, what about me? What about our—" I can't even say it.

He walks ahead, slowly, stiffly, like he's walking toward death.

***

We're in the hotel room, and he smokes one cigarette after the other. He goes to my guitar, touches it, but he won't look at me. We're playing a game of charades, and I try to guess what he's thinking, what he wants. I no longer think of what I want, only to survive this madness. He takes off his sports jacket, opens the top button of his stiffly pressed shirt, then walks in a trance to the bed. He stands with his back to me, a hand reaching out. I slowly go to him.

He aggressively pulls back the bedspread to the cool white sheets below. His hand opens to invite mine. I slip my hand into his, and for a moment, I feel him in his hand. With my other hand, I gently touch his back. I hear him gasp, a tiny crack he lets open. He turns and wraps around me and kisses me with a strange hunger, like he's never kissed before or will ever kiss again. We slide onto the bed, but we're different. We don't know each other, or we've become terribly old; there's hardly blood in our veins. He turns away, as if to punish me. Punishing me by withholding his best self, the Luca I loved. He turns back around. All the color drains from his face.

"You could come with me," he says. "My father can arrange for you to have a job on the ship as a chambermaid. You have only to say yes."

"A maid?" I gasp, sitting up in the bed. "What are you talking about?"

"We can be together on the ship. My father can get you a job."

"As a chambermaid? I am not a maid. I'm a—"

"That's the only job you can get. Just say yes, and I will tell him."

"Luca, please." I tug at him, still lying there. But he remains limp and empty. "I can't be a chambermaid. I never once saw those maids on the ship. They work in the shadows, like slaves. You'd never respect me, or even see me." Of all the reckless things I've done, there's no way I could take this job. And he knows it. Is this a test? "Luca, your father decided this, didn't he?"

"You know nothing. Nothing!"

"You're punishing me, because of the—"

"I gave you money, but not for that."

His voice is mean, but his body remains limp. There's no fight in him. I, who never had one, can't imagine how a father could do this. How wrong I was with my *Sound of Music* fantasy of being welcomed by his family. What fools we were to think we could be stronger than the world. It's clear something is so terrifying for Luca to confront that he'd rather smother his soul—and mine—then challenge it. A poison he's ingested that's killing everything, the dream of our life in Rome, the children we could have, and the music we would make. In an instant, everything is slaughtered.

Luca gets up, like a ghost. He still won't look at me. "I must get home. My father is waiting."

"But?" I say, with one last feeble attempt at salvaging our lives. "Wasn't I going to meet your family?"

"You cannot meet my family. Ever!"

"Luca, wait, we can—"

"No, we can't. We can't anything. I will come get you in the morning and take you to the train station."

He seems to vanish into the air. I blink, and there's not a sign of him anywhere. It's then that I realize he never brought a suitcase—he never intended to stay.

Nothing remains, just the burned scent of my foolish, foolish dreams.

# 27.

## CINQUE TERRE, 2002

SINCE THEY HUMMED together on the way to Pieter's, Simone hasn't stopped singing. She has, it turns out, a strong voice, and Grace welcomes her eagerly into the singing group. They bring Zoe along, and there's enough willing hands on the farm to keep an eye on the child while they rehearse.

The days before the performance, Grace wants to practice as much as possible, so with Gino still away and Pieter in Holland, Joanna, Simone, and Zoe stay over at the farm. Simone, at first suspicious, quickly takes to the international community. She dramatically tells the group how she's let go of her acting career, with years living in Tanzania, but still hungers for the smell of the greasepaint and the roar of the crowd. Her strong presence and energy, mixed with Joanna's musical skills, brings the group to a new level.

The director had expected a small audience to try out her new concept, yet with Simone branding herself *the ancient one come back to life* in posters all over Cinque Terre, she's created such a hoopla that the show is sold out. Once very famous, no one wants to miss this rare opportunity to see and hear her, *live*.

On performance day, Joanna is a bag of nerves. Just the thought of having to start the show makes her blood rush from her head. So woozy, she can barely stand, let alone sing. By the time she reaches Simone's, she's sure she's going to have a heart attack, her pulse racing that fast. With her old folks, it was easier; besides, most of them were deaf and loved her no matter how she sounded. Simone hasn't heard from Gino, but Joanna won't be surprised if he comes to the show, compounding her anxiety. The whole of Cinque Terre seems to be coming.

The moment Joanna enters the apartment, she picks Zoe up and does a manic waltz around the room.

"Hey, hey," Simone calls out. "Don't use it up! Savor the nervous energy. You must savor it. I told you, you'll be all right."

"I can't breathe!"

"You'll be fine."

Out on the street, Simone walks like a *grande dame* with regal dignity and purpose. "It's going to be very interesting tonight at the church," she whispers to Joanna, her face bright with mischief. "It's rather *pagan* what we're planning to do. Like witches dancing around the pyre. I'm not sure Vernazza is ready for such a show in their place of worship."

"Then why are we doing it there?" Joanna asks, her voice pinching. She hadn't thought of this element, this unusual performance. It makes her even more nervous.

"It's the biggest space, for one thing," Simone explains, "and a chance for the church to earn some money, which they will, now that it's sold out. They're pretending not to care, to be modern, but I'm curious." Simone rubs her hands together, like she single-handedly crafted this brew.

When they arrive, Joanna feels her throat clamp even more, as if her whole existence is at stake. She'll never find the right tone—or any tone! Will never be able to start the group or lead them in the big closing number, the song she's written. "I can't do it," she whispers, clutching Simone. "I'm going to be sick."

"No, you're not. You will be fine. Just keep looking at me, and I'll carry you. I'm on fire. I *love* the stage."

## LUCA OF THE SEA, 1976

It is late, no sign of Luca returning. The hotel is quiet, everyone asleep. I take my diary and walk out of the hotel onto the grassy knoll overlooking the sea. The stars are brilliant overhead. It's a deep plunge to the sea below, and I could, like Byron, toss myself overboard—another hopeless romantic lost into the lapping waves of the Mediterranean. But I don't. Or maybe I'm no longer here. I don't know anything, yet my mind is clear and calm and somehow reasonable. I tear the corner of the page of my diary, with Luca's number on it, into tiny pieces, then open my hand and let the wind take the ashes of my once beloved. I feel a strange relief, like I'm free, like the girl who loved him has vanished. She was troublesome and confusing, better to let her go. She and her impossible dreams.

I have no idea what tomorrow will bring. But no one will see me, and no one will judge me, so it will hardly matter. A corner of my brain feels bad about my friend Amy; she will never get to meet me in Rome—because the only thing I know for sure is that I'm getting out of here as soon as I can. Italy is nothing like how I thought it would be. I'm not afraid, though, and that, too, feels odd. Like I've slipped out of myself, into some higher creature who knows exactly what to do.

I don't remember going to sleep, yet I wake in bed when the door opens. It's very early. Luca stands there, quiet and small. Not a word of explanation. His voice is soft; he isn't angry. "Here," he says, giving me a one-way ticket to Rome. "We must leave."

I get dressed and gather my things. He carries my bag and I carry my guitar, and we drive to the station. He follows me to the platform. We move like cutout dolls or puppets controlled by an invisible master. He doesn't smoke, just stands there, getting smaller and smaller. It's only when the train enters the station and I've climbed onboard that he speaks.

"You love too many things," he says, "and you will always love the music more than you love me."

The train pulls away before I think of what I could have said. Before any part of me returns. *You're wrong, Luca, so very wrong. I could have loved you AND the music.* But I can never tell him because I will never *ever* see him again. I didn't memorize his number before ripping it up last night, so I can't contact him. Besides, what would be the point? I could never work on the ship. And he could never, so it seems, stand up to his father.

I look out the window as the train passes through open fields of dry, parched land. I wish I could cry, but I can't. All I notice is the wind blowing into the empty train compartment and the scent of lavender and pine.

# 28.

## CINQUE TERRE, 2002

THE YOUNG DIRECTOR gathers them together at the altar of the church for a pep talk. It's six o'clock, one hour before the show is set to start. "Remember," she says, "just listen to each other. Listen first, then react. That's all you have to do."

She leads the singers onto the podium and shows them where to stand. They come to the edge right before the statue of Mary, leaving enough room for the dancers. With the ten singers cramped in a row, Joanna feels the unexpected touch of the statue behind her. She tries to garner courage from this, this connection. *Mary, please help me!* All six dancers do a few movements, checking the space, and then the director asks them all to lie down. With a gentle voice, she guides them in a chakra-style warm-up. Joanna is glad to be flat on her back, wishes she could stay there for the entire show.

"We will be entering a sacred space," the director says. "Let yourself become a channel, nothing more."

*I can't do it,* Joanna thinks in a growing state of panic. *I have got to get out of here.* Once they're backstage, with the director urging them not to dissipate the *sacred* energy, she can't breathe.

The doors open and the audience piles in. Joanna hears the

endless footsteps, a full church like Christmas Eve. Joanna tests her voice, but she's hoarse like sandpaper. Simone is by her side, smiling encouragingly. "Just look at me. Keep looking at me."

After what seems like forever, the director gets them all to jiggle, to awaken the *kundalini*, the latent female energy, she tells them, stored at the base of the spine. "Don't try to relax, but go deeper into whatever you're feeling. No such thing as being too nervous. Use all of it. Embrace all of it." Joanna has never learned to do this, that instead of fighting to be rid of the nervousness, *use* it, like fuel, like power.

With a hush, the lights go dim and the director leads them onstage. They're all to breathe three rounds in dynamic intention, and then the healing group, with Joanna in the lead, will start. There's a loaded stillness in the church. Joanna's legs tremble; she feels faint, spooked by the saints and crosses and the bleeding Jesus.

She shoots a panicked look at Simone, who steps forward and begins. Not exactly the correct key, but close enough for the others to join in. At last, Joanna gets a smidgen of voice as the dancers initiate their choreographed improvisation, and the show takes off. The audience, who've been holding their breath, let out an audible sigh of delight.

The show will be a series of exchanges, a conversation. Sometimes the dancers move in silence, only their feet making sound. Sometimes in response to the healing group's improvised music. The director from below the podium gives these cues. Clearly and effectively, with no hesitation. Her level of concentration is astounding, seductive, and little by little, Joanna forgets her nerves and enters the magic realm of creation. The audience seems captivated. No one coughs or sneezes; not a soul gets up for the entire performance.

The last piece is Joanna's song, the one the healing group practiced most. She stares at the director, waiting for her cue. The dancers start to move percussively, creating a six-eight rhythm, a

Celtic repetitive drone. Now the director nods to Joanna. She has only a few lines to sing alone before the others join in and the dancers take off in an explosion of movement. Joanna reaches the heel of her foot back and touches the stone base of Mary. *Please, please help me.* This moment *is* the crucible of her life, all or nothing. If she's not able to sing now, then she will never ever sing again! She lets a full and deep breath in, and with that blessed connection to Mary, a sound comes. The *good* voice, the full voice, powerful and free, bursts out of her. When the majesty of the other voices mixes in, her body is alive with vibration.

> *It's you, your love, that gives my spirit breath.*
> *It's you, your love, that takes me into light.*
> *It's you, just you, who breathes within my heart.*
> *It's you, just you, who guides me through the night.*
> *You must, she said, believe we're not alone.*
> *The wind, the sun, the silent undertow.*
> *Is old, it's older than all words.*
> *So trust, please trust, that I am really here.*

Everything she's ever felt, known, seen, or desired is pouring out of her. The sound flows like a Gregorian chant. The others join in, their voices stronger than in any rehearsal. Their faces flushed, their bodies as one powerful being. The reaction in the audience heightens the intensity, and they sing even fuller until Joanna feels she might explode. Except she doesn't. She expands. The sound vibrating through her ignites the entire church. The dancers leap and swish and move with grace and beauty. When the song finishes, when the last dancer falls still, the audience holds its breath; no one claps. No one dares break this moment of awe.

The director stares at Joanna. There was nothing more they'd rehearsed. Still, the director, with an invisible wand, makes a sweeping movement straight to Joanna. All at once, she feels a swell within her, giving birth to a new melody. This is no longer her, but *Mary*. She's entirely filled with Mary. Something explosive begins. Joanna is no longer human, wings spread across her back; the sound grows roots in and through her. She's a channel, and all she must do is get out of the way again and again, with each breath. The director's face lights up with a glorious *Yes!* The dancers leap into a new improvisation; the singers give over to what they previously had no idea they possessed. The ensemble melds together in stunning coordination. The audience gasps and breaks into cheers. This is living art, a visitation from the great spirits, a meshing together of performers and audience and spirit into a vibrant form.

Then it is over. The show is over. And when the last tone no longer resonates against the ancient church walls, the crowd bursts into thunderous applause. Pagan or not, this was from a higher power. They stand up and stamp their feet and clap even more and cry out, *Bis! Bis! Ancora!* The director, who'd hoped for a positive response, hadn't prepared for this reaction. She turns to the audience and begins to clap a rhythm and then invites them to join in, which they enthusiastically do. Joanna, no longer surprised as the connection is so powerfully in her, starts a tone with a simple *"ah,"* no other vowels, just the *"ah."* The audience, on fire, catches this invitation and joins in. No one can keep still. When they reach an ecstatic peak, the director brings the sound to an end, and the show is over.

After another deafening round of applause, the audience begins to file out. Slowly, the performers leave the podium. Joanna hates for the moment to end; she could live the rest of her life singing like this. She turns to face the statue of Mary. "Thank you," she whispers. *"Grazie mille."*

She feels an intense gaze upon her. Slowly, she turns and sees one last person standing in the audience. She can't distinguish his face in the darkness, only that she's never seen him before. He comes forward, an older man with graying sideburns and glasses tinted yellow. Joanna still doesn't recognize him, but he seems to know her.

Just then, one of the young dancers runs out from behind the podium. "Papa!" she cries. He wraps his arms around her, speaking in Italian. It sounds like high praise. Joanna walks over in a daze to give the dancer a hug. The young girl says, "Papa, this is Joanna."

"Joanna?" he repeats slowly, and then again. "Joanna, is that really you?" His voice has thickened. It's hoarse and rough, but it's that deep voice she could never forget.

"Luca?" She gasps.

"Yes, it's me." Though he's only said these few words, his English sounds surer, more confident than she remembered.

## LUCA OF THE SEA, 1976

When the train arrives in Rome, I'm tempted to leave my guitar at the station, as it's my music, not the red dress, that's ruined everything. Maybe Luca was testing me to see if I truly loved him, and just having my guitar was sign enough for him that I didn't love him enough. Maybe there never was a job on a ship, and I failed the test because he was right—I couldn't be without the music. I walk out onto the busy streets of Rome, without a clue where to go. I will have to find a hostel for the night. I will have to make a plan.

A car is following me. "Go away," I yell.

"*Amore mio.*" The driver waves for me to stop. I hate him. I hate all Italian men. He keeps following me; his tiny car fits into every street I turn down. My body shakes; I can't run fast with my canvas bag and guitar.

"Go away!" I shout again. "Leave me alone!"

Still, he follows me. I run into a piazza with no cars. He jumps out of his and runs after me. I rush to an outside café, where I hear two men speaking English. "Please," I beg them, "let me sit here." The two Englishmen notice the interloper chasing me.

"Sure," the younger one says in a cockney accent. I sit, covered in sweat. "They're a pest, those Italian men," the older one says. "Not like us civilized English."

I look back and see the man with his hands in the air, but he doesn't come farther. "Thank you," I say. Because I have to, I instantly trust these men, these friendly, not at all handsome, strangers. Like guardian angels. It hasn't hit fully, my plight, only that I haven't much money.

"A cup of tea, milady?" the younger one says.

When the tea comes, the older one, Martin, speaks. "You remind me of my daughter," he says with gentle concern. It feels so nice, this caring, that my limbs begin slowly uncurling. "She once got herself in such a fix. I'm guessing the reason why you came here isn't working out."

Not able to name it, I nod. "But I can't go back to New York."

"Have you ever been to England?" Martin says in a fatherly voice. "They speak English there, and you could easily get a job." I nod again, as I will need a job. "We're leaving soon. We're *lorry* drivers, truck drivers where you come from. I happen to have bunk beds in mine, as my daughter sometimes travels with me. Five days across Europe, and it won't cost you a penny. It's a long drive, and I'd welcome the company. I promise, I won't touch you."

Martin stays true to his word. The first two days of the journey, I stay cocooned on the second bunk, writing in my diary. Then, on the third day, it hits fully that I've lost Luca forever.

# 29.

## CINQUE TERRE, 2002

JOANNA CAN'T STOP staring at him; she can barely form words. Has she, from thinking so much about Luca recently, conjured his appearance? "Your daughter is a lovely dancer."

"Ah, yes." Luca smiles so she sees his dimples. "She doesn't take after her father. You remember, I hated to dance." He turns to his daughter and says something in Italian. The girl looks shyly to Joanna. They only met twice for a combined rehearsal, so Joanna doesn't really know any of the dancers.

"It's many weeks since I saw my daughter," Luca says. "She is studying in Milan, and I live in Rome. You remember I wanted to live there."

"I remember." Joanna had thought, if she ever saw him again, she'd feel anger. But she doesn't. It's more curiosity.

"My daughter will leave early tomorrow," Luca says. "I never thought I'd see you again. Can we meet for a coffee tomorrow before I have to go?" There he is again, her Luca, her young Luca emerging from under this older man's face. "Joanna, you will never know. So much of my life, I have thought of you. But you, you look exactly the same, maybe even better." His hand brushes the side of her cheek, sending a shiver through her body. "You will have time tomorrow?" Luca asks. Joanna can't say a word beyond a soft yes.

***

She stands outside the church for what feels like an eternity, then heads back to Simone's apartment. They'd planned to have dinner together. Simone will be wondering where she is. Joanna passes the entrance to Gino's restaurant. The outer terrace is closed for the season, yet with the mild night, the entrance door is open. Luca and his daughter sit at a table by the window. Joanna watches him, still not believing. She again sees a flash of his young self, but he seems so different. Her Luca of the past is evaporating. Like when they open caves with ancient art, the oxygen destroys the image. In the twilight between dream and reality, her *Luca of the Sea*, the one she cherished, despite all the hurt, is dissolving. He must have felt her gaze, for, suddenly, he stares at her through the window, says something to his daughter, points to the menu, and comes outside. They move away from the door so no one can see them.

"Where are you staying?" he asks, lighting a cigarette.

"Up there." She points.

"I stay in the hotel, around the corner." He takes a serious pull from his cigarette. "Yes," he says, "I still smoke and drink, but not so much champagne as we once did. Do you remember?"

Joanna smiles. "All that expensive champagne you'd bring."

"I can't believe I'm here with you."

"Me too," she says, feeling wave after wave of something tingling in her skin. God, in *her* mysterious ways. Wasn't it enough to have sung as she did in the performance? Why send Luca on the same night?

"I really want to see you," he says. "So much I need to tell you. Please, can we meet later tonight?"

"Not here," she says. She sees Gino helping in the restaurant.

She can't let him see her with Luca. Two worlds crashing. She must keep them apart. "There's an internet café close to the station that stays open," she says. "We can meet there."

Luca takes a few last puffs of his cigarette, crushes it on the ground, then looks at his watch. "Shall we meet at ten thirty?"

*\*\*\**

As if someone suddenly replaced the batteries of her movable self, she not only moves but runs. Runs all the way to Simone's, with a heart ready to explode.

Simone has already put Zoe to bed and has prepared a simple supper of salad and minestrone. "What took you so long?" Simone asks. Yet she's too excited to wait for an answer and gushes on. Joanna half listens to Simone's flood of words about the concert, moving her spoon through the soup, unable to eat. Simone finally notices her odd state. "Why aren't you hungry? How can you not be hungry? I already had two bowls."

"He's here." Joanna gasps.

"Who?"

"The man I told you about, Luca. The big love from my past."

"*Mamma mia!*" Simone circles her hands.

"His daughter was one of the dancers."

"The life can be so strange, no? Will you see him again?"

"Yes. Later tonight."

"You sure you want to stir up all that? If he has a daughter, that probably means he has a wife and a whole other life, without you."

"He was the one who recognized *me*. He could have walked away. Maybe this is my chance to finally find out what happened in the end. I never told you about that, the last time I saw him."

Simone makes a face. "We should never wake sleeping dogs, but it's your life."

"I need to go . . . I *have* to go."

He's already waiting outside the café when she arrives.

"Is there another place we could go?" he asks. "Maybe more private?"

Joanna can't imagine bringing him to her room, so she leads them to the road behind the station. It is dark and silent. Not many trains run so late.

"I've thought of you so often," he says. It surprises and pleases her to imagine him thinking of *her*. "Do you remember I played the drums?" Puckering in his lips, he goes on. "Lately, I've started playing again. And then I thought of you and that night on the ship, the night I played for you."

It stuns her, that he'd never forgotten that night as well. She swoons, slightly off balance, like she's stepping off the ship. He reaches to steady her. The feel of his touch, so familiar, the warmth of him, his scent, it all brings her back.

"You remember," he says, "I had a difficult time with my father? Maybe I could have done something with my music, like you. But in the end, he won. I did what he wanted. He taught me to thirst for power, not music. But you, tonight, the show! You sang so beautifully. You know, it's not my kind of music. I prefer Led Zeppelin. But you were great. I heard your voice so strong. That's when I knew it was you."

"I haven't performed in years. I had lost my music—"

"No, *bella*. You never lost it." Luca speaks as if he alone possesses the truth. But it isn't the truth. And this time, she will tell him. Yet he isn't listening; perhaps he never listened. He turns away to light another cigarette. Maybe she, too, never really listened.

"How do *you* remember it?" Luca asks.

"You met me at the station in Rome, and you had a fancy sports car, and we drove to Sorrento and then—"

"I am sure we had a day in Rome, then a day in Positano."

Joanna is certain that isn't how it happened, but maybe that's how he needs to remember it. They both shrug, not wanting to ruin this magical reunion with details.

Luca looks at her. "You have aged so well. Not like me. I drink and smoke too much."

"And your wife?" Joanna asks. "Where is she?"

"Home with our other child. I have two." Joanna feels a lump in her throat.

"You remember I wasn't easy. My wife, she struggles hard with me."

"Because you were meant to play the drums," Joanna says with a forced laugh.

"It was only you who thought that." He takes a slow drag of his cigarette. "Do you remember Marco? You met him the night before you met me."

Joanna is shocked he should recall that detail. "Yes," she says. "How did you know?"

"Marco was the famous lover onboard. I was sick the first night of your cruise, so I couldn't go down to meet the new passengers. The next night after I met you and you chose *me*, he couldn't believe it. Marco thought he was the hero man." Luca lets out a gruff laugh, a smoker's laugh. "I was the new one onboard, much younger than him. And you gave him up for me!" Luca taps his chest proudly. Joanna also laughs, which breaks a bit of the tension.

"I never slept with him!"

"Well, that's not what he told us."

"It was you I fell in love with."

"And I with you." Luca grins, and she sees his dimples once again, his irresistible dimples. She feels a sudden urge to touch his cheek.

"Why didn't you call me after that night in Sorrento?" he asks. "I thought you would call."

"You're kidding? After the way we ended? How could I have possibly called?"

"I had no idea you were coming!" Luca says. "Then, out of the blue, you phone me at my family's house to tell me you were at the station. We were about to eat Sunday lunch, and my father was furious that I had to leave to meet you. I didn't expect you."

*You didn't expect me? We were going to get married!* She's sure they'd had a flurry of letters all summer, and she definitely wrote him the details of her flight. Could it be that her last letters confirming everything had never arrived, or that Luca's father destroyed them? Still, she refuses to believe he didn't know she was coming. She changed her whole world for him. Surely, he knew that!

She wants desperately to ask him about the job on the ship. Had he just made that up to test her? Not wanting to ruin this bizarre reunion, she plays it safe. "Do you remember the beautiful beaches you took me to?"

"Yes." Luca smiles, his dimples again deepening.

"Did you take many other girls there?"

"A few," Luca says, and then with a firm voice adds, "but it's you I most remember." Luca flicks his wrist to check his watch. Before he can say anything, Joanna steers them in the direction back to the station.

"There is something very big I have to tell you," he says, veering for control. "Can we still meet tomorrow for the coffee?"

"Can't you tell me now?" Joanna asks, anxious to know, afraid he won't be there in the morning.

"No, we must go to bed. It's maybe dangerous to stay too long in the night. Even if we are no longer the young boy and girl who drank champagne, they are still in us. The magic fire might reignite between us, and if we blow life to that fire, it could devastate our lives now. Maybe it can happen that we become friends . . . eh?" Luca says with a crooked smile. "The boy from your past, he could never have had such a request, no?"

Joanna resents the assumptions he's making, and yet she knows if she remains with him in the darkness by the half moonlight, she'll have to touch him, reach for him, maybe even kiss him.

"Please come tomorrow," he says. "I have much to tell you. Do you remember I wrote poetry? I still do. One is bursting in me now. Can I read it to you tomorrow? Will you hear my silly poem?"

Joanna nods.

"Good," he says. Then, with a soft brush of his hand on her cheek, adds, "*Ciao, bella*." Then he disappears.

## LUCA OF THE SEA, 1976

For the rest of the journey to London, I swap between crying my eyes out and talking nonstop. I end up telling Martin, the driver, everything, every single detail. He listens with empathy, and our last day together, crossing the channel to Dover, he makes me listen. And I do.

"You think you won't be able to live with this misery you feel. You think your life is over. But it isn't. Not if you learn to force your limbs into action. You're young, you've been heartbroken, but you aren't dead. This is what you're going to do. You're going to get up every day, find a job in London, and do your life. All of us who fall in love are fools, but we're also lucky. Carry that love with you, but remember there's no one big love, not really, no happily ever after. Only a bit of humor in the day."

Martin smiles at me. "You remember when we slept the night at the big lorry stop, and the next morning, when you entered the breakfast room? It makes you laugh to remember, doesn't it? You were a good little actress. I'll never live down this trip!"

I smile to remember how he told me that morning that they'd all think we'd been having sex this whole trip. They'd never believe we've traveled platonically. "Let's not disappoint them. Walk into that breakfast room with those several hundred drivers and make them think we've been having the most incredible sex." And I did. I strutted in like a satisfied woman. All the looks I got! And Martin. The looks of envy, the thumbs-up.

"We made their morning," Martin says, "and gave them something juicy to think on for the next hundred kilometers."

I think now, walking the cold and rainy streets of London, how Martin helped me heal. Helped me realize that most people, including myself and probably Luca, never want the truth. We're created to imagine things. Like walking into the breakfast room with those hundreds of drivers staring at me. Easy to create a persona that they all expected. This is what I'll do. Create a persona of what people want and get through the rest of my life.

\*\*\*

After a year in London, enough time to bury my shame and earn enough money, *and* refine my persona, I return to New York. To a job in the Bronx, in a good nursing home. And my mother, in one of her good moments, has promised not to taunt me over my lost love. She keeps to her word, and we never mention Luca again.

Stranger still, a year later, on my way home from work, I run into Mr. Karpel, my inspiring geology professor who I haven't seen since graduation. He asks if I have time for dinner, to catch up, and I do. I'm not seeing anyone, couldn't handle falling in love again. But Mr. Karpel, who now, no longer his student, wants me to call him Stuart, feels like home.

It takes some time to get used to calling him Stuart, but we humans can get used to anything. And Martin, the kind lorry driver, was right; you can, without a big love, have a life, a fine life.

# 30.

## CINQUE TERRE, 2002

THE NEXT MORNING, Luca and Joanna are having coffee by the brick steps outside the café. She dares not face him, nor sit too close. She watches the way his thumb moves a ring around his finger. Luca also seems to look past her, focusing on the distance. It's he who speaks first. "I worked on the ship a few more years," he says, taking a sip of his espresso. "Then, would you believe it, I went north to deal with oil platforms. Luca the businessman! That's why my English is so good!" He laughs. But it's a strange laugh, one she doesn't recognize. She thinks of the life she'd imagined with him, the life of music and poetry. A life they'd never have had after all. "You look surprised," he says. "I happen to be very good at it. Maybe too good."

"It's just that—" She can't say it. That it was Luca the *anarchist*, the one raging against the system, the materialistic world, who she wanted to spend her life with. Not the man sitting beside her. She hates to admit she's judging him, but she is. His shiny shoes and tailored suit, the exclusive leather case he carries. In the past, his fancy clothing seemed exotic. Now she can't help but see this was his choice. His father might have been powerful, but clearly Luca had wanted that life. Strange to fathom that while Stuart fought to keep fossil fuels in the ground, Luca was working to extract them. She glances anew at his face, the sculpted lines carved around his eyes and brow telling the story of his life, a very different story than she'd once dreamed of.

He checks his watch, shifting restlessly on the brick steps. "I don't want to make excuses. I just want you to know what happened to the boy you loved. You can see I have money, too much. They teach us wrong in this life that it's only money and power we need and must have. But—and this is what I have to tell you—something very big happened to me not long ago. You see, once you're in that life, you have to keep running. It made me sick, very sick, and I almost died. I don't know the English term for it. And then, she came to me and helped me through."

Joanna waits while he pauses. "Who came to you?" she asks.

"You can't know how amazing it was to see you last night in the church, right in front of *her*!"

"At the concert?"

"Yes. Just behind where you stood, she was there, weeping." Luca's eyes glaze over.

"*Mary?*"

"*Sì, Maria.*" He nods. "She is good to me, too good. I don't deserve such kindness. And now she leads me to you, so I get the chance to explain why the Luca you knew couldn't live anymore." He flicks his wrist, that movement she knew so well, to look at his watch, then cups his hand around his chin. "I have to make a phone call. This is—" He suddenly stops as if even he, a man she's never seen cry, can barely gain control. "This is a precious gift that I meet you. You can wait?"

How peculiar to even ask her that. Hasn't she waited her whole life? To hear him speak his own language, Italian, to feel the vibration of his words. All of it so strange.

When he gets off the phone, he smiles that he's arranged more time. Then he makes a funny show of being an old man, again sitting beside her at the steps. He puts one hand gently on her thigh, not as a lover but as a holy man living apart from the world. "Please, can I tell you? I'm sure you have wondered all these years what really happened. It was terrible what I did. But you have to know, I had such fear of you. Of what you could make me do, make me feel."

Gino just then comes out to set the tables. He's smoking a cigarette and looks up at her. She smiles at him, but he turns away. She tries to send a signal to Gino that this is important, she's hearing the end of her story, the question she's waited thirty years to resolve. Luca notices Gino. "He likes you, that young man."

Joanna signals to Gino that she will explain. Gino looks at her sadly, but no longer with anger. Then he goes back inside the restaurant.

"You know him?" Luca says. "I'm not surprised. You're still beautiful, Joanna. You haven't changed at all. The day we wrote our names in the sand, your name still rides high on the waves. I am sure of it. Yes, I was terrible, but never strong enough to sink you. You were always so much higher than me, because I needed to destroy. Can you understand? Come. Finish your coffee and let's walk. He makes me nervous, that young man."

They walk to the other side of the station, where they'd been the previous night. Luca stands close beside her; she feels the intense heat of his body.

"When I was sick," he says, "I began to realize my father wasn't as smart or as strong as I'd always imagined, and I could no longer blame him. As I recovered, I was forced to find a way to remedy the wrong things I'd done. It's not easy. Maria is helping, but she has a hard job." He makes a scowl, a grimace she recognizes. "Joanna, can you imagine my surprise when I saw you last night? I went early this morning to that church, to pray to her." He sucks in his lips, as if trying to swallow something down. "She told me that after this, this gift of our meeting, we must never meet again. I think you understand, now that you see me. I can never give you *him*, that boy, that Luca I stole from you. Don't you see? I was too scared of my father. I let him control me. Not even Maria can bring that boy back. He is dead. I killed him."

It's coming too fast, and she has no idea how to respond or even how she feels.

"I must leave soon." His voice is softer now, more like she remembers. Like the wind rolling off the sea. He takes a paper from his pocket. "Can I read you the poem I wrote last night?" He brushes his hand through his hair, clears his throat, and begins, "I have tried to translate it: '*Piccola Joanna, the rustle of the trees that accompany tonight, your sweet dance while the wings of autumn have left forever. The old man weeps and suffers for the sins of the boy, and a single voice is raised to the sky in prayer.*'"

He puts away the paper and lights another cigarette.

"It's beautiful," she says, moved by the gentle cadence of his words. "But why were you afraid of me?"

"I was young and . . . and *the love*. I didn't know what to do with the love, how to depend on it. I didn't dare let in the tender things, like love or music; it made me too soft."

"Things could've changed," she blurts out.

"No," he says, putting out his cigarette, this one only half-smoked, as if to emphasize the finality. "I don't think so. But miracles do happen—no? I come to see my daughter dance, and you don't know the fights we had about her dancing. And *who* is in the show but *you*. I never thought I should see you again. Do not think what has occurred is an accident. It was thirty years in the making. I needed that time. I am afraid my father continued to control me for many years." They have come to a rise in the street where you can see the Mediterranean. It is still and calm like glass.

"She's out there, you know," Luca says, pointing. "Our *Leonardo*. Sunk to the bottom of the sea."

*The sinking of the Leonardo da Vinci*. It comes to her again, that it wasn't just her life and her dreams that had sunk. But the myth of what we think we need to be happy and the price we're willing to pay for that illusion.

"After you left," Joanna says, "all those years ago in Sorrento, I could hardly play music, hardly wrote songs again."

"I don't believe you. I saw you last night." He says it again, and this time she hears it. "You never lost your music." Maybe he's right, that she never lost it. That day in Sorrento, it was her guitar more than the dress that had triggered him. And his final words, that she *loved the music more than him,* suddenly made sense. He'd asked her then that if she loved him, really loved him, then she should give up her music just as he gave up his. That was the dare, to follow him as a chambermaid onto the ship. If she'd loved him *enough,* she would have gone anywhere and done anything to be with him.

They hear the rumble of the nearing train. "*Mamma mia,*" he cries. "Why can't the time for once hold still? I should take this train, but I can't go yet." He makes another phone call, another flood of commanding Italian. "I will pay for this, with angry colleagues later, but I can't leave, not yet."

\*\*\*

They sit and order in the local osteria, and she realizes they've rarely had a real meal out together, and never a happy one. He looks at the wine bottles lining the wall. She shakes her head no. He orders a glass for himself.

"When I was sixteen," he says, "I loved the drums more than anything. My father was furious. He had to show me once and for all what is the life, the true life. He sent me off for the summer as the ship's dishwasher. I know, when you met me at twenty-four, I worked as a navigator, but my first job at sixteen was terrible. We weren't poor. This was not for the money, but the lesson.

"On the ship was a girl from your country. We met in secret in the night. I told her I was the first officer of the ship. But she found out I was a dishwasher and wanted nothing more to do with me. She was the first girl I loved. How could she be that stupid? My father was right. The people of the world are mostly blind. After that summer, I was very confused. And then, a few years later, I met you. The love I had for you—" He stops now and moves his hand for emphasis. His eyes glaze over. "I was a coward for the love, and I needed you to be absolute. I couldn't take a chance to be wrong again. I still had to win in that other world too. Forgive me, Joanna. I tried the impossible, to have both worlds, but in the end, I lost the Luca of the heart."

He goes on. "And, our different cultures—American, Italian. You had no family, mine was very traditional . . . and the way you dressed. Still, it was just an excuse. Can't you see, at the same time, I was afraid you *could* give me that love, but that would mean rejecting everything of my life. My parents would never accept you, even if I bought you the best clothing."

He pauses, like he's tasting the words he's just said, seeing if something is missing. He pushes away the mostly uneaten meal and asks for the bill. "If only you had called me again, our history might have been different."

Joanna again crashes through her memory. She could never have contacted him, not after how he'd left her. Has he forgotten what really happened?

"But you, you never lost the stars in your eyes. Will you walk me to the station?"

*** 

Standing on the platform, awaiting his train, she notices something different in his eyes. A mist of sadness, an existential sorrow. That he'd hurt her *and* himself and needs her forgiveness. Maybe she needs that as well. They search each other in the wilderness across time.

"Please know," Luca says, "I do want to see you again. But we mustn't. It would ruin our lives."

*Your life,* Joanna can't help but think.

"Don't go yet," he says. "Please stay until the train comes."

"Did you know?" she finally asks, touching her belly. "That I was—"

"Eh?" Again, the swirl of hands in the air. He doesn't need to answer. She could never have arrived in Rome with a bursting belly; no way would his parents have welcomed her. Their love could never have worked out, no matter what she'd done or what dress she'd worn. She feels a heady mix of sadness and acceptance and a strange wave of forgiveness.

"I often dreamt it was a girl," Joanna says. "A wild redheaded girl." Luca cups her face in his hands, and a million feelings charge through her. She wills them not to kiss; she can't live on if they kiss and he leaves *again*. But they don't.

Yet what he does seems worse, like a tease. "*Piccola bambina.* Shall we cut a path outside the world and return to our beautiful beach? Perhaps it is waiting." He sighs with frustration. "I wish you could speak Italian. It is too hard to say what I want with my poor English."

"*Che pensicri?*" Joanna says. "Is that correct for what you are thinking?"

"Not quite," he says. "It should be *pensi*. Maybe one day you'll speak Italian. We have a plan with the sea, you remember? We will meet in the next life, when Luca is finished fighting in this one. But you, you don't fight. You are pure. Do you know that? You still have the stars in your eyes."

The train blows in on a mighty gust. Luca steps onboard and finds a seat. He taps on the window and waves goodbye. The train, with a sound as hard as steel, pulls away.

Joanna collapses onto a bench like a weary old woman. This time, it's really finished. She will never see him again. She wants to hate him but feels a strange gratitude. He's given her a glimpse of the truth. Ah, *the life*. She smiles, remembering how often Luca said those words.

A melody starts in her head. Such a hokey song, she laughs out loud. And with borrowed breath on the upsurge of song, on the empty platform, she lets her voice out: *Try to remember when life was so tender* . . .

Of all the songs to pick, remarkable for her mind to have chosen that one, from *The Fantasticks*. A play about lovers who return to each other, bruised but enlightened, what she'd secretly hoped would happen with Luca one day. A silly, fantastical play about what rarely happens in the world and probably why the play keeps running forever. We all yearn for a happy ending.

The song lightens her mood enough to start moving again. She returns to her apartment, gets her guitar, and heads straight to Simone's.

Zoe is playing on the ground when she gets there. Joanna takes the guitar from the case, tunes it, and starts playing. Simone had planned to leave, to take care of some chores, but seeing Joanna in this intense state, she comes over and joins in. They haven't sung just the two of them since that walk to Pieter's place, and it feels wonderful.

Only vowels, no words. They sing, following each other, as if weaving soft healing ropes of macramé. Zoe crawls onto Simone's lap. Joanna keeps on in a trance until the improvisation ends. Then Zoe squirms to be let down. Balancing onto Simone's leg, she goes to Joanna and caresses her thigh. Joanna takes off her guitar, leans it against the table, and lifts Zoe onto her lap. The little girl begins to roll her hands and, in her search for familiar vowels, sings, "*Round and round, round and round.*" Joanna takes the cue, thinking her heart will burst hearing the little girl's attempt at words. That Zoe could make the world move again. *The wheels on the bus go round and round, round and round, round and round.*

# EPILOGUE

I T'S LATE WHEN Joanna hears a knock, assuming it's someone to ask her to stop playing, as she's been unable to stop singing since returning from Simone's. But it's Gino at her door. He smiles at her, his head cocked to one side, hands deep in his pockets.

"I never heard you sing like that," Gino says. "Like how you did at the church. It was beautiful. Like how you're singing now. I don't know what happens to me when you sing." He sighs deeply. "I love it. I know it's late, but can you sing me one more?"

It isn't the only difference with Luca, that Gino truly likes the kind of music she plays, yet it's a crucial difference.

When she finishes the song, Gino sits beside her at the little table, her notes and papers scattered about. He touches her arm gently, so unlike his hungry touch from their early days. Everything seems closer and yet farther away.

"Joanna," he whispers. "Talk to me." She looks up. She doesn't know what to say and, without the protective shroud of song, remains silent.

"The man I saw you with," Gino asks. "Was that the one you told me about, from the *Leonardo*?"

She nods.

"How did he know to come here to find you?"

"He didn't come here for me. His daughter was in the show last night."

"*È vero?*" Gino says, stroking her cheek. "You look like a young girl."

"I don't feel young," Joanna says. "I feel ancient."

"But you're still here."

"Simone said you'd gone fishing."

"Yes," he says, waving his hand in the air. "I went fishing for my life. Maybe like you."

This is good, Joanna realizes. Good to hear about him, to think of someone else.

"I saw her," Gino says, hesitating. "Eloise. I saw her in Milan."

"I thought she went away."

"No. She isn't going anywhere, not anymore." Gino strains his body back, his brow wrinkling tight.

"What do you mean?"

"When I left, she was, how you say . . . not there. Her eyes were open, but she wasn't there."

"Gino, what happened?"

"She was in the hospital." He leans over, like he's getting sick. "I found out by accident. She didn't tell anyone. Only a friend of mine knew. She was too skinny. Then she couldn't eat. The last day, she was . . . how do you say . . . in a coma, I think."

"My God, Gino. Does she want to see Zoe?"

He shakes his head. "It's too late. She never wanted to return to this town. Now she won't, not anymore. She won't . . . anything anymore. She's gone, Joanna. She's gone."

"I am so sorry."

"Mmm," he murmurs. "I had one day to speak with her, when she was still a little bit *there*. She was very weak, like a dying bird. She had no strength to fight me. I never saw her like that, so fragile, so broken."

"This stupid world we live in," Joanna says, thinking of the misery

Eloise must have gone through. "Why do we get it so wrong?"

"Not everyone gets it so wrong," Gino says, his voice cracking. Joanna can't imagine how hard it's been for him. She mustn't compare, but she can't help it. Luca is alive; he is well and strong and still busy with his fight. Eloise lost hers.

"I saw it in Simone, the minute I came back," Gino continues. "She is so beautiful now. Simone, more than seventy years, yet the most alive in all the town. I know the people here, like my mother, they think Simone is in bed with the devil. But I saw her so changed, so healthy, so young. It was you who gave her that."

"Not just me," Joanna says. "It was the music."

Gino makes a clicking sound with his tongue, as if emphasizing that he's still right. He gets up, goes to the glass door, and peers out into the darkness of the garden.

"It's final now," he says. "Zoe will stay with Simone. Eloise left it all complete. But Simone, she still wants me to help."

"Do you want that?" Joanna asks. "What if you meet someone else? What if you want your own children?"

"The world, the life, maybe this, maybe that. I am here, and Eloise is gone." He is crying now.

"Oh, Gino."

He looks at her. "What about your love? Will you go to him now that you've found him again? He isn't dead."

"No," she says with a heavy sigh. "We won't meet again."

"Are you sure? I saw how he looked at you."

"I'm sure. He lives in Rome and is married with a family."

"So what!" Gino shrieks. "That man who did this to Eloise, *he* was married."

"I won't ever see him again." There, she's said it, those labored words finally out in one go. Gino touches her shoulder now, with kindness.

"Joanna, I'm so tired."

"Me too," she says.

"Can I stay here next to you and just hold you?"

They lie on top of the covers on the bed, wrapping tightly in each other's arms. She strokes his head as he gently weeps, his hair matted down from the strain of these emotional days. She, too, lets the tears fall; it feels good to let them go.

She thinks of love. Of the many shades and sizes of love, of passion and consequence, of purpose and responsibility. Of the absolute love that Luca and maybe she had been so afraid of yet yearned for. That if love didn't come on high seas of emotion, it wasn't real. But now she wonders if love can also ride on a calm sea, if the waves need not always crash and destroy.

Looking at Gino, as he falls asleep, she thinks of the many nights she'd watched Stuart sleep, whatever book he'd been reading spread open across his chest. She'd gingerly remove the book, lower his pillows, and shut off his bedside light. All so gentle and quiet. That, too, was love. She had loved Stuart, and he had loved her, in his way. Even if he never spoke with fancy words, nor waxed poetic, never looked at her deeply or strongly like Luca. Perhaps that was more in the Italian repertoire than the Midwestern. But Stuart had retained the soft probing warmth in his eyes until the last of his days, and she had, after all, loved him, really loved him.

Luca may have found mercy and forgiveness with his Maria, but he was not *of* her. Maybe that had always been his fight, and what he had to punish Joanna for. Maybe there isn't one definitive, absolute, *real* love. It shifts and changes all the time, just as water and air, just as the shape of clouds and snowflakes. But Luca, she suspects, would have tormented her with his jealousy. That what he deemed as her *purity* was just this, that Maria or the angels or whatever form the kindly spirits take lived more inside her than in him. That is what he both loved and hated in her. And what she, so young and frightened in their time together, could never see or understand. You have to allow the angels in. Joanna, in her foolish innocence, had never understood she had this gift, and she had never lost it.

And why Luca always said she had stars in her eyes.

Maybe this is what she's learning in her remarkable time in Italy. To allow *this*, this openness, so the angels can live within her, even if she doesn't always feel it or understand. It's this willingness to be vulnerable, to not know, that lets the angel in.

Gino's sleeping form gives comfort and company, warmth and wonder. And now, she, too, so very tired, gives over to sleep. She doesn't have to know anything else that will follow, doesn't have to worry about what will happen when they wake. Only that she's eager and ready to live, in whatever constellation it will reveal itself.

# ABOUT THE AUTHOR

DEBORAH JEANNE WEITZMAN travels the world as a writer, teacher, performer, and adventurer. She leads workshops in the Alexander Technique, vocal activation, movement, and creative expression. An ASCAP award-winning songwriter, her recordings—*Briefly Mine, For the Feel of the Wind, Beneath Your Moon*, and others—are available online. She is the author of the memoir *Pandora Learns to Sing* and the musical *Island in the Storm*. *The Sinking of the Leonardo da Vinci* is her first novel. Originally from New York City, she lives with her husband between Norway and Greece.

www.deborahjeanne.com